The Watchful Gods

WESTERN LITERATURE SERIES

Other Books by Walter Van Tilburg Clark

THE OX-BOW INCIDENT

THE CITY OF TREMBLING LEAVES

THE TRACK OF THE CAT

The Watchful Gods

AND OTHER STORIES

Walter Van Tilburg Clark

Foreword by Ann Ronald

UNIVERSITY OF NEVADA PRESS
RENO & LAS VEGAS

WESTERN LITERATURE SERIES

The Watchful Gods and Other Stories was originally published in the
United States by Random House, Inc., New York, and simultaneously
in Canada by Random House of Canada, Limited, Toronto. The University
of Nevada Press edition is published by arrangement with the Estate of
Walter Van Tilburg Clark. A foreword by Ann Ronald has been added.

University of Nevada Press, Reno, Nevada 89557 USA

www.unpress.nevada.edu

Cover design by Carrie House

Library of Congress Cataloging-in-Publication Data

Clark, Walter Van Tilburg, 1909–1971.

The watchful gods, and other stories / Walter Van Tilburg Clark ;

foreword by Ann Ronald. — University of Nevada Press pbk. ed.

p. cm. — (Western literature series)

ISBN 0-87417-601-8 (pbk. : alk. paper)

1. West (U.S.) — Social life and customs — Fiction. I. Title.

II. Series.

PS3505.L376W3 2004

813′.52–dc22   2004004206

The paper used in this book meets the requirements of American National
Standard for Information Sciences—Permanence of Paper
for Printed Library Materials, ANSI Z.48-1984. Binding materials were
selected for strength and durability.

University of Nevada Press Paperback Edition, 2004
This book has been reproduced as a digital reprint.

for A. E. Hill

Contents

When Walter Van Tilburg Clark began publishing novels and short stories, his writing was hailed as an antidote to the formula western. *The Ox-Bow Incident* (1940) turned conventional cowboy expectations upside down, questioning both the psychology of violence and the integrity of frontier justice in a complex narrative of men and women caught up by the enthusiasms of a lynch mob. Clark's next novel, *The City of Trembling Leaves* (1945), was more serene. This somewhat autobiographical portrayal of a young man growing to maturity is especially appreciated by Nevada readers for its depiction of 1920s Reno, while at the same time it follows the escapades of a sensitive, artistic youth in an urban western setting rather than those of a callow gunfighter out on the lone prairie. With *The Track of the Cat* (1949), Clark continued his background portraiture of Nevada scenery but returned to the more profound philosophical concerns found in *The Ox-Bow Incident.* Although some critics found too much obtuse symbolism in *The Track of the Cat,* I appreciate its provocative dualities. The interior and intuitive complexities of good and evil are a far cry from the exterior and rather simplistic white hats and black described in other western fiction being written at the time.

Simultaneously, Clark was producing short fiction that echoed the same themes that characterize his longer works. Beginning in the early 1930s, these stories appeared in such important venues as *Accent, Atlantic Monthly, Rocky Mountain Review, Tomorrow, Virginia Quarterly Review,* and *Yale Review.* A year after he published *The Track of the Cat,* the best of his stories were brought together in a collection called *The Watchful Gods and Other Stories* (1950). Like the rest of his books, this one was reasonably well received. The *Saturday Review of Literature,* for example, favorably compared Clark's short fiction with Ernest Hemingway's, William Faulkner's, and Eudora Welty's first collections of stories. Harvey Swados, in the *Nation,* called Clark "a sensitive and cultivated writer, as much at home with knowledgeable outdoor men and their natural world, as with intellectuals and academicians." Swados also praised "a prose style that is wiry, masculine, and mature," with "its own evocative power." Jean Garrigue, in the *New Republic,* wrote that "the best stories in this book . . . are told with the effortless charm of campfire yarns." Although some readers, like Bernard De Voto, complained about some of the stories, most reviewers looked forward to more such western tales.

What followed, instead, was silence. For twenty years after *The Watchful Gods and Other Stories,* Clark published nothing whatsoever. He continued to write but refused to send anything to his agent. He would begin a novel, then discard it after fifty pages, draft a poem, turn it into a short story, then reject them both. Many of those embryonic efforts now are stored in the Getchell Library's Special Collections Department at the University of Nevada, Reno. After perusing them, I would say that Clark was a harsh but consistent critic of his own prose. Between the publication of the short-story collection in 1950 and his death in 1971, his only literary accomplishment was an edited set of Alfred Doten's Virginia City diaries.

With such a long hiatus, Clark's reputation faded and the sales of his books diminished. Many of today's readers, in fact, no longer recognize his name. While *The Ox-Bow Incident* remains a classic anti-western text, and while scholars and critics of the American West continue to praise Clark's contributions to the field, *The Watchful Gods and Other Stories* has been out of print for nearly three decades. With the publication of Jackson J. Benson's new Clark biography, it is time to reprint Clark's short fiction. These are fine stories, ten quite diverse evocations of nature, man, and the primal interactions between the two. All together, the tales lend credence to an opinion like John R. Milton's, that Walter Clark "did perhaps more than anyone else to define (in his fiction) the mode of perception, the acquisition of knowledge, and the style which we tend to call western" (197) in the literary rather than formulaic sense of the word.

The lead story, "The Watchful Gods," foregrounds those themes most important to Clark and sets a dramatic tone that draws the reader immediately into the action. Like *The City of Trembling Leaves*, the narrative features a young man stepping out on the road to maturity. On the day of his twelfth birthday, Buck receives from his father the gun he covets. Succeeding adventures with the .22-caliber rifle bring Buck face to face with the fragile, intricate web that connects humanity with other bioconstituents of the natural world. A recalled encounter with a rattlesnake and the purposeful shooting of a tiny rabbit take Buck rapidly from innocence to experience.

Overseeing that process are the mystical forces of "the watchful gods," a complex of imagined impotence and power that accompanies anyone exploring Clark's western terrain. Multiple gods of fog, of medieval romance, of myth, of mystique, of maturity, of good, and of evil come into play.

Buck "had lost the bright gods," Clark writes, "and he had not been accepted by the dark. He was in no soul's land and in its isolation his own soul was withdrawn, small and heavy as a stone within him, and closed about his evil deed. No wonder it could not take wing and make heralding music. That was the whole of reality now, the little stone inside, and outside the cold, dark ravine and the inescapable watcher" (268). Buck, in Clark's terms, is on his way to the subconscious, unconscious haunts of manhood. Max Westbrook, in his Twayne examination of Walter Van Tilburg Clark's accomplishments, argues convincingly that the overriding concept in Clark's fiction is the notion of "sacrality." Synthesizing Mircea Eliade's sense of the sacred and its connection with the real, adding an overlay of Jungian symbolic images, blending these together with Robinson Jeffers's intimations of an inherent natural force, Clark's distillation of sacrality enables him to create characters who contact primordial reality through archetypes, men who seek unity through the unconscious, boys who experience the multiple meanings of sacred space.

By untangling Clark's struggles with his own personal ontology, Westbrook shows how to unravel the physical and psychological encounters created by this complicated author. Westbrook sees "The Watchful Gods" as an early compendium of Clark's metaphysics, "a fictive study of sacred unity" (113), where a series of sacred and profane impulses propels Buck through a particular initiation sequence. The resulting narrative is a "genuine testimony to his [Buck's] recognition of the primary authority of the dictates of the unconscious. He is beginning," Westbrook concludes, "to learn the discipline of the inner debate" (124). So, too, is Walter Clark. "The Watchful Gods" is a tightly controlled exploration of the inner self within the rich parameters of the outer world.

"The Fish Who Could Close His Eyes," the penultimate story in this collection, pursues the same ends from a rather different point of view. Tad Manson is an adult with the thought processes of a child. At the aquarium where he works, Tad encounters the realities of scientific research and the consequent destruction of innocence when his favorite fish meets with an untimely demise. Like Lenny Small in John Steinbeck's *Of Mice and Men,* Clark's misfit ignorantly effects his own heartbreak. Even if Tad cannot articulate personal culpability, the reader certainly comprehends the point Clark means to make about this character's unilateral interactions with his complicated surroundings and about his inability to connect.

Tad's brand of innocence is replicated in "Hook," the story of an orphaned hawk's struggles to survive in a world of nature red in tooth and claw. Some readers fault "Hook" for its anthropomorphic rendition of a mere creature, but in fact Clark is designing a far-ranging symbolic entity that can soar and fall both literally and figuratively. The germ of the story comes from Robinson Jeffers's 1929 poem, "Hurt Hawks," though Jeffers's bird's final encounter with humanity is a noble

one whereas Clark's raptor meets mankind on less ma-
jestic and more enigmatic terms. I think Clark's rendition, which leaves the reader with a profound sense of
irony, is not only more philosophically provocative but
offers one more version of Clark's sacrality. Encounters
between and connections among contemporary humans
and animals are occasions for the stirring of ancient
memories long suppressed. Westbrook would say that
the power of this story lies "in its dramatic presentation
of archetypal energies" (133). I agree, and I would add
that "Hook" is my personal favorite of all Clark's stories.

"The Indian Well" effectively works with sacred energies, too. Jim Suttler, a prospector down on his luck, set-
tles with his burro at an isolated oasis haunted regularly
by a variety of decidedly real wild animals. In rapid suc-
cession, Suttler encounters a rattlesnake, a roadrunner,
cliff swallows, bluebirds, lizards, a red-and-white range
cow and calf, a host of jackrabbits, a coyote. After an
extended idyllic interlude, a cougar arrives, bringing an
apparent source of evil to this new-world garden. When
the cougar kills Suttler's precious burro, the lonely man
stirs himself into a sacred rage. Without giving the plot
away, let me say that the story ends as it begins, with only
animals left to drink the precious water and with no
long-lasting human impact at all. In this case, at least,
man's interaction with a sacred space results in nothing
but the primordial disinterestedness of nature: "After a
month the antelope returned. The well brimmed, and
in the gentle sunlight the new aspen leaves made a tiny
music of shadows" (148).

The story's ending gives some indication of the power
of Clark's prose when he describes the natural world

in metaphysical or ontological terms. The story's pan-
oramic beginning sets that scene: "The pictograph of a
starving, ancient journey, cut in rock above the basin, a
sun-warped shack on the south wing of the canyon, and
an abandoned mine above it, were the last minute and
contemporary tokens of man's participation in the cycles
of the well's resistance, each of which was an epitome
of centuries, and perhaps of the wars of the universe"
(125). Jim Suttler's vignette, iterating man's inconse-
quential behavior, reveals one more example of man's
efforts to control and then his inability to cohere with
his natural surroundings.

"The Portable Phonograph" takes human behavior
one step further, picturing an empty world after a mil-
lennial catastrophe. "High in the air there was wind, for
through the veil of the dusk the clouds could be seen
gliding rapidly south and changing shapes. A sensation
of torment, of two-sided, unpredictable nature, arose
from the stillness of the earth air beneath the violence
of the upper air" (179). The hanging violence, the veil
of dusk, and a sense of torment permeate this tragic
story, until the only harbingers of hope appear. An
aged phonograph, some old scarred records, and man's
symphonic memories become symbols of what has been
lost and what might still be found. "The individual, delectable presences swept into a sudden tide of unbearably beautiful dissonance, and then continued fully the
swelling and ebbing of that tide, the dissonant inpourings, and the resolutions, and the diminishment, and
the little, quiet wavelets of interlude lapping between"
(186). In the emptiness of this new world order, music
brings the only sacred connection available to the story's

unfortunate characters. But even that, the reader finds, is not sufficient.

Three other stories in this collection muse about the dissonances of civilized existence, too. "Why Don't You Look Where You're Going?" is perhaps the most outrageous. Set on the ocean's empty expanses, it describes a confrontation between an enormous passenger liner and a tiny sailboat crewed by a single man. The passengers themselves demonstrate what Clark might call the paucity of modernity; the lone crewman, his fist raised against the forces bearing down upon him, represents self-expression and defiance, apparently the only options left when someone is faced with indifferent and unbeatable odds. Critics who don't care for Clark's methodology—"the purpose vanishes in a cloud of not-quite-clear suggestions," said Joseph Henry Jackson in the *San Francisco Chronicle*—have been unkind when assessing the relative success of stories like this one. As a parable of Clark's frustrations with contemporary society, however, and as an existential rendering of the writer's lot, the story works quite well.

"The Rapids" introduces another powerless character, but this time Clark places the nameless man in a situation where he can shape his own destiny at least for a time. While it is true that the purpose of "The Rapids" may be somewhat unclear, that is exactly the point. The man repetitiously floats, swims, and rafts down the same set of rapids, over and over again, until his wife and the pressures of ordinary life pull him back from his adventure. "Well, what on earth *were* you doing out there?" his wife asks repeatedly (63), and remains "unpleasantly silent" (64). Like the author, the husband remains silent, too. I see this story as one more example of Clark's expression of man's ego when someone, however feebly, attempts to find some sort of unity with the sacred world.

The title character in "The Anonymous," however, doesn't even make an attempt. He suddenly appears at an Indian school, a young man sent there to be taught about literature and history and the arts. His mysterious background puzzles the teacher, as does the fellow's obvious disdain for deliberating about anything he might be learning. Rather than think about humanistic concepts and continuities, the young man memorizes facts. Here, Clark not only indicts the educational system but also exposes those cultural pressures that turn potential students into automatons. The "anonymous" student believes that, by acquiring a façade of culture, he can successfully marry into contemporary society. Clark does not disabuse him; nor does the teacher.

Two remaining tales in *The Watchful Gods and Other Stories* return the reader to the natural world, as Clark moves his characters away from the machinations of modernity and places them closer to the land. Even the tone changes from a narrative distancing to a more personal interaction with the environment. "The Buck in the Hills" dissects a hunting party, tacitly evaluating the reasons why certain men kill in certain ways and why other men respond as they do. The narrative ends in a blizzard, but the effect of the weather is to bring about a profound association between the narrator and the land. "Snow makes a hush that's even harder to talk in than the clear silence. There was something listening behind each tree and rock we passed, and something waiting among the taller trees down slope, blue through the falling snow" (109). That something is analogous to a "watchful god."

"The Wind and Snow of Winter" also predicates a season of closure, but this time the denouement is reminiscent of "The Portable Phonograph." Mike Braneen returns to civilization after a long prospecting foray, only to find that nothing has remained the same. The stores and the saloon are shut down, his friends and acquaintances are gone, whatever was once familiar has changed, winter is descending with ghostly speed. "The light was still there, although the fire was dying out of it, and the snow swarmed across it more quickly" (43). With no tangible explanation of such irrevocable change, Clark intimates that here is one more example of the disjuncture between the inner man and the outer world, one more indication of the inevitable failure to find whatever one is seeking. That the main character is an itinerant prospector surely underscores the will-o-the-wisp nature of the quest. "I wanted to make my story a kind of *in memoriam* to this vanished, or nearly vanished, breed" (Laird, 125), the author once wrote. For me, Mike Bradeen's time-warped encounter provides a thematic summary of the important motifs in the other tales, offers another fictive study of unity and disunity, and acts as a saddened counterpart to the collection's title story, "The Watchful Gods."

Walter Van Tilburg Clark never solved the nightmare of his own equivocations. His silence after the publication of *The Watchful Gods and Other Stories* attests to vacillations of his imagination. In a letter to his editor, Saxe Cummins, Clark summarized his ambitions for the lead story, originally titled "The Little Gods, The Watchful

Gods." I wish to recapitulate "in capsule form," he explained, the history of the race from primitive anthropomorphism, through classicism and Christianity, into "a complete unity of mysticism" (Laird, 188). Clark was bound to be stymied, I think, by such a mammoth undertaking.

Nonetheless, "The Watchful Gods" and the nine other stories included here are worthwhile reading because they reveal several crucial characteristics of this complicated writer's imagination. When Buck experiences "the timid, used up feeling of his whole body, within which some great change was rolling and growing by itself, silently as a new fog bank rises from the ocean horizon, and no more comfortingly" (303), Clark's writing profoundly assesses the frustrations, the awful dead ends, and the intriguing possibilities of modern existence. Even when struggling with stylized characters and unfulfilled themes, Clark's presentations replicate the very machinations that characterize the core of his dilemma. How, he asks over and over, are we to connect man's psychical energies with the wonderous sacralities of the natural world? He tries to answer with this collection, an encapsulation of both the sacred unities and the mystic disunities of Walter Van Tilburg Clark. No longer parochially western—although his best writing is always set in the West—the stories operate as a kind of corollary to his novelistic achievements. Together, they provide a preternatural road map to the twisting routes traced so intricately in *The Ox-Bow Incident, The City of Trembling Leaves,* and *The Track of the Cat.*

Ann Ronald
RENO, NEVADA

Works Cited and Consulted

Benson, Jackson J. *The Ox-Bow Man: A Biography of Walter Van Tilburg Clark.* Reno: University of Nevada Press, 2004.

Clark, Walter Van Tilburg. *The Watchful Gods and Other Stories.* Reno: University of Nevada Press, 2004.

De Voto, Bernard. Review of *The Watchful Gods and Other Stories. New York Times,* 24 September 1950.

Erisman, Fred, and Richard W. Etulain. *Fifty Western Writers: A Bio-Bibliographical Sourcebook.* Westport, Conn.: Greenwood Press, 1982.

Garrigue, Jean. Review of *The Watchful Gods and Other Stories. Saturday Review of Literature,* 30 September 1950.

Jackson, Joseph Henry. Review of *The Watchful Gods and Other Stories. San Francisco Chronicle,* 18 October 1950.

Laird, Charlton, ed. *Walter Van Tilburg Clark: Critiques.* Reno: University of Nevada Press, 1983.

Milton, John R. *The Novel of the American West.* Lincoln: University of Nebraska Press, 1980.

Ronald, Ann. *Reader of the Purple Sage: Essays on Western Writers and Environmental Literature.* Reno: University of Nevada Press, 2003.

Swados, Harvey. Review of *The Watchful Gods and Other Stories. Nation,* 7 October 1950.

West, R. B. Review of *The Watchful Gods and Other Stories. New Republic,* 25 December 1950.

Westbrook, Max. *Walter Van Tilburg Clark.* New York: Twayne, 1969.

The Watchful Gods

Hook

HOOK, the hawks' child, was hatched in a dry spring among the oaks beside the seasonal river, and was struck from the nest early. In the drouth his single-willed parents had to extend their hunting ground by more than twice, for the ground creatures upon which they fed died and dried by the hundreds. The range became too great for them to wish to return and feed Hook, and when they had lost interest in each other they drove Hook down into the sand and brush and went back to solitary courses over the bleaching hills.

Unable to fly yet, Hook crept over the ground, challenging all large movements with recoiled head, erected, rudimentary wings, and the small rasp of his clattering beak. It was during this time of abysmal ignorance and continual fear that his eyes took on the first quality of a hawk, that of being wide, alert and challenging. He dwelt, because of his helplessness, among the rattling brush which grew between the oaks and the river. Even in his thickets and near the water, the white sun was the dominant presence. Except in the dawn, when the land wind stirred, or in the late afternoon, when the sea wind became strong enough to penetrate the half-mile inland to this turn in the river, the sun was the major force, and everything was dry and motionless under it. The brush, small plants and trees alike husbanded the little moisture at their hearts; the moving creatures waited for dark, when sometimes the sea fog came over and made a fine, soundless rain which relieved them.

The two spacious sounds of his life environed Hook at this time. One was the great rustle of the slopes of yellowed wild wheat, with over it the chattering rustle of the leaves of the California oaks, already as harsh and individually tremulous as in autumn. The other was the distant whisper of the foaming edge of the Pacific, punctuated by the hollow shoring of the waves. But these Hook did not yet hear, for he was attuned by fear and hunger to the small, spasmodic rustlings of live things. Dry, shrunken, and nearly starved, and with his plumage delayed, he snatched at beetles, dragging in the sand to catch them. When swifter and stronger birds and animals did not reach them first, which was seldom, he ate the small, silver fish left in the mud by the failing river. He watched, with nearly chattering beak, the quick, thin lizards pause, very alert, and raise and lower themselves, but could not catch them because he had to raise his wings to move rapidly, which startled them.

Only one sight and sound not of his world of microscopic necessity was forced upon Hook. That was the flight of the big gulls from the beaches, which sometimes, in quealing play, came spinning back over the foothills and the river bed. For some inherited reason, the big, ship-bodied birds did not frighten Hook, but angered him. Small and chewed-looking, with his wide.

already yellowing eyes glaring up at them, he would stand in an open place on the sand in the sun and spread his shaping wings and clatter his bill like shaken dice. Hook was furious about the swift, easy passage of gulls.

His first opportunity to leave off living like a ground owl came accidentally. He was standing in the late afternoon in the red light under the thicket, his eyes half-filmed with drowse and the stupefaction of starvation, when suddenly something beside him moved, and he struck, and killed a field mouse driven out of the wheat by thirst. It was a poor mouse, shriveled and lice ridden, but in striking, Hook had tasted blood, which raised nest memories and restored his nature. With started neck plumage and shining eyes, he tore and fed. When the mouse was devoured, Hook had entered hoarse adolescence. He began to seek with a conscious appetite, and to move more readily out of shelter. Impelled by the blood appetite, so glorious after his long preservation upon the flaky and bitter stuff of bugs, he ventured even into the wheat in the open sun beyond the oaks, and discovered the small trails and holes among the roots. With his belly often partially filled with flesh, he grew rapidly in strength and will. His eyes were taking on their final change, their yellow growing deeper and more opaque, their stare more constant, their challenge less desperate. Once during this transformation, he surprised a ground squirrel, and although he was ripped and wing-bitten and could not hold his prey, he was not dismayed by the conflict, but exalted. Even while the wing was still drooping and the pinions not grown back, he was excited by other ground squirrels and pursued them futilely, and was angered by their dusty escapes. He realized that his world was a great arena for killing, and felt the magnificence of it.

The two major events of Hook's young life occurred in the same day. A little after dawn he made the customary essay and succeeded in flight. A little before sunset, he made his first sustained flight of over two hundred yards, and at its termination struck and slew a great buck squirrel whose thrashing and terrified gnawing and squealing gave him a wild delight. When he had gorged on the strong meat, Hook stood upright, and in his eyes was the stare of the hawk, never flagging in intensity but never swelling beyond containment. After that the stare had only to grow more deeply challenging and more sternly controlled as his range and deadliness increased. There was no change in kind. Hook had mastered the first of the three hungers which are fused into the single, flaming will of a hawk, and he had experienced the second.

The third and consummating hunger did not awaken in Hook until the following spring, when the exultation of space had grown slow and steady in him, so that he swept freely with the wind over the miles of coastal foothills, circling, and ever in sight of the sea, and used without struggle the warm currents lifting from the slopes, and no longer desired to scream at the range of his vision, but intently sailed above his shadow swiftly climbing to meet him on the hillsides, sinking away and rippling across the brush-grown canyons.

That spring the rains were long, and Hook sat for hours, hunched and angry under their pelting, glaring into the fogs of the river valley, and killed only small, drenched things flooded up from their tunnels. But when the rains had dissipated, and there were sun and sea wind again, the game ran plentiful, the hills were thick and shining green, and the new river flooded about the boulders where battered turtles climbed up to shrink and sleep. Hook then was scorched by the third hunger. Ranging farther, often forgetting to kill and eat, he sailed for days with growing rage, and woke at night clattering on his dead tree limb, and struck and struck and struck at the porous wood of the trunk, tearing it away. After days, in the draft of a coastal canyon miles below his own hills, he came upon the acrid taint he did not know but had expected, and sailing down it, felt his neck plumes rise and his wings quiver so that he swerved unsteadily. He saw the un-mated female perched upon the tall and jagged stump of a tree that had been shorn by storm, and he stooped, as if upon game. But she was older than he, and wary of the gripe of his importunity, and banked off screaming, and he screamed also at the intolerable delay.

At the head of the canyon, the screaming pursuit was crossed by another male with a great wing-spread, and the light golden in the fringe of his plumage. But his more skillful opening played him false against the ferocity of the twice-balked Hook. His rising maneuver for position was cut short by Hook's wild, upward swoop, and at the blow he raked desperately and tumbled off to the side. Dropping, Hook struck him again, struggled to clutch, but only raked and could not hold, and, diving, struck once more in passage, and then beat up, yelling triumph, and saw the crippled antagonist side-slip away, half-tumble once, as the ripped wing failed to balance, then steady and glide obliquely into the cover of brush on the canyon side. Beating hard and stationary in the wind above the bush that covered his competitor, Hook waited an instant, but when the bush was still, screamed again, and let himself go off with the current, reseeking, infuriated by the burn of his own wounds, the thin choke-thread of the acrid taint.

On a hilltop projection of stone two miles inland, he struck her down, gripping her rustling body with his talons, beating her wings down with his wings, belting her head when she whimpered or thrashed, and at last clutching her neck with his hook and, when her coy struggles had given way to stillness, succeeded.

In the early summer, Hook drove the three young ones from their nest, and went back to lone circling above his own range. He was complete.

2

Throughout that summer and the cool, growthless weather of the winter, when the gales blew in the river canyon and the ocean piled upon the shore, Hook was master of the sky and the hills of his range. His flight became a lovely and certain thing, so that he played with the treacherous currents of the air with a delicate ease surpassing that of the gulls. He could sail for hours, searching the blanched grasses below him with telescopic eyes, gaining height against the wind, descending in mile-long, gently declining swoops when he curved and rode back, and never beating either wing. At the swift passage of his shadow within their vision, gophers, ground squirrels and rabbits froze, or plunged gibbering into their tunnels beneath matted turf. Now, when he struck, he killed easily in one hard-knuckled blow. Occasionally, in sport, he soared up over the river and drove the heavy and weaponless gulls downstream again, until they would no longer venture inland.

There was nothing which Hook feared now, and his spirit was wholly belligerent, swift and sharp, like his gaze. Only the mixed smells and incomprehensible activities of the people at the Japanese farmer's home, inland of the coastwise highway and south of the bridge across Hook's river, troubled him. The smells were strong, unsatisfactory and never clear, and the people, though they behaved foolishly, constantly running in and out of their built-up holes, were large, and appeared capable, with fearless eyes looking up at him, so that he instinctively swerved aside from them. He cruised over their yard, their gardens, and their bean fields, but he would not alight close to their buildings.

But this one area of doubt did not interfere with his life. He ignored it, save to look upon it curiously as he crossed, his afternoon shadow sliding in an instant over the chicken-and-crate-cluttered yard, up the side of the unpainted barn, and then out again smoothly, just faintly, liquidly rippling over the furrows and then over the stubble of the grazing slopes. When the season was dry, and the dead earth blew on the fields, he extended his range to satisfy his great hunger, and again narrowed it when the fields were once more alive with the minute movements he could not only see but anticipate.

Four times that year he was challenged by other hawks blowing up from behind the coastal hills to scud down his slopes, but two of these he slew in mid-air, and saw hurtle down to thump on the ground and lie still while he circled, and a third, whose wing he tore, he followed closely to earth and beat to death in the grass, making the crimson jet out from its breast and neck into the pale wheat. The fourth was a strong flier and experienced fighter, and theirs was a long, running battle, with brief, rising flurries of striking and screaming, from which down and plumage soared off.

Here, for the first time, Hook felt doubts, and at moments wanted to drop away from the scoring, burning talons and the twisted hammer strokes of the strong beak, drop away shrieking, and take cover and be still. In the end, when Hook, having outmaneuvered his enemy and come above him, wholly in control, and going with the wind, tilted and plunged for the death rap, the other, in desperation, threw over on his back and struck up. Talons locked, beaks raking, they dived earthward. The earth grew and spread under them amazingly, and they were not fifty feet above it when Hook, feeling himself turning toward the underside, tore free and beat up again on heavy, wrenched wings. The other, stroking swiftly, and so close to down that he lost wing plumes to a bush, righted himself and planed up, but flew on lumberingly between the hills and did not return. Hook screamed the triumph, and made a brief pretense of pursuit, but was glad to return, slow and victorious, to his dead tree.

In all these encounters Hook was injured, but experienced only the fighter's pride and exultation from the sting of wounds received in successful combat. And in each of them he learned new skill. Each time the wounds healed quickly, and left him a more dangerous bird.

In the next spring, when the rains and the night chants of the little frogs were past, the third hunger returned upon Hook with a new violence. In this quest, he came into the taint of a young hen. Others too were drawn by the unnerving perfume, but only one of them, the same with which Hook had fought his great battle, was a worthy competitor. This hunter drove off two, while two others, game but neophytes, were glad enough that Hook's impatience would not permit him to follow and kill. Then the battle between the two champions fled inland, and was a tactical marvel, but Hook lodged the neck-breaking blow, and struck again as they dropped past the treetops. The blood had already begun to pool on the gray, fallen foliage as Hook flapped up between branches, too spent to cry his victory. Yet his hunger would not let him rest until, late in the second day, he drove the female to ground among the laurels of a strange river canyon.

When the two fledglings of this second brood had been driven from the nest, and Hook had returned to his own range, he was not only complete, but supreme. He slept without concealment on his bare limb, and did not open his eyes when, in the night, the heavy-billed cranes coughed in the shallows below him.

3

The turning point of Hook's career came that autumn, when the brush in the canyons rustled dryly and the hills, mowed close by the cattle, smoked under the wind as if burning. One midafternoon, when the black clouds were torn on the rim of the sea and the surf flowered white and high on the rocks, raining in over the low cliffs, Hook rode the wind diagonally across the river mouth. His great eyes, focused for small things stirring in the dust and leaves, overlooked so large and slow a movement as that of the Japanese farmer rising from the brush and lifting the two black eyes of his shotgun. Too late Hook saw and, startled, swerved, but wrongly. The surf muffled the reports, and nearly without sound, Hook felt the minute whips of the first shot, and the astounding, breath-breaking blow of the second.

Beating his good wing, tasting the blood that quickly swelled into his beak, he tumbled off with the wind and struck into the thickets on the far side of the river mouth. The branches tore him. Wild with rage, he thrust up and clattered his beak, challenging, but when he had fallen over twice, he knew that the trailing wing would not carry, and then heard the boots of the hunter among the stones in the river bed and, seeing him loom at the edge of the bushes, crept back among the thickest brush and was still. When he saw the boots stand before him, he reared back, lifting his good wing and cocking his head for the serpent-like blow, his beak open but soundless, his great eyes hard and very shining. The boots passed on. The Japanese farmer, who believed that he had lost chickens, and who had cunningly observed Hook's flight for many afternoons, until he could plot it, did not greatly want a dead hawk.

When Hook could hear nothing but the surf and the wind in the thicket, he let the sickness and shock overcome him. The fine film of the inner lid dropped over his big eyes. His heart beat frantically, so that it made the plumage of his shot-aching breast throb. His own blood throttled his breathing. But these things were nothing compared to the lightning of pain in his left shoulder, where the shot had bunched, shattering the airy bones so the pinions trailed on the ground and could not be lifted. Yet, when a sparrow lit in the bush over him, Hook's eyes flew open again, hard and challenging, his good wing was lifted and his beak strained open. The startled sparrow darted piping out over the river.

Throughout that night, while the long clouds blew across the stars and the wind shook the bushes about him, and throughout the next day, while the clouds still blew and massed until there was no gleam of sunlight on the sand bar, Hook remained stationary, enduring his sickness. In the second evening, the rains began. First there was a long, running patter of drops upon the beach and over the dry trees and bushes. At dusk there came a heavier squall, which did not die entirely, but slacked off to a continual, spaced splashing of big drops, and then returned with the front of the storm. In long, misty curtains, gust by gust, the rain swept over the sea, beating down its heaving, and coursed up the beach. The little jets of dust ceased to rise about the drops in the fields, and the mud began to gleam. Among the boulders of the river bed, darkling pools grew slowly.

Still Hook stood behind his tree from the wind, only gentle drops reaching him, falling from the upper branches and then again from the brush. His eyes remained closed, and he could still taste his own blood in his mouth, though it had ceased to come up freshly. Out beyond him, he heard the storm changing. As rain conquered the sea, the heave of the surf became a hushed sound, often lost in the crying of the wind. Then gradually, as the night turned toward morning, the wind also was broken by the rain. The crying became fainter, the rain settled toward steadiness, and the creep of the waves could be heard again, quiet and regular upon the beach.

At dawn there was no wind and no sun, but everywhere the roaring of the vertical, relentless rain. Hook then crept among the rapid drippings of the bushes, dragging his torn sail, seeking better shelter. He stopped often and stood with the shutters of film drawn over his eyes. At midmorning he found a little cave under a ledge at the base of the sea cliff. Here, lost without branches and leaves about him, he settled to await improvement.

When, at midday of the third day, the rain stopped altogether, and the sky opened before a small, fresh wind, letting light through to glitter upon a tremulous sea, Hook was so weak that his good wing trailed also to prop him upright, and his open eyes were lusterless. But his wounds were hardened, and he felt the return of hunger. Beyond his shelter, he heard the gulls flying in great numbers and crying their joy at the cleared air. He could even hear, from the fringe of the river, the ecstatic and unstinted bubblings and chirpings of the small birds. The grassland, he felt, would be full of the stirring anew of the close-bound life, the undrowned insects clicking as they dried out, the snakes slithering down, heads half erect, into the grasses where the mice, gophers and ground squirrels ran and stopped and chewed and licked themselves smoother and drier.

With the aid of this hunger, and on the crutches of his wings, Hook came down to stand in the sun beside his cave, whence he could watch the beach. Before him, in ellipses on tilting planes, the gulls flew. The surf was rearing again, and beginning to shelve and hiss on the sand. Through the white foam-writing it left, the long-billed pipers twinkled in bevies, escaping each wave, then racing down after it to plunge their fine drills into the minute double holes where the sand crabs bubbled. In the third row of breakers two seals lifted sleek, streaming heads and barked, and over them, trailing his spider legs, a great crane flew south. Among the stones at the foot of the cliff, small red and green crabs made a little, continuous rattling and knocking. The cliff swallows glittered and twanged on aerial forays.

The afternoon began auspiciously for Hook also. One of the two gulls which came squabbling above him dropped a freshly caught fish to the sand. Quickly Hook was upon it. Gripping it, he raised his good wing and cocked his head with open beak at the many gulls which had circled and come down at once toward the fall of the fish. The gulls sheered off, cursing raucously. Left alone on the sand, Hook devoured the fish and, after resting in the sun, withdrew again to his shelter.

4

In the succeeding days, between rains, he foraged on the beach. He learned to kill and crack the small green crabs. Along the edge of the river mouth, he found the drowned bodies of mice and squirrels and even sparrows. Twice he managed to drive feeding gulls from their catch, charging upon them with buffeting wing and clattering beak. He grew stronger slowly, but the shot sail continued to drag. Often, at the choking thought of soaring and striking and the good, hot-blood kill, he strove to take off, but only the one wing came up, winnowing with a hiss, and drove him over onto his side in the sand. After these futile trials, he would rage and clatter. But gradually he learned to believe that he could not fly, that his life must now be that of the discharged nestling again. Denied the joy of space, without which the joy of loneliness was lost, the joy of battle and killing, the blood lust, became his whole concentration. It was his hope, as he charged feeding gulls, that they would turn and offer battle, but they never did. The sandpipers, at his approach, fled peeping, or, like a quiver of arrows shot together, streamed out over the surf in a long curve. Once, pent beyond bearing, he disgraced himself by shrieking challenge at the businesslike heron which flew south every evening at the same time. The heron did not even turn his head, but flapped and glided on.

Hook's shame and anger became such that he stood awake at night. Hunger kept him awake also, for these little leavings of the gulls could not sustain his great body in its renewed violence. He became aware that the gulls slept at night in flocks on the sand, each with one leg tucked under him. He discovered also that the curlews and the pipers, often mingling, likewise slept, on the higher remnant of the bar. A sensation of evil delight filled him in the consideration of protracted striking among them.

There was only half of a sick moon in a sky of running but far-separated clouds on the night when he managed to stalk into the center of the sleeping gulls. This was light enough, but so great was his vengeful pleasure that there broke from him a shrill scream of challenge as he first struck. Without the power of flight behind it, the blow was not murderous, and this newly discovered impotence made Hook crazy, so that he screamed again and again as he struck and tore at the felled gull. He slew the one, but was twice knocked over by its heavy flounderings, and all the others rose above him, weaving and screaming, protesting in the thin moonlight. Wakened by their clamor, the wading birds also took wing, startled and plaintive. When the beach was quiet again, the flocks had settled elsewhere, beyond his pitiful range, and he was left alone beside the single kill. It was a disappointing victory. He fed with lowering spirit.

Thereafter, he stalked silently. At sunset he would watch where the gulls settled along the miles of beach, and after dark he would come like a sharp shadow among them, and drive with his hook on all sides of him, till the beatings of a poorly struck victim sent the flock up. Then he would turn vindictively upon the fallen and finish them. In his best night, he killed five from one flock. But he ate only a little from one, for the vigor resulting from occasional repletion strengthened only his ire, which became so great at such a time that food revolted him. It was not the joyous, swift, controlled hunting anger of a sane hawk, but something quite different, which made him dizzy if it continued too long, and left him unsatisfied with any kill.

Then one day, when he had very nearly struck a gull while driving it from a gasping yellowfin, the gull's wing rapped against him as it broke for its running start, and, the trailing wing failing to support him, he was knocked over. He flurried awkwardly in the sand to regain his feet, but his mastery of the beach was ended. Seeing him, in clear sunlight, struggling after the chance blow, the gulls returned about him in a flashing cloud, circling and pecking on the wing. Hook's plumage showed quick little jets of irregularity here and there. He reared back, clattering and erecting the good wing, spreading the great, rusty tail for balance. His eyes shone with a little of the old pleasure. But it died, for he could reach none of them. He was forced to turn and dance awkwardly on the sand, trying to clash bills with each tormentor. They banked up quealing and returned, weaving about him in concentric and overlapping circles. His scream was lost in their clamor, and he appeared merely to be hopping clumsily with his mouth open. Again he fell sideways. Before he could right himself, he was bowled over, and a second time, and lay on his side, twisting his neck to reach them and clappering in blind fury, and was struck three times by three successive gulls, shrieking their flock triumph.

Finally he managed to roll to his breast, and to crouch with his good wing spread wide and the other stretched nearly as far, so that he extended like a gigantic moth, only his snake head, with its now silent scimitar, erect. One great eye blazed under its level brow, but where the other had been was a shallow hole from which thin blood trickled to his russet gap.

In this crouch, by short stages, stopping repeatedly to turn and drive the gulls up, Hook dragged into the river canyon and under the stiff cover of the bitter-leafed laurel. There the gulls left him, soaring up with great clatter of their valor. Till nearly sunset Hook, broken spirited and enduring his hardening eye socket, heard them celebrating over the waves.

When his will was somewhat replenished, and his empty eye socket had stopped the twitching and vague aching which had forced him often to roll ignominiously to rub it in the dust, Hook ventured from the protective lacings of his thicket. He knew fear again, and the challenge of his remaining eye was once more strident, as in adolescence. He dared not return to the beaches, and with a new, weak hunger, the home hunger, enticing him, made his way by short hunting journeys back to the wild wheat slopes and the crisp oaks. There was in Hook an unwonted sensation now, that of the ever-neighboring possibility of death. This sensation was beginning, after his period as a mad bird on the beach, to solidify him into his last stage of life. When, during his slow homeward passage, the gulls wafted inland over him, watching the earth with curious, miserish eyes, he did not cower, but neither did he challenge, either by opened beak or by raised shoulder. He merely watched carefully, learning his first lessons in observing the world with one eye.

At first the familiar surroundings of the bend in the river and the tree with the dead limb to which he could not ascend, aggravated his humiliation, but in time, forced to live cunningly and half-starved, he lost much of his savage pride. At the first flight of a strange hawk over his realm, he was wild at his helplessness, and kept twisting his head like an owl, or spinning in the grass like a small and feathered dervish, to keep the hateful beauty of the wind-rider in sight. But in the succeeding weeks, as one after another coasted his beat, his resent-ment declined, and when one of the raiders, a haughty yearling, sighted his up-staring eye, and plunged and struck him dreadfully, and failed to kill him only be-cause he dragged under a thicket in time, the second of his great hungers was gone. He had no longer the true lust to kill, no joy of battle, but only the poor desire to fill his belly.

Then truly he lived in the wheat and the brush like a ground owl, ridden with ground lice, dusty or muddy, ever half-starved, forced to sit for hours by small holes for petty and unsatisfying kills. Only once during the final months before his end did he make a kill where the breath of danger recalled his valor, and then the danger was such as a hawk with wings and eyes would scorn. Waiting beside a gopher hole, surrounded by the high, yellow grass, he saw the head emerge, and struck, and was amazed that there writhed in his clutch the neck and dusty coffin-skull of a rattlesnake. Holding his grip, Hook saw the great, thick body slither up after, the tip an erect, strident blur, and writhe on the dirt of the gopher's mound. The weight of the snake pushed Hook about, and once threw him down, and the rising and falling whine of the rattles made the moment terrible, but the vaulted mouth, gaping from the closeness of Hook's gripe, so that the pale, envenomed sabers stood out free, could not reach him. When Hook replaced the grip of his beak with the grip of his talons, and was free to strike again and again at the base of the head, the struggle was over. Hook tore and fed on the fine, watery flesh, and left the tattered armor and the long, jointed bone for the marching ants.

When the heavy rains returned, he ate well during the period of the first escapes from flooded burrows, and then well enough, in a vulture's way, on the drowned creatures. But as the rains lingered, and the burrows hung full of water, and there were no insects in the grass and no small birds sleeping in the thickets, he was constantly hungry, and finally unbearably hungry. His sodden and ground-broken plumage stood out raggedly about him, so that he looked fat, even bloated, but underneath it his skin clung to his bones. Save for his great talons and clappers, and the rain in his down, he would have been like a handful of air. He often stood for a long time under some bush or ledge, heedless of the drip, his one eye filmed over, his mind neither asleep or awake, but between. The gurgle and swirl of the brimming river, and the sound of chunks of the bank cut away to splash and dissolve in the already muddy flood, became familiar to him, and yet a torment, as if that great, ceaselessly working power of water ridiculed his frailty, within which only the faintest spark of valor still glimmered. The last two nights before the rain ended, he huddled under the floor of the bridge on the coastal highway, and heard the palpitant thunder of motors swell and roar over him. The trucks shook the bridge so that Hook, even in his famished lassitude, would sometimes open his one great eye wide and startled.

5

After the rains, when things became full again, bursting with growth and sound, the trees swelling, the thickets full of song and chatter, the fields, turning green in the sun, alive with rustling passages, and the moonlit nights strained with the song of the peepers all up and down the river and in the pools in the fields, Hook had to bear the return of the one hunger left him. At times this made him so wild that he forgot himself and screamed challenge from the open ground. The fretfulness of it spoiled his hunting, which was now entirely a matter of patience. Once he was in despair, and lashed himself through the grass and thickets, trying to rise when that virgin scent drifted for a few moments above the current of his own river. Then, breathless, his beak agape, he saw the strong suitor ride swiftly down on the wind over him, and heard afar the screaming fuss of the harsh wooing in the alders. For that moment even the battle heart beat in him again. The rim of his good eye was scarlet, and a little bead of new blood stood in the socket of the other. With beak and talon, he ripped at a fallen log, and made loam and leaves fly from about it.

But the season of love passed over to the nesting season, and Hook's love hunger, unused, shriveled in him with the others, and there remained in him only one stern quality befitting a hawk, and that the negative one, the remnant, the will to endure. He resumed his patient, plotted hunting, now along a field of the Japanese farmer, but ever within reach of the river thickets.

Growing tough and dry again as the summer advanced, inured to the family of the farmer, whom he saw daily, stooping and scraping with sticks in the ugly, open rows of their fields, where no lovely grass rustled and no life stirred save the shameless gulls, which walked at the heels of the workers, gobbling the worms and grubs they turned up, Hook became nearly content with his shard of life. The only longing or resentment to pierce him was that which he suffered occasionally when forced to hide at the edge of the mile-long bean field from the wafted cruising and the restive, down-bent gaze of one of his own kind. For the rest, he was without flame, a snappish, dust-colored creature, fading into the grasses he trailed through, and suited to his petty ways.

At the end of that summer, for the second time in his four years, Hook underwent a drouth. The equinoctial period passed without a rain. The laurel and the rabbitbrush dropped dry leaves. The foliage of the oaks shriveled and curled. Even the night fogs in the river canyon failed. The farmer's red cattle on the hillside lowed constantly, and could not feed on the dusty stubble. Grass fires broke out along the highway, and ate fast in the wind, filling the hollows with the smell of smoke, and died in the dirt of the shorn hills. The river made

no sound. Scum grew on its vestigal pools, and turtles
died and stank among the rocks. The dust rode before
the wind, and ascended and flowered to nothing between the hills, and every sunset was red with the dust
in the air. The people in the farmer's house quarreled,
and even struck one another. Birds were silent, and only
the hawks flew much. The animals lay breathing hard
for very long spells, and ran and crept jerkily. Their
flanks were fallen in, and their eyes were red.

At first Hook gorged at the fringe of the grass fires on
the multitudes of tiny things that came running and
squeaking. But thereafter there were the blackened
strips on the hills, and little more in the thin, crackling
grass. He found mice and rats, gophers and ground-
squirrels, and even rabbits, dead in the stubble and
under the thickets, but so dry and fleshless that only a
faint smell rose from them, even on the sunny days. He
starved on them. By early December he had wearily
stalked the length of the eastern foothills, hunting at
night to escape the voracity of his own kind, resting
often upon his wings. The queer trail of his short steps
and great horned toes zigzagged in the dust and was
erased by the wind at dawn. He was nearly dead, and
could make no sound through the horn funnels of his
clappers.

Then one night the dry wind brought him, with the
familiar, lifeless dust, another familiar scent, trouble-
some, mingled and unclear. In his vision-dominated
brain he remembered the swift circle of his flight a year
past, crossing in one segment, his shadow beneath him,
a yard cluttered with crates and chickens, a gray barn
and then again the plowed land and the stubble. Travel-

ing faster than he had for days, impatient of his shrunken sweep, Hook came down to the farm. In the dark wisps of cloud blown among the stars over him, but no moon, he stood outside the wire of the chicken run. The scent of fat and blooded birds reached him from the shelter, and also within the enclosure was water. At the breath of the water, Hook's gorge contracted, and his tongue quivered and clove in its groove of horn. But there was the wire. He stalked its perimeter and found no opening. He beat it with his good wing, and felt it cut but not give. He wrenched at it with his beak in many places, but could not tear it. Finally, in a fury which drove the thin blood through him, he leaped repeatedly against it, beating and clawing. He was thrown back from the last leap as from the first, but in it he had risen so high as to clutch with his beak at the top wire. While he lay on his breast on the ground, the significance of this came upon him.

Again he leapt, clawed up the wire, and, as he would have fallen, made even the dead wing bear a little. He grasped the top and tumbled within. There again he rested flat, searching the dark with quick-turning head. There was no sound or motion but the throb of his own body. First he drank at the chill metal trough hung for the chickens. The water was cold, and loosened his tongue and his tight throat, but it also made him drunk and dizzy, so that he had to rest again, his claws spread wide to brace him. Then he walked stiffly, to stalk down the scent. He trailed it up the runway. Then there was the stuffy, body-warm air, acrid with droppings, full of soft rustlings as his talons clicked on the board floor. The thick, white shapes showed faintly in the darkness.

Hook struck quickly, driving a hen to the floor with one blow, its neck broken and stretched out stringily. He leaped the still pulsing body, and tore it. The rich, streaming blood was overpowering to his dried senses, his starved, leathery body. After a few swallows, the flesh choked him. In his rage, he struck down another hen. The urge to kill took him again, as in those nights on the beach. He could let nothing go. Balked of feeding, he was compelled to slaughter. Clattering, he struck again and again. The henhouse was suddenly filled with the squawking and helpless rushing and buffeting of the terrified, brainless fowls.

Hook reveled in mastery. Here was game big enough to offer weight against a strike, and yet unable to soar away from his blows. Turning in the midst of the turmoil, cannily, his fury caught at the perfect pitch, he struck unceasingly. When the hens finally discovered the outlet, and streamed into the yard, to run around the fence, beating and squawking, Hook followed them, scraping down the incline, clumsy and joyous. In the yard, the cock, a bird as large as he, and much heavier, found him out and gave valiant battle. In the dark, and both earthbound, there was little skill, but blow upon blow, and only chance parry. The still squawking hens pressed into one corner of the yard. While the duel went on, a dog, excited by the sustained scuffling, began to bark. He continued to bark, running back and forth along the fence on one side. A light flashed on in an uncurtained window of the farmhouse, and streamed whitely over the crates littering the ground.

Enthralled by his old battle joy, Hook knew only the burly cock before him. Now, in the farthest reach of the window light, they could see each other dimly. The Japanese farmer, with his gun and lantern, was already at the gate when the finish came. The great cock leapt to jab with his spurs and, toppling forward with extended neck as he fell, was struck and extinguished. Blood had loosened Hook's throat. Shrilly he cried his triumph. It was a thin and exhausted cry, but within him as good as when he shrilled in mid-air over the plummeting descent of a fine foe in his best spring.

The light from the lantern partially blinded Hook. He first turned and ran directly from it, into the corner where the hens were huddled. They fled apart before his charge. He essayed the fence, and on the second try, in his desperation, was out. But in the open dust, the dog was on him, circling, dashing in, snapping. The farmer, who at first had not fired because of the chickens, now did not fire because of the dog, and, when he saw that the hawk was unable to fly, relinquished the sport to the dog, holding the lantern up in order to see better. The light showed his own flat, broad, dark face as sunken also, the cheekbones very prominent, and showed the torn-off sleeves of his shirt and the holes in the knees of his overalls. His wife, in a stained wrapper, and barefooted, heavy black hair hanging around a young, passionless face, joined him hesitantly, but watched, fascinated and a little horrified. His son joined them too, encouraging the dog, but quickly grew silent. Courageous and cruel death, however it may afterward sicken the one who has watched it, is impossible to look away from.

In the circle of the light, Hook turned to keep the dog in front of him. His one eye gleamed with malevo-

lence. The dog was an Airedale, and large. Each time
he pounced, Hook stood ground, raising his good wing,
the pinions newly torn by the fence, opening his beak
soundlessly, and, at the closest approach, hissed furiously, and at once struck. Hit and ripped twice by the
whetted horn, the dog recoiled more quickly from several subsequent jumps and, infuriated by his own cowardice, began to bark wildly. Hook maneuvered to watch
him, keeping his head turned to avoid losing the foe
on the blind side. When the dog paused, safely away,
Hook watched him quietly, wing partially lowered,
beak closed, but at the first move again lifted the wing
and gaped. The dog whined, and the man spoke to him
encouragingly. The awful sound of his voice made Hook
for an instant twist his head to stare up at the immense
figures behind the light. The dog again sallied, barking,
and Hook's head spun back. His wing was bitten this
time, and with a furious side-blow, he caught the dog's
nose. The dog dropped him with a yelp, and then,
smarting, came on more warily, as Hook propped himself up from the ground again between his wings.
Hook's artificial strength was waning, but his heart still
stood to the battle, sustained by a fear of such dimension
as he had never known before, but only anticipated
when the arrogant young hawk had driven him to cover.
The dog, unable to find any point at which the merci-
less, unwinking eye was not watching him, the parted
beak waiting, paused and whimpered again.

"Oh, kill the poor thing," the woman begged.

The man, though, encouraged the dog again, saying,
"Sick him; sick him."

The dog rushed bodily. Unable to avoid him, Hook

was bowled down, snapping and raking. He left long slashes, as from the blade of a knife, on the dog's flank, but before he could right himself and assume guard again, was caught by the good wing and dragged, clattering, and seeking to make a good stroke from his back. The man followed them to keep the light on them, and the boy went with him, wetting his lips with his tongue and keeping his fists closed tightly. The woman remained behind, but could not help watching the diminished conclusion.

In the little, palely shining arena, the dog repeated his successful maneuver three times, growling but not barking, and when Hook thrashed up from the third blow, both wings were trailing, and dark, shining streams crept on his black-fretted breast from the shoulders. The great eye flashed more furiously than it ever had in victorious battle, and the beak still gaped, but there was no more clatter. He faltered when turning to keep front; the broken wings played him false even as props. He could not rise to use his talons.

The man had tired of holding the lantern up, and put it down to rub his arm. In the low, horizontal light, the dog charged again, this time throwing the weight of his forepaws against Hook's shoulder, so that Hook was crushed as he struck. With his talons up, Hook raked at the dog's belly, but the dog conceived the finish, and furiously worried the feathered bulk. Hook's neck went limp, and between his gaping clappers came only a faint chittering, as from some small kill of his own in the grasses.

In this last conflict, however, there had been some

minutes of the supreme fire of the hawk whose three hungers are perfectly fused in the one will; enough to burn off a year of shame.

Between the great sails the light body lay caved and perfectly still. The dog, smarting from his cuts, came to the master and was praised. The woman, joining them slowly, looked at the great wingspread, her husband raising the lantern that she might see it better.

"Oh, the brave bird," she said.

The Wind and the

Snow of Winter

IT WAS near sunset when Mike Braneen came onto the last pitch of the old wagon road which had led into Gold Rock from the east since the Comstock days. The road was just two ruts in the hard earth, with sagebrush growing between them, and was full of steep pitches and sharp turns. From the summit it descended even more steeply into Gold Rock, in a series of short switchbacks down the slope of the canyon. There was a paved highway on the other side of the pass now, but Mike never used that. Cars coming from behind made him uneasy, so that he couldn't follow his own thoughts long, but had to keep turning around every few minutes, to see that his burro, Annie, was staying out on the shoulder of the road, where she would be safe. Mike didn't like cars anyway, and on the old road he could forget about them, and feel more like himself. He could forget about Annie too, except when the light, quick tapping of her hoofs behind him stopped. Even then he didn't really break his thoughts. It was more as if the tapping were another sound from his own inner machinery, and when it stopped, he stopped too, and turned around to see what she was doing. When he began to walk ahead again at the same slow, unvarying

pace, his arms scarcely swinging at all, his body bent a
little forward from the waist, he would not be aware
that there had been any interruption of the memory or
the story that was going on in his head. Mike did not
like to have his stories interrupted except by an idea of
his own, something to do with his prospecting, or the
arrival of his story at an actual memory which warmed
him to close recollection or led into a new and more
attractive story.

An intense, golden light, almost liquid, fanned out
from the peaks above him and reached eastward under
the gray sky, and the snow which occasionally swarmed
across this light was fine and dry. Such little squalls had
been going on all day, and still there was nothing like
real snow down, but only a fine powder which the wind
swept along until it caught under the brush, leaving the
ground bare. Yet Mike Braneen was not deceived. This
was not just a flurrying day; it was the beginning of
winter. If not tonight, then tomorrow, or the next day,
the snow would begin which shut off the mountains, so
that a man might as well be on a great plain for all he
could see, perhaps even the snow which blinded a man
at once and blanketed the desert in an hour. Fifty-two
years in this country had made Mike Braneen sure
about such things, although he didn't give much
thought to them, but only to what he had to do because
of them. Three nights before, he had been awakened by
a change in the wind. It was no longer a wind born in
the near mountains, cold with night and altitude, but a
wind from far places, full of a damp chill which got
through his blankets and into his bones. The stars had
still been clear and close above the dark humps of the

mountains, and overhead the constellations had moved slowly in full panoply, unbroken by any invisible lower darkness, yet he had lain there half awake for a few minutes, hearing the new wind beat the brush around him, hearing Annie stirring restlessly and thumping in her hobble. He had thought drowsily, "Smells like winter this time," and then, "It's held off a long time this year, pretty near the end of December." Then he had gone back to sleep, mildly happy because the change meant he would be going back to Gold Rock. Gold Rock was the other half of Mike Braneen's life. When the smell of winter came, he always started back for Gold Rock. From March or April until the smell of winter, he wandered slowly about among the mountains, anywhere between the White Pines and the Virginias, with only his burro for company. Then there would come the change, and they would head back for Gold Rock.

Mike had traveled with a good many burros during that time, eighteen or twenty, he thought, although he was not sure. He could not remember them all, but only those he had had first, when he was a young man and always thought most about seeing women when he got back to Gold Rock, or those with something queer about them, like Baldy, who'd had a great, pale patch, like a bald spot, on one side of his belly, or those who'd had something queer happen to them, like Maria. He could remember just how it had been that night. He could remember it as if it were last night. It had been in Hamilton. He had felt unhappy, because he could remember Hamilton when the whole hollow was full of people and buildings, and everything was new and active. He had gone to sleep in the empty shell of the Wells Fargo Building, hearing an old, iron shutter banging against the wall in the wind. In the morning, Maria had been gone. He had followed the scuffing track she made on account of her loose hobble, and it had led far up the old, snow-gullied road to Treasure Hill, and then ended at one of the black shafts that opened like mouths right at the edge of the road. A man remembered a thing like that. There weren't many burros that foolish. But burros with nothing particular about them were hard to remember, especially those he'd had in the last twenty years or so, when he had gradually stopped feeling so personal about them, and had begun to call all the jennies Annie and all the burros Jack.

The clicking of the little hoofs behind him stopped, and Mike stopped too, and turned around. Annie was pulling at a line of yellow grass along the edge of the road.

"Come on, Maria," Mike said, patiently. The burro at once stopped pulling at the dead grass and came on up toward him, her small, black nose working, the ends of the grass standing out on each side of it like whiskers. Mike began to climb again, ahead of her.

It was a long time since he had been caught by a winter, too. He could not remember how long. All the beginnings ran together in his mind, as if they were all the beginning of one winter so far back that he had almost forgotten it. He could still remember clearly, though, the winter he had stayed out on purpose, clear into January. He had been a young man then, thirty-five or forty or forty-five, somewhere in there. He would have to stop and try to bring back a whole string of memories about what had happened just before, in order to remember just how old he had been, and it wasn't worth the trouble. Besides, sometimes even that system didn't work. It would lead him into an old camp where he had been a number of times, and the dates would get mixed up. It was impossible to remember any other way, because all his comings and goings had been so much alike. He had been young, anyhow, and not much afraid of anything except running out of water in the wrong place; not even afraid of winter. He had stayed out because he'd thought he had a good thing, and he had wanted to prove it. He could remember how it felt to be out in the clear winter weather on the mountains, the pinon trees and the junipers weighted down with feathery snow, and making sharp, blue shadows on the white slopes. The hills had made blue shadows on one another too, and in the still air his pick had made the beginning of a sound like a bell's. He knew he had been young, because he could remember taking a day off now and then, just to go tramping around those hills, up and down the white and through the blue shadows, on a kind of holiday. He had pretended to his common sense that he was seriously prospecting, and had carried his hammer, and even his drill along, but he had really just been gallavanting, playing colt. Maybe he had been even younger than thirty-five, though he could still be stirred a little, for that matter, by the memory of the kind of weather which had sent him gallavanting. High-blue weather, he called it. There were two kinds of high-blue weather, besides the winter kind, which didn't set him off very often, spring and fall.

In the spring it would have a soft, puffy wind and soft, puffy white clouds which made separate shadows that traveled silently across hills that looked soft too. In the fall it would be still, and there would be no clouds at all in the blue, but there would be something in the golden air and the soft, steady sunlight on the mountains, that made a man as uneasy as the spring blowing, though in a different way, more sad and not so excited. In the spring high-blue a man had been likely to think about women he had slept with, or wanted to sleep with, or imaginary women made up with the help of newspaper pictures of actresses or young society matrons, or of the old oil paintings in the Lucky Boy Saloon, which showed pale, almost naked women against dark, sumptuous backgrounds, women with long hair or braided hair, calm, virtuous faces, small hands and feet and ponderous limbs, breasts and buttocks. In the fall high-blue, though it had been much longer since he had seen a woman or heard a woman's voice, he was more likely to think about old friends, men, or places he had heard about, or places he hadn't seen for a long time. He himself thought most often about Goldfield the way he had last seen it in the summer in nineteen-twelve. That was as far south as Mike had ever been in Nevada. Since then, he had never been south of Tonopah. When the high-blue weather was past, though, and the season worked toward winter, he began to think about Gold Rock. There were only three or four winters out of the fifty-two when he hadn't gone home to Gold Rock, to his old room at Mrs. Wright's, up on Fourth Street, and to his meals in the dining room at the International House, and to the Lucky Boy, where he could talk to

Tom Connover and his other friends, and play cards, or have a drink to hold in his hand while he sat and remembered.

This journey had seemed a little different from most, though. It had started the same as usual, but as he had come across the two vast valleys, and through the pass in the low range between them, he hadn't felt quite the same. He'd felt younger and more awake, it seemed to him, and yet, in a way, older too, suddenly older. He had been sure that there was plenty of time, and yet he had been a little afraid of getting caught in the storm. He had kept looking ahead to see if the mountains on the horizon were still clearly outlined, or if they had been cut off by a lowering of the clouds. He had thought more than once, how bad it would be to get caught out there when the real snow began, and he had been disturbed by the first flakes. It had seemed hard to him to have to walk so far, too. He had kept thinking about distance. Also the snowy cold had searched out the regions of his body where old injuries had healed. He had taken off his left mitten a good many times, to blow on the fingers which had been frosted the year he was sixty-three, so that now it didn't take much cold to turn them white and stiffen them. The queer tingling, partly like an itch and partly like a pain, in the patch of his back that had been burned in that old powder blast, was sharper than he could remember its ever having been before. The rheumatism in his joints, which was so old a companion that it usually made him feel no more than tight-knit and stiff, and the place where his leg had been broken and torn when that ladder broke in ninety-seven, ached, and had a pulse he could count. All of this made him believe that he was walking more slowly than usual, although nothing, probably not even a deliberate attempt, could actually have changed his pace. Sometimes he even thought, with a moment of fear, that he was getting tired.

On the other hand, he felt unusually clear and strong in his mind. He remembered things with a clarity which was like living them again, nearly all of them events from many years back, from the time when he had been really active and fearless and every burro had had its own name. Some of these events, like the night he had spent in Eureka with the little, brown-haired whore, a night in the fall in eighteen eighty-eight or nine, somewhere in there, he had not once thought of for years. Now he could remember even her name. Armandy she had called herself; a funny name. They all picked names for their business, of course, romantic names like Cecily or Rosamunde or Belle or Claire, or hard names like Diamond Gert or Horseshoe Sal, or names that were pinned on them, like Indian Kate or Roman Mary, but Armandy was different.

He could remember Armandy as if he were with her now, not the way she had behaved in bed; he couldn't remember anything particular about that. In fact he couldn't be sure that he remembered anything about that at all. There were others he could remember more clearly for the way they had behaved in bed, women he had been with more often. He had been with Armandy only one night. He remembered little things about being with her, things that made it seem good to think of being with her again. Armandy had a room upstairs in a hotel. They could hear a piano playing in a club across the street. He could hear the tune, and it was one he knew, although he didn't know its name. It was a gay tune that went on and on the same, but still it sounded sad when you heard it through the hotel window, with the lights from the bars and hotels shining on the street, and the people coming and going through the lights, and then, beyond the lights, the darkness where the mountains were. Armandy wore a white silk dress with a high waist, and a locket on a gold chain. The dress made her look very brown and like a young girl. She used a white powder on her face that smelled of violets, but this could not hide her brownness. The locket was heart-shaped, and it opened to show a cameo of a man's hand holding a woman's hand very gently, their fingers laid out long together, and just the thumbs holding, the way they were sometimes on tombstones. There were two little gold initials on each hand, but Armandy wouldn't tell what they stood for, or even if the locket was really her own. He stood in the window, looking down at the club from which the piano music was coming, and Armandy stood beside him, with her shoulder against his arm, and a glass of wine in her hand. He could see the toe of her white satin slipper showing from under the edge of her skirt. Her big hat, loaded with black and white plumes, lay on the dresser behind them. His own leather coat, with the sheepskin lining, lay across the foot of the bed. It was a big bed, with a knobby brass foot and head. There was one oil lamp burning in the chandelier in the middle of the room. Armandy was soft spoken, gentle and a little fearful, always looking at him to see what he was thinking. He stood with his arms folded. His arms felt big and strong

upon his heavily muscled chest. He stood there, pretending to be in no hurry, but really thinking eagerly
about what he would do with Armandy, who had something about her which tempted him to be cruel. He
stood there, with his chin down into his heavy, dark
beard, and watched a man come riding down the middle
of the street from the west. The horse was a fine black,
which lifted its head and feet with pride. The man sat
very straight, with a high rein, and something about
his clothes and hat made him appear to be in uniform,
although it wasn't a uniform he was wearing. The man
also saluted friends upon the sidewalks like an officer,
bending his head just slightly, and touching his hat
instead of lifting it. Mike Braneen asked Armandy who
the man was, and then felt angry because she could tell
him, and because he was an important man who owned
a mine that was in bonanza. He mocked the airs with
which the man rode, and his princely greetings. He
mocked the man cleverly, and Armandy laughed and
repeated what he said, and made him drink a little of
her wine as a reward. Mike had been drinking whisky,
and he did not like wine anyway, but this was not the
moment in which to refuse such an invitation.

Old Mike remembered all this, which had been completely forgotten for years. He could not remember what
he and Armandy had said, but he remembered everything else, and he felt very lonesome for Armandy, and
for the room with the red, figured carpet and the brass
chandelier with oil lamps in it, and the open window
with the long tune coming up through it, and the young
summer night outside on the mountains. This loneliness
was so much more intense than his familiar loneliness

that it made him feel very young. Memories like this had come up again and again during these three days. It was like beginning life over again. It had tricked him into thinking, more than once, "Next summer I'll make the strike, and this time I'll put it into something safe for the rest of my life, and stop this fool wandering around while I've still got some time left," a way of thinking which he had really stopped a long time before.

It was getting darker rapidly in the pass. When a gust of wind brought the snow against Mike's face so hard that he noticed the flakes felt larger, he looked up. The light was still there, although the fire was dying out of it, and the snow swarmed across it more thickly. Mike remembered God. He did not think anything exact. He did not think about his own relationship to God. He merely felt the idea as a comforting presence. He'd always had a feeling about God whenever he looked at a sunset, especially a sunset which came through under a stormy sky. It had been the strongest feeling left in him until these memories like the one about Armandy had begun. Even in this last pass, his strange fear of the storm had come on him again a couple of times, but now that he had looked at the light and thought of God, it was gone. In a few minutes he would come to the summit and look down into his lighted city. He felt happily hurried by this anticipation.

He would take the burro down and stable her in John Hammersmith's shed, where he always kept her. He would spread fresh straw for her, and see that the shed was tight against the wind and snow, and get a measure of grain for her from John. Then he would go

up to Mrs. Wright's house at the top of Fourth Street,
and leave his things in the same room he always had, the
one in front, which looked down over the roofs and
chimneys of his city, and across at the east wall of the
canyon, from which the sun rose late. He would trim
his beard with Mrs. Wright's shears, and shave the
upper part of his cheeks. He would bathe out of the blue
bowl and pitcher, and wipe himself with the towel with
yellow flowers on it, and dress in the good, dark suit and
the good, black shoes with the gleaming box toes, and
the good, black hat which he had left in the chest in
his room. In this way he would perform the ceremony
which ended the life of the desert and began the life of
Gold Rock. Then he would go down to the International House, and greet Arthur Morris in the gleaming
bar, and go into the dining room and eat the best supper
they had, with fresh meat and vegetables, and new-made
pie, and two cups of hot, clear coffee. He would be served
by the plump, blonde waitress who always joked with
him, and gave him many little extra things with his first
supper, including the drink which Arthur Morris always sent in from the bar.

At this point Mike Braneen stumbled in his mind,
and his anticipation wavered. He could not be sure that
the plump, blonde waitress would serve him. For a moment he saw her in a long skirt, and the dining room of
the International House, behind her, had potted palms
standing in the corners, and was full of the laughter and
loud, manly talk of many customers who wore high
vests and moustaches and beards. These men leaned
back from tables covered with empty dishes. They
patted their tight vests and lighted expensive cigars. He
knew all their faces. If he were to walk down the aisle

between the tables on his side, they would all speak to him. But he also seemed to remember the dining room with only a few tables, with oil cloth on them instead of linen, and with moody young men sitting at them in their work clothes, strangers who worked for the highway department or were just passing through, or talked mining in terms which he did not understand or which made him angry.

No, it would not be the plump, blonde waitress. He did not know who it would be. It didn't matter. After supper he would go up Canyon Street under the arcade to the Lucky Boy Saloon, and there it would be the same as ever. There would be the laurel wreaths on the frosted-glass panels of the doors, and the old sign upon the window, the sign that was older than Tom Connover, almost as old as Mike Braneen himself. He would open the door and see the bottles and the white women in the paintings, and the card tables in the back corner and the big stove and the chairs along the wall. Tom would look around from his place behind the bar.

"Well, now," he would roar, "look who's here, boys. Now will you believe it's winter?" he would roar at them.

Some of them would be the younger men, of course, and there might even be a few strangers, but this would only add to the dignity of his reception, and there would also be his friends. There would be Henry Bray with the gray walrus moustache, and Mark Wilton and Pat Gallagher. They would all welcome him loudly.

"Mike, how are you, anyway?" Tom would roar, leaning across the bar to shake hands with his big, heavy, soft hand with the diamond ring on it.

"And what'll it be, Mike? The same?" he'd ask, as if

Mike had been in there no longer ago than the night before.

Mike would play that game too. "The same," he would say.

Then he would really be back in Gold Rock; never mind the plump, blonde waitress.

Mike came to the summit of the old road and stopped and looked down. For a moment he felt lost again, as he had when he'd thought about the plump, blonde waitress. He had expected Canyon Street to look much brighter. He had expected a lot of orange windows close together on the other side of the canyon. Instead there were only a few scattered lights across the darkness, and they were white. They made no communal glow upon the steep slope, but gave out only single, white needles of light, which pierced the darkness secretly and lonesomely, as if nothing could ever pass from one house to another over there. Canyon Street was very dark too. There it went, the street he loved, steeply down into the bottom of the canyon, and down its length there were only the few street lights, more than a block apart, swinging in the wind and darting about that cold, small light. The snow whirled and swooped under the nearest street light below.

"You are getting to be an old fool," Mike Braneen said out loud to himself, and felt better. This was the way Gold Rock was now, of course, and he loved it all the better. It was a place that grew old with a man, that was going to die some time too. There could be an understanding with it.

He worked his way slowly down into Canyon Street, with Annie slipping and checking behind him. Slowly, with the blown snow behind them, they came to the first built-up block, and passed the first dim light showing through a smudged window under the arcade. They passed the dark places after it, too, and the second light. Then Mike Braneen stopped in the middle of the street, and Annie stopped beside him, pulling her rump in and turning her head away from the snow. A highway truck, coming down from the head of the canyon, had to get way over onto the wrong side of the street to pass them. The driver leaned out as he went by, and yelled, "Pull over, Pop. You're in town now."

Mike Braneen didn't hear him. He was staring at the Lucky Boy. The Lucky Boy was dark, and there were boards nailed across the big window that had shown the sign. At last Mike went over onto the board walk to look more closely. Annie followed him, but stopped at the edge of the walk and scratched her neck against a post of the arcade. There was the other sign, hanging crossways under the arcade, and even in that gloom Mike could see that it said Lucky Boy and had a Jack of Diamonds painted on it. There was no mistake. The Lucky Boy sign, and others like it under the arcade, creaked and rattled in the wind.

There were footsteps coming along the boards. The boards sounded hollow, and sometimes one of them rattled. Mike Braneen looked down slowly from the sign and peered at the approaching figure. It was a man wearing a sheepskin coat with the collar turned up around his head. He was walking quickly, like a man who knew where he was going, and why, and where he had been. Mike almost let him pass. Then he spoke.

"Say, fella—"

He even reached out a hand as if to catch hold of the man's sleeve, though he didn't touch it. The man stopped, and asked, impatiently, "Yeah?" and Mike let the hand down again slowly.

"Well, what is it?" the man asked.

"I don't want anything," Mike said. "I got plenty."

"O.K., O.K.," the man said. "What's the matter?"

Mike moved his hand toward the Lucky Boy. "It's closed," he said.

"I see it is, Dad," the man said. He laughed a little. He didn't seem to be in quite so much of a hurry now.

"How long has it been closed?" Mike asked.

"Since about June, I guess," the man said. "Old Tom Connover, the guy that ran it, died last June."

Mike waited for a moment. "Tom died?" he asked.

"Yup. I guess he'd just kept it open out of love of the place anyway. There hasn't been any real business for years. Nobody cared to keep it open after him."

The man started to move on, but then he waited, peering, trying to see Mike better.

"This June?" Mike asked finally.

"Yup. This last June."

"Oh," Mike said. Then he just stood there. He wasn't thinking anything. There didn't seem to be anything to think.

"You know him?" the man asked.

"Thirty years," Mike said. "No, more'n that," he said, and started to figure out how long he had known Tom Connover, but lost it, and said, as if it would do just as well, "He was a lot younger than I am, though."

"Hey," said the man, coming closer, and peering again. "You're Mike Braneen, aren't you?"

"Yes," Mike said.

"Gee, I didn't recognize you at first. I'm sorry."

"That's all right," Mike said. He didn't know who the man was, or what he was sorry about.

He turned his head slowly, and looked out into the street. The snow was coming down heavily now. The street was all white. He saw Annie with her head and shoulders in under the arcade, but the snow settling on her rump.

"Well, I guess I'd better get Molly under cover," he said. He moved toward the burro a step, but then halted. "Say, fellow . . ."

The man had started on, but he turned back. He had to wait for Mike to speak.

"I guess this about Tom's mixed me up."

"Sure," the man said. "It's tough, an old friend like that."

"Where do I turn up to get to Mrs. Wright's place?"

"Mrs. Wright's?"

"Mrs. William Wright," Mike said. "Her husband used to be the foreman in the Aztec. Got killed in the fire."

"Oh," the man said. He didn't say anything more, but just stood there, looking at the shadowy bulk of old Mike.

"She's not dead too, is she?" Mike asked slowly.

"Yeah, I'm afraid she is, Mr. Braneen," the man said. "Look," he said more cheerfully. "It's Mrs. Branley's house you want right now, isn't it? Place where you stayed last winter?"

Finally Mike said, "Yeah. Yeah, I guess it is."

"I'm going up that way. I'll walk up with you," the man said.

After they had started, Mike thought that he ought

to take the burro down to John Hammersmith's first,
but he was afraid to ask about it. They walked on down
Canyon Street, with Annie walking along beside them
in the gutter. At the first side street they turned right
and began to climb the steep hill toward another of
the little street lights dancing over a crossing. There
was no sidewalk here, and Annie followed right at their
heels. That one street light was the only light showing
up ahead.

When they were half way up to the light, Mike
asked, "She die this summer too?"

The man turned his body half around, so that he
could hear inside his collar.

"What?"

"Did she die this summer too?"

"Who?"

"Mrs. Wright," Mike said.

The man looked at him, trying to see his face as they
came up toward the light. Then he turned back again,
and his voice was muffled by the collar.

"No, she died quite a while ago, Mr. Braneen."

"Oh," Mike said finally.

They came up onto the crossing under the light, and
the snow-laden wind whirled around them again. They
passed under the light, and their three lengthening
shadows before them were obscured by the innumerable tiny shadows of the flakes.

The Rapids

WHERE THE unpaved road curved over the top of the hill and descended to the river, a man appeared, walking by himself. He was thin, and wore spectacles, and his legs, when they showed through the flapping wings of his red and blue dressing gown, were very white. He carried a towel in one hand. Walking carefully, for his slippers were thin, he came down between the fir trees, then between the alders and the willows, and stood at the edge of the river.

Four terraces of red rock lay diagonally across the river at this point, but they were tilted away from him, so that the heavy water gushed all on the farther side, and narrowed until, from the lowest ledge, it jetted forth in a single head, making a big, back-bellying bubble rimmed with foam in the pool below. Closer to him, eddies from the main stream came over the terraces at intervals, making thin, transparent falls a foot or two high. Swarms of midget flies danced against these falls, keeping just free of the almost invisible mist which blew from them.

Climbing cautiously from the bank to the rocks, the man walked out onto the second terrace, which was the broadest, and had a gentle incline. He bent over and felt of the rock. It was warm with sun. He took off his dressing gown and sat down. Then he fished in the pocket of the gown, drew out a piece of soap, and put it beside the towel. Finally he pulled off his slippers and placed them on the edge of the towel, to hold it down if the wind blew. After this preparation, he sat with his arms around his knees and stared at the running water.

The sun felt good on his back. He wondered if he dared to remove his shorts, but the bridge from his road lay across the river close above him, so he decided not to. Also there was a building on the opposite bank at the point where the river jumped out into the pool. There were only two and a half walls of the building standing, and the windows had been out of those for a long time. Vines grew over the gray-tan stones and into the windows, and nothing was left of the roof. Still, it was a building, four stories high. So he kept on his shorts and sat in the sun and looked at the building, remembering the bit of its history he had heard. It had been a mill, way back toward the days of the Revolution. Since then this part of the country had failed. There were only small, poor farms in it now, and the remnants of villages. It gave him a queer feeling to look through the empty windows and see trees growing inside, and the steep, green bank behind them. The ruin was old for America. He was used to seeing empty mills that weren't ten years old. This one went a long way back.

After a time the draft in the river canyon felt chilly in spite of the sun. The man removed his spectacles with both hands, placed them on his dressing gown, picked up the cake of soap, and approached the nearest of the little falls. Standing beside it, with his feet in the shallow basin of turning water, he shivered before the breath of the river. Timidly he began to wash, laving his forearms and the back of his neck, determinedly splashing a palmful of water over his white chest and belly. Encouraged, he wet himself all over and rubbed on the soap vigorously, ducking his head into the fall and then working up a great lather on it, like a shining white wig. When he was well soaped, he couldn't open his eyes. Feeling for the rim of the fall, he moved gingerly, for the basin was slimy. Having come close enough, he squatted under the fall and let it drive the soap down from him until he could open his eyes and see the iridescent trail of the soap, like an oil mark, draining away from him down the gutter of rock. All of this time he moved his arms as much as he dared, because the water was cold.

Back out in the sun, he realized that he would have to do more. He had been too cramped in the basin, and much of his body was still greasy with soap. He walked carefully down the terrace toward the pool, gripping the stone with his toes, for his wet feet were uncertain. They left a trail of increasingly perfect tracks from the small puddle where he had stood beside his dressing gown to the last print at the edge of the terrace, which showed each toe faintly but distinctly, and the ball, the arch, and the heel—clearly a man's foot.

After hesitating, he let himself down over the edge until the cool water was about his shins. Then he stood on slimy stone like that in the basin. On all fours, he moved slowly, crabwise, along this submerged ledge, and slid off into deeper water. This was at the center of the pool, and the water was quiet, moved only by a side flow circling the pool from the falls, and occasionally by a light wind-ripple along the surface. Awkwardly, and with some splashing, he rubbed himself under water until the last slickness of soap was gone and his hands adhered to his thighs. Then he paddled aimlessly in the pool for a few minutes, treading water and observing himself below. His arms and legs appeared dwarfed and misshapen, his hands and feet immense and square. All of him that was under water looked yellow, and was hairy with particles of the slime he had stirred getting in. Altogether, he was a much more powerful and formidable man, seen through the glass of the pool. He began to feel adventurous.

He noticed that the green darkness of the pool paled on the side across from the ledges. A sub-aqueous, changeable gold was visible there under the black surface reflection of the forest on the hill. He paddled toward it, keeping his head above water and feeling before him with his hands. When he came to rest, balanced on his hands, he was on a sunken sand-bar—the dam which made the pool. The sand was coarse and white, and felt clean to his touch after the scum in the basin and on the ledge. Letting his feet down, he planted them firmly and walked up the incline of the sand-bar, feeling himself emerge into gusty air. At last he was on top, the water ankle-deep. Looking down from this eminence, he saw a boat farther along the ridge of the bar. It lay bottom up, and was so water-logged that it had ground into the sand until no part of it but the very center of the bottom was above water. Now and then a wind-ripple passed over even that.

The man was excited by the discovery. He waded to the boat and attempted to turn it right side up. The vacuum under it, or simply its weight, held it solidly. He was angered, and put forth all his thin might in repeated efforts, standing upright between tries, to breathe deeply and let the blood subside from his head. To the best of his efforts the boat rocked, and straining, he raised the gunwale as far as his knee. This encouraged him, but when he lifted again, the boat came no higher, and then remained passively immovable. He had to let it fall back into the water, where it rolled lightly, splashing around its shape like a stubborn live thing, run aground, but insisting upon its element. The man's feet had been driven down into the sand until he could not lift well from his position. Freeing himself, he climbed onto the crest of the bar again and stood with his legs apart, glaring at the boat. He considered leaving it and relinquishing himself to placid floating in the pool, whence he could eye the useless boat disdainfully. But when the blood in his temples ceased pounding, he had a cunning thought. Moving down into the water until he was on the outer side of the boat, he slid it backwards off the bar. Once it floated free, he could get his shoulder under it. This stratagem succeeded. The boat rolled bulkily over, sending out a wave which broke on the sand-bar.

"That fixes you," the man said aloud.

However, the water in the boat was level with the water in the pool. Only a portion of the prow and of the square stern protruded. The man found that tilting the boat let in as much water as it let out. He laid hold of a chain at the prow and drew the boat onto the crest

of the bar. It followed him with lumbering unwilling-
ness. On the bar, a great deal more of it stood above
water, and by teetering it fore and aft, he drove several
belches of water out over the stern. Still the boat would
not rise. The man climbed into it and began to scoop
with both hands. The water flew in silver sheets, spread
into silver drops, and splattered on the pool, but more
of it fell through his hands than went overboard. He
stood up and looked around. On a flat rock at the west
edge of the pool, there sat a shining two-quart tin can.
He clambered out of the boat, went down into the
water, paddled industriously across, hoisted himself up
the irregular rock steps, and procured the can.

Shortly he had all but an inch or two of water out of
the boat. That persisted because of three little leaks,
through which he could see minute streams gliding
steadily in. He pushed the boat, with the can in it, off
the sand-bar, and kicking noisily, propelled it to shore.
Here he pulled grass and made small wads of it, with
the heads standing up in tufts. These plugged the leaks
quite effectively, and the man began to hum to himself
while he bailed out the last water.

The boat, clumsy and flat-bottomed, with two bowed
planks forming each side, had been battered downstream in the flood of the spring rains. Much of the
orange paint had been beaten from it, and the single
thwart had been torn out, leaving four rusty nails pro-
jecting from each scar. The man searched out a squarish
stone and hammered the nails down, humming more
loudly. He was formulating a daring plan. He would
work the boat around in front of the falls, where the
big bubble bellied, and see how far he could go down

the stony rapids below the pool. A man taking a risk like that couldn't have nails sticking out where they'd rake his legs if he had to move quickly.

At last he drifted on the pool, keeping the can with him. "Quite a boat," he maintained in a clear voice, and then, argumentatively, but with satisfaction, "I say it's quite a boat."

The boat, dull with the water it had soaked up, rode low and heavily. It refused to be coerced by hand paddling, and cruised, half sidewards, out into the middle of the pool, where it spun slowly three times in the circular current and then headed—or rather tailed—for the stagnant backwash between the shore boulders and the terrace of red rock. The man ceased humming and paddled frantically with his hands, first on one side and then on the other, for the boat was too wide for him to reach water on both sides at once. The boat turned completely around once more, and continued to back toward the extremely green scum in the crevice. The man abandoned himself, held onto the sides, and rode in backwards, muttering. The boat bumped gently, grated along the stone, stirred sinuously, and succeeded in wedging itself. The man sat and observed the pond scum with aversion.

Then he saw a long bamboo pole caught under a ledge. His spirits rose. The pole was within reach, and by bruising his knees a little, slithering on the wet mossiness of the boat, he grasped it. It was heavy, and rotten from enduring the river and from its long hiding in the pool, but having it, he felt confident again. "You'll do," he told the pole. He stood erect, and brandished it in both hands, like a cudgel. "Swell pole." He pressed it firmly against the holding rock, and leaned on it. The boat gave way and swam sluggishly out through the scum. The man, still standing, was immensely elated. "And now, Mr. Boat," he cried.

Maintaining his heroic erectness, he jabbed at rocks along the side and bottom, and brought the boat circuitously toward the back-rolling bubble. As he poled, he hummed grandly, even venturing some open-mouthed tra-las. Approaching the bubble more closely, he became quiet and knelt, preparatory to sitting. In this position, he watched the waterfall steadily. Coming very close, he was suddenly alarmed by the rapid streaming-away of the foam toward the rocks where the water jumped at a hundred points and turned white, like a miniature surf in a cross-rip. He made a spasmodic thrust with the pole. The boat swung sedately around, slid its stern directly under the fall, lifted its snout, and sank backwards. The man clung amazed until the water was under his chin, and then, with a shout, let go and struck out wildly to avoid the rise of the boat.

He continued to swim, growing calmer, until he bumped on the sand-bar and could stand up in the water. Thence he saw his boat lodged against a rock below the bar, the waters protesting around it. The sight enraged him. He remained angry until he had secured the boat, bailed it out, recovered his pole, and returned round the edge of the pool to the fall. Then he swore at the fall to keep his temper up, and this time managed to enter the current just below the bubble. He sat down quickly, nervous because of the speed he expected, believing all at once that his pole was useless. But the boat was too water-logged. Slow and stately it turned upon the stream, let the anxious waters divide about it, coasted past the sand-bar, knocked gently from one rock to another at the head of the shallow rapids, and came to rest between two of them. The man relaxed and took his hands from the sides. "Well," he said, "Well, well."

Thereafter he became pink over his whole body from the exertion of dragging his boat back to the pool. He scraped his feet among the stones of the river bed and never noticed. He took three more rides, going a little farther each time, as he became acquainted with the most prominent rocks. He was so confident on the fifth ride that during the burdensome start he sat with his pole in his hands and regarded the world before him.

In the canyon below the rapids, where the rocky shores grew into cliffs with dense cedar and spruce forests above them, was a splendid curve which hid the lower river. Over the cliff and the forest, a great, rounded thunderhead swelled voluminously out of the west and darkened the trees. It appeared to fill the sky, and its upper bosses were bright with sun. The man felt this cloud to be a recognition of the dimension of his undertaking, and gazed at it with stern exultation.

In the late afternoon a woman came over the hill on the road. When she first appeared, irritation was in her walk. The clouds had spread far east and were no longer gilded. The wind kept blowing her hair.

Part way down, she stopped, and stood with her hands on her hips. "For goodness sake," she exclaimed. "For goodness sake, what does that man think he's doing?" She stared. "And yelling his head off like a lunatic," she exclaimed.

The man was just launching out from the jade-colored, white-streaked, back-bellying bubble. He was standing upright in the orange boat, the bamboo pole held aloft like a spear. As he gravitated toward the rapids, his mouth could be seen to open tremendously and repeatedly. He waved his left arm in accompaniment. Faintly, even over the wind and the rush of the falls, the woman could hear the words. "Sailing, sailing," roared the man in the boat. He shook his spear. "Sailing, sailing," he roared, until the boat stumbled and knocked him to his knees. Even then his mouth opened and closed in the same way. Only when the boat stalled, with a white fan of water behind it, did he close his mouth. Then he scrambled out, grabbed the chain on the prow, and dragged, tugged and jerked the boat up the slope of rock and froth.

When the boat was in the pool again, he commenced at once to climb into it and to work his mouth. "Sailing, sailing," he bellowed.

The woman said, "Gracious heavens, he's absolutely crazy," and recovered herself. She advanced to the edge of the rock and yelled at the man. He was then half-way over the stern and kicking valiantly. The woman yelled, "John!" She leaned forward and stuck her chin out when she yelled. The man lay perfectly still for an instant, half-way over the stern. Then he slid back into the water and held onto the stern with one hand. He looked across at the woman. "Yes?" he asked.

The woman could see his mouth move. She looked angry but relieved, and eased her voice a little. "D. L. called you," she cried. "He wants you back in town."

"Bother D. L.," the man said to himself.

"What's that you said?" cried the woman.

"I said all right," the man yelled suddenly.

The woman put one hand on her hip. "He called hours ago. He'll be wild."

The man let go of the boat reluctantly and paddled across to the terrace. The woman stood where she was, waiting. The man drew himself out of the water slowly, with great care for his battered toes. Crab-wise he ascended the slimy, submerged rock and crawled up onto the red rock in the wind. Cautiously he walked across the red rock to the spot where he had left his things. His tracks grew more distinct as he went.

"For goodness sake, get a move on," the woman called up at him.

His thin, unmuscular body was turning blue in the wind. Bending stiffly, he removed his slippers from the towel, straightened up, and began to wipe himself. He sat down to wipe his feet, and was tender of his toes. He put his spectacles on, using both hands. Then he stood up and donned the red and blue dressing gown and the leather slippers. He wobbled on one leg at a time while putting on his slippers, and screwed his face up while each rubbed over his toes. He searched a moment for the cake of soap. When he found it, he put it in his pocket and, carrying his towel in one hand, descended carefully to where the woman was waiting.

"What on earth were you doing out there?" she asked. But having seen what he was doing, she went on. "D. L. called up hours ago. How on earth did I know I'd have to come way down here after you? How could I know you'd be . . ."

They went on up the road.

"Well, I'm sure I don't know what you were doing," said the woman. "You're so cold your teeth are chattering."

The man was avoiding sharp pebbles in the road, and said nothing. His peeled knees worked in and out of the opening of the dressing gown, which occasionally fled out behind him on the wind.

"How would I know you'd take all afternoon?" asked the woman sharply. "D. L. will be wild. And all because —well, what on earth *were* you doing out there?"

"Oh, I don't know," said the man. "I found an old boat."

The woman was unpleasantly silent.

"I was just fooling around with an old boat," the man explained, and again, "That's all I was doing, just fooling around with an old boat I found."

The wind on top of the hill was unexpectedly sustained. The woman, holding down her hair with both hands, made no reply. The man had to clutch at his dressing gown tightly, to keep it from streaming out and leaving him uncovered.

The Anonymous

It was June and summer quiet when Peter Carr's long shadow first appeared through the open door of my classroom. I still feel that foreboding came with it. I said, "Come in," without looking up, and he came in and stood in front of my desk. I could hear that he was wearing high-heeled boots.

It was over a hundred outside, and in my shirtsleeves, with my tie pulled loose, I was sweating over a pile of papers in a smell of floor oil, chalk, and dust from the quad. The Indian children, in their secret way, had all anybody has, but it didn't get into their papers. Their papers were terrible. I made the last marks carefully, so as not to appear angry when I looked up.

"Señor Gates?" he asked.

I was shocked. It was not only the "Señor," or even the deep, gentle voice in this place of arid voices. It was the accent.

"Yes," I said.

"I am so sorry to interrupt," he said, and the accent was confirmed. He spoke like a Boston clergyman who has taken up light satire as a defense. He implied that it was amusing to apologize for interrupting nothing. I took him in while I asked what I could do for him. He was exotic for these parts, with his new, creased Levis, skin-tight, blue silk shirt with scarlet trim, and new, black sombrero. His belt and hat band were made of linked silver conchas, and he wore on one wrist an old silver bracelet as wide as my hand, and on a finger of the other hand a silver ring with a large matrix turquoise. His long hair was tied in a club on his neck, and bound with a scarlet band. He was thin, and exceedingly straight, and had a long, narrow face and aristocratic hands. His eyes were rather intentionally direct as he smiled at my examination, a faint, even uncertain smile, but with that same quality of light ridicule.

"The Señora at the office told me I should come to you to arrange for a room and meals, and for instruction also."

"You're coming to the school?" I asked. I showed my surprise. We often got them as old as he was, perhaps twenty, but his voice and manner suggested something far beyond us.

"That seems at present necessary, Señor," he said, smiling again.

"Oh, does it?" I thought.

"The arrangement is for personal instruction, I believe," he said.

He didn't miss my look. "Apart from the usual classes, Señor."

I couldn't be sure of the contempt. Already I felt that the way he said things wasn't his own.

"You don't come from this territory?"

"Scarcely, Señor."

"We've never given special instruction here," I said finally. "I doubt if we'd have what you want."

"The arrangement has been made with Señor Cuyler," he told me.

I stared at him while I wondered what Cuyler figured to get out of this.

"You're Navajo, aren't you?" I asked him.

"Si, Señor. Navajo."

"Then why—?"

When I didn't go on, he said gently, "I have permission, Señor."

I didn't understand. The Navajos are a proud people, and our students were mostly Piutes, the children of pine-nut pickers and third-rate ranch hands. At that time, before the national government began asking people who knew Indians, our job looked to me useless or worse. When they left us they went back to a degraded reservation life, or the most menial of ranch work, or nothing. There were curfews against them in the towns, and the white ranchers were always trying to get the rights to what little workable land they had left. The school was what you might have expected, a handful of ugly, frame buildings in the middle of a barren valley, cold and windy in the winter, hot and windy in the summer, and always dusty unless there was snow down. Still, I could see we wouldn't get anywhere on our present track. I stood up.

"What's your name, son?" I asked him.

"I may be called Peter Carr, Señor."

"But you're not, is that it?"

He smiled, but wouldn't say anything.

"Well, come along, Peter Carr," I said. "I'll show you where you sleep."

We walked across the quad, squinting in the light and

dust. A group of the smaller boys watched us from the shadow of a building, and I felt the heartbreak I always felt when I saw them, the smallest ones, with their cropped heads and blue overalls, standing on the edge of things, watching. Never mind the new young man. Time was dying quietly here anyway, without resistance or hope, in the sunlight, in the rustle of little poplars. He wouldn't matter in the long run.

The boys slept in a long, second-storey hall with two rows of cots, a bare floor, and windows too high to see out of. I pointed out a cot to Peter Carr.

"That will be yours. I'll show you where to get bedding."

"Thank you, Señor, but I have brought my own blankets."

"So you'll lie in style," I thought. But there was no rule.

"If I might have a place to put my things, Señor. Where they will be safe. I will sleep outside for the time being."

"You'll sleep here," I told him. "They all do."

"But here, Señor, they must all see one another, and breathe one another's sleep." He wasn't insulted. He was explaining decency to me.

"If anyone sleeps out, they'll all want to," I said.

"Is this rule because of the girls, Señor?" he inquired with malicious gravity. "Where do the girls sleep, Señor?"

I resented the kind of watch we had to keep myself. The thought made me sharp. "You'll find that out for yourself, I imagine," I said, and was at once ashamed. I would never have said that to one of the boys of whom it might have been true.

"Across the quad," I apologized. "Pretty much the same as this."

I took him down to Reilly, the master of the boy's dormitory. I wanted to find out what the office knew about him. I couldn't place him yet, and I was afraid he'd make trouble when the older students came back in the fall, though I couldn't guess yet whether they'd be with him or against him. I told him I'd talk with him about his work in Reilly's room after supper. There was another duty, though. I'd left it till the last.

"You may wear those clothes," I told him, as if making a concession, "but you'll have to have your hair cut like the other boys, and leave your jewelry with Mr. Reilly."

He looked at me quietly, and then at Reilly, and then slowly took off all the silver, without looking at it, and laid it on the bare center table.

"I'll keep them safe for you," Reilly said. Reilly was a stocky, freckled red-head with a broken nose. He was a machine man, like Cuyler, but a good hand with the boys, strict but fair. I could tell he was stung, but knew Peter Carr wouldn't suffer for it.

"Of course," Peter Carr said. There was a noticeable hiatus where there should have been the Señor he was lavishing on me. Reilly's jaw set, and he looked at me. I didn't say anything. I tried not to show anything either. I had a feeling we'd need independent judgments.

I went across to the office. Cuyler was away, as usual, keeping his connections warm, but his secretary, Mrs. Grayborg, was in. He had to keep her to keep the place

going, even in its rut, though she wasn't his ideal as a
secretary, being a thin, neat, middle-aged widow with
spectacles. She always surprised you when she spoke.

Mrs. Grayborg's first impression must have been
much like mine. She was very dry about Peter Carr. He
had entered, she told me, by special arrangement with
some people Cuyler had met in Reno. There was influence somewhere, she said, banging Cuyler's rubber
stamp onto some letter he had probably never seen.
What it was, she added, no one had seen fit to inform
her. I knew it was true if she said so. Mrs. Grayborg and
I had no secrets about the school. He was not a reservation Indian, she went on. He came from some ranch
outside Albuquerque. He would stay just one year, to
learn all he could, which was apparently expected to be
a great deal, and if she was any judge, he was likely to
receive some rather remarkable privileges. I knew she
was only too good a judge.

"Which is going to make it nice for you and Tom,"
she said, rolling paper and carbon vigorously into the
typewriter. Tom was Reilly.

"Isn't it?" I said.

The typewriter began to rattle. "Personal tutoring,"
she said.

"So Mr. Carr informed me," I said, lighting a cigarette.

"Señor Carr," she said.

I sat down on the bench against the wall. "You don't
have any idea what it's all about?" I asked. "What the
boy's going to do, that begets this cultural urge?"

"Not the slightest," she said. "Not even," she said,
whanging the carriage back, "a dependable suspicion."

"It *must* be a state matter." I said.

"It must," she agreed.

"But as for what he's going to do here . . ." she said, ripping the paper off the roller, and at once inserting another sheet.

"I imagine Mr. Carr will tell me himself," I said.

"Señor Carr," she corrected again. "I imagine he will."

I'd have to find him out gradually and accidentally, I judged. I finished my cigarette and went back to my papers.

Peter Carr came to Reilly's room at exactly the time I had set, with his hair still uncut. He wouldn't sit down. I believe he felt that such informality would seem like a premature accession. I took a chair by the window, and lit my pipe.

"What do you want to study?" I asked him.

He had it by rote. "I wish to read and write English, to know what a gentleman should about music, literature, art and the histories of European nations, and to understand mathematics and business methods." It was then that I got the first inkling that more than his manner was borrowed, but at the moment I was so shocked by the confession of illiteracy that I missed the important revelation.

"To read and write?" I asked.

He nodded gravely.

"You speak your own tongue, of course; and Spanish?"

"I do not know Navajo, Señor," he said. "It is of no use. Of Spanish, but a few words." He explained blandly. "It is a language of such courtesy. It makes

those who come to the ranch feel important. Then they
are easily happy."

I felt my face burning, but as far as I could tell in
the dusk, he was serious.

"You have never lived with your own people?"

"With the Navajos? No, Señor."

"You can drop the Señor," I said.

"As you wish."

"And how long do you intend to work at these
studies?"

"Until I have mastered them, Señor."

I looked at him.

"I am sorry," he said, bowing slightly. "I have used
the word so long." And after a moment, "You would
judge the time better than I. I had thought a year, perhaps."

"A whole year for that?" I inquired lightly.

"If it seems necessary," he said.

"It might be," I admitted. "And you wish to work by
yourself?"

"Of course." He nearly said the Señor, so it was an
honest habit.

We talked about books and hours for a short time,
and about his previous work, which was none. Then I
returned to my room. I wanted to get him straight, but
didn't, then, or until the end. The answer was so simple
and single that I couldn't find it in the tangled mass of
his apparently irreconcilable traits, Indian and codfish
aristocracy, ignorance and delicacy, egotism and ill-veiled
timidity, superficiality and mystery. I finally made myself go to sleep because it was getting worse.

Mrs. Grayborg was right about Peter's privileges.

Cuyler not only let him keep his hair, but ordered his jewelry returned. Except for cancelled authority, I didn't mind the hair; he would be the queer. The jewelry was another thing. It wouldn't matter with the little ones who stayed in the summer, who would no more be jealous of him than of me, but to the older ones, when they returned, it would be a notable distinction. I wouldn't ask favors of Peter Carr, but short of that, I did what I could, made a ceremony of returning the ornaments, and told him how the others would feel. He listened attentively, thanked me for returning them, and was wearing them the next day. He even added, at times, a ceremonial necklace of huge silver beads and claws, with a double crescent pendant. That finished him with Reilly, who after that kept asking me how my new girl was getting along. I didn't like it, either, but I wasn't so sure what it meant. It seemed to me he was not merely being obstinate, but rather observing a pledge of some moral significance.

Yet he continued to deny his Navajo heritage when I tried to break the tedium of alphabet and copying exercises by drawing him out on their customs and ritual and art. He declared, almost savagely, that they, and all they stood for, were dead. It was a sore point with him, as if he were less certain of it than of most of his queer code.

Gradually I let him lead me into the talk he wanted, the life of European societies, important historical events, the names of and recognizable keys to famous works of music, art and literature. But even here he wanted facts, just facts; he was an insatiable sink for facts, and never put facts together, never saw a direction, never thought, just remembered. When I would try to make him draw a heap of facts into a theory or a trend, he would take my theories as facts too, and come up days later with one of them worked neatly into his assiduous parlor conversation and stated as dogmatically as he would say Columbus discovered America in 1492. It made me sick to hear my way of thinking begin to come out of him pat, sharing the honor of devotion with that detestable voice I had heard from the start. I let it go, and stuck to his drills, to pointing out identifying themes in master compositions played on my terrible little portable and identifying figures or groupings in my pile of bad art prints, and to the undigested facts, only trying to keep enough related facts together so that his practice conversations wouldn't sound like quiz programs. Only once in a while he would suddenly fall silent in the middle of his execrable but beautifully voiced parrotings, and stare for a long time through the window at the empty quad, so that I felt sick with pity for him, felt that he also knew his hollowness, and the futility of the facts he had chosen to dump into it. The rest of the time he was a Santa Fé poster which had unfortunately learned to talk. Outside of his work, I tried to forget him.

He made problems, though, that wouldn't let me forget him. About six weeks after his arrival, something came up which looked to me really serious. He'd been living in a separate cabin which we'd need again in the fall. That was bad enough. Now there was a new bungalow going up in the grove, quite a place for one boy, to judge by the foundations and the plans the contractor showed me, which called for a bedroom, a bath with separate shower, a kitchen, a study with built-in bookcases, and a living room with a big plate-glass window like a showcase front, looking up at the Sierra, which was all we had to look at, or the best. A dozen workers were going strong on it on the west edge of the grove, which was really just a clump of big cottonwoods across the entrance road from the main quad, but a place marked and of the elect in the minds of our students, not only because they were the only trees on the place except a scattering of half-dead poplars and aspens, but because, until now, Cuyler's own residence had stood alone on its eastern edge.

I went to the office. Oh, yes, Mrs. Grayborg said, the bungalow was for Peter Carr. It would, she declared, banging a ledger down on the desk, guarantee him some privacy from the common herd. Since he was unusually sensitive, she said, making a forcible entry with a stub pen, it was necessary that he have some protection, as well as quiet in which to pursue his studies. She completed the entry with a dash which splattered the ink so she could pound the blotter.

"Cuyler didn't say that?" I asked.

"Well, I certainly didn't," she said.

I went back to see Cuyler on one of those rare days when he was in. It was no use. He just stood there, his plump, almost caricatured political self, and chewed a cigar and stared at me through his heavy glasses. Probably fresh from being put in his place, he had just finished, as his heavy breathing and bright look showed, putting Mrs. Grayborg in hers. She was staring at her typewriter with a tired, stupefied look. He listened to me with that bright look, of patiently waiting to say something that mattered.

"Has Peter been making trouble?" he asked me, chewing the cigar into the other corner of his mouth, and patting his belly with both hands, preparatory to downing me.

"No," I said, "but this layout of his will. This isn't a private school, and I'm not a private tutor."

Cuyler withdrew his cigar and stared at me steadily. "Who asked you what it is?"

"Don't worry," I said. "I know what it is. And what's he doing here anyway? We can't give him anything he couldn't get better a dozen other places, if he has that much to spend. And without making a hundred other kids feel like mud."

"They are mud," Cuyler said. "If you don't shoot your mouth off, they'll never know the difference. They'll never even think he's one of them. And he's not. I happen to know."

He paused to let me understand how intimately he knew.

"I happen to know his connections," he said.

"Would you mind giving me some idea?" I asked.

"I most certainly would. You're a bigot, Gates. You've got no tolerance. If you knew who's behind him, he wouldn't have a prayer with you."

"I don't see how he's going to anyway, unless I get some idea what he's after."

"He told you, didn't he?"

"Everything but why, and that's everything, in his case. I'm just guessing."

"What he wants to tell you is enough. Never mind guessing.

"And as for their being mud," he blocked me, "they

are mud. If you'd get rid of your half-baked parlor notions, and get out and see how they really live . . ."

"I've seen," I told him. I'd been on the reservations,
and in the pine-nut camps and fishing shelters fifty times
to his accidental one, and he knew it.

"While, as for taking care of any little jealousies that
may arise, I think that's my province," Cuyler said, as
if finally.

"One might think so."

"Now, you listen to me, Gates." He planted his feet
apart, removed his cigar again, and pointed it at me.
"You're hired to teach; to teach, and to carry out arrangements as handed to you. Just that. Peter Carr's
arrangements are according to my orders. That's enough
for you."

Then he made one of those oily shifts I most de-
tested. I believe he thought them subtle, these conclu-
sions intended to soothe without weakening his position.

"Peter's friends have reasons of their own for sending him to an Indian school, good reasons, in my opinion, and actually, Gates, you yourself are the chief
reason they chose this one. You don't find many Indian
schools with a teacher who has three college degrees.
You know that. And I'm sure you'll find Peter worth
your time. Maybe," he said, looking bright again,
"maybe in more ways than one."

I tried to go on, but he waved an affable hand. "Some
other time, Gates. I'm up to my ears, and I have to get
back to see Senator Miles this evening. If there's any
trouble, just come to me. But there won't be."

"You're up to Mrs. Grayborg's ears, you mean," I

thought. Actually, all I got out of it was that Peter had friends.

I was still hot about the mess being prepared for Reilly and me, when another incident occurred, which gave me a new angle on Peter Carr, or his friends. I believe now that it revealed the friends more than Peter, but perhaps, with time, I've romanticized Peter a little myself.

I was working on my old Ford in a patch of shade behind the tool shed. I was half-way under the hood, and didn't see Peter Carr when he came.

"A little difficulty, Mr. Gates?"

"No," I said, without looking up. "Plenty."

"You seem to have a great deal of trouble with that car, Mr. Gates."

"It's that kind of a car."

"Do you like that sort of work?" he asked. There was a tone in his voice like a cat walking in water.

"I do not," I said.

"I should think you'd let a mechanic do it."

"First get it to the mechanic."

After a moment he said, "It's a rather inexpensive car, isn't it?"

I stood up and looked at him. I was sweating and greasy, and there he stood, just in the edge of the shadow, cool in all his silver and a white silk blouse that made his hands and face look like well-carved mahogany. He was smoking a long Russian cigarette.

"Well, it's no Rolls-Royce," I said, and turned back.

He began to tell me seriously what a fine car the Rolls-Royce was. He spoke of the pleasure of driving an Hispano-Suiza too, and even had a good word for the Cadillac and Packard.

"I know all that," I said. "But this is what I've got. It's a six-year-old Ford."

"But for a man with your interests," he said. "The continual annoyance."

I gave up, sat down on the running board and lit a cigarette myself, while he related to me with delicate gravity the experience of an acquaintance of his, a man with tastes much like mine, and similarly in straitened circumstances, those were his words, who had solved the problem with a reconditioned Pierce-Arrow. Toward the end, because I kept looking at him, his exposition was less confident.

"I couldn't let this go," I told him. "It's bone of my bone and flesh of my flesh and most of my spare time. You have to love anything that's this much trouble, after six years."

This was too much for him. Neither in his natural self, if there were such, nor in the personality he had selected, was there enough humor to be sure what I meant. He hung around for a minute, not saying anything, and then wandered away. I wondered what this new glimpse promised for the fall. I was constantly wondering, at this time, what would happen in the fall, and almost hoping, I believe, that it would be enough to shake Cuyler, though I knew that would end by shaking Reilly and me.

Actually, I think it helped. Cuyler was right in spite of himself. Peter Carr was so perfectly isolated in his donned conceit that he offered little to keep animosity alive. The bungalow was finished by the time school began, and he had moved into it, along with three truck-loads of over-stuffed furniture, Navajo rugs and leather-bound classics, which he had insisted I list for him, and which he was already reading for hours each day, his parroted facility in speech having brought him along rapidly after the first painful steps, though in the same infuriating way, remembering facts and memorized opinion taken as fact, and nothing else. With regular classes again, and helping Reilly on the football field, I moved Peter's hours to the evening, and since he studied most of the day, and ran alone for exercise, he didn't cross the other students much.

They were curious when they first saw him, of course. He was in full panoply, crossing the quad toward my classroom. I was standing in the door, and saw them watching him in little groups, the boys sober-faced and intent, thinking pretty deadly things, I guessed, and many of the girls giggling.

One of the girls danced out a few steps from her group, and gave him a languishing look, and then pillowed one cheek on her two hands and gazed after him soulfully. At this pantomime, her friends wriggled in ecstasy. Even among the boys there were slow grins. The girl was Jenny Jackson. I looked to see if Jim Blood was among the boys, and he was, sitting on a step of the dorm, his massive shoulders hunched over, and his big, flat face turned at Peter Carr too, and grinning a little. It was a good beginning; better than a serious one, anyway.

Actually there was only one complication, and that had to do with Jenny, and so with Jim Blood, which might, with a more normal climax, have caused plenty of trouble.

Jenny was a very pretty and pert Shoshone girl, considerably more intelligent and sensitive than most of her schoolmates, and with the drawing power of a doe in the spring. I don't mean she was loose. She wasn't; she set a high value on herself. But in a delicate way she had the urge, and the charms that derive from it. She was the cause, I suspected, of a lot of dreaming in the monastic dormitory, but because of Jim Blood, the dreams didn't even get as far as conversation.

Jim wasn't Jenny's choice. She was his. He couldn't get anywhere with her, but he marked her off, and his sign was enough. Jim was older than most of the boys, older than Peter, I'd guess, and besides being very powerful, the school's best athlete, he was a vindictive, silent sort, whose little humor was malicious. Not that he was openly a bully. He'd never had a fight at the school. But fundamentally he was dangerous.

Perhaps, at first, Jenny saw in Peter Carr's separateness nothing more than a hope of escaping Jim Blood, though later it was certainly more than that. Whatever she saw, after the first two or three weeks she began to make an open play for Peter. She watched him constantly, and knew his whole routine, I think. She kept crossing him on the quad, standing near him at the football games, and especially taking late afternoon walks that would intercept him when he came in from his long runs on the desert. When that wasn't enough, she began to come to my classroom in the evenings, with excuses about borrowing books or getting help with assignments. She came two or three times a week, as often as she felt it safe to ask for a pass from the matron. They weren't hard to get. Jenny was a good student, good enough so we were thinking of college for her, and she'd never caused any trouble.

She was quick to understand Peter. When she found him in agony over childish rudiments, punctuation, arithmetic, spelling, she didn't stay, but when we were talking, she would often sit for an hour, listening. I doubt if she saw, then at least, through the worldly pose into the terrible emptiness of the boy. She would watch him intently as he gave me back, in flawless periods, that stored tripe, and sometimes I would see her soft, rather round mouth, silently shaping words after him. She began to borrow my copies of some of the books he was reading, and finally, after some weeks, even to enter tentatively into the talk. I found her a pleasing antidote. Unlike Peter, everything she wanted was to help form an opinion, and though her entries were timid, her inalienable, whimsical pertness got into her speech as into her movements.

As far as Peter Carr was concerned, though, she wasn't there. He would wait patiently until she was done, which was never long under this silent pressure, and then take up the conversation as if nothing had been said since my last remark or his. I wondered how she bore up under this freezing, but you can't tell, perhaps it was even a stimulus. She quickly learned to speak only to me, but she continued to come and sit with us, and listen to Peter, and watch him.

Why it happened so suddenly, when it did happen, I will never understand. He may have been more responsive elsewhere, though I doubt that. Perhaps her active imagination had built the situation up falsely. Perhaps she was applying a desperation measure to the only opportunity offered. Certainly that part of Peter's encouragement which I witnessed was very slight.

She had come in early that evening, and we were talking about *Laughing Boy*, which I had given her to read, behind Cuyler's back. She had decided Peter was a kind of Laughing Boy. It was the first time she'd talked to me about Peter, and I'd underrated her penetration. Or perhaps I hadn't. Perhaps she had missed the Laughing Boy. I'll never be sure, because Peter came in before I could start digging, and afterwards, of course, she would never open up to me either.

Peter said good evening to Jenny. That much he always did. All she said was good evening too, but he looked at her again after she'd said it. Since she was already there, we didn't mention his drill work, but drifted into our conversation. It was the usual talk, but there was an important difference that charged it with a kind of warm inspiration usually wholly lacking. Twice Peter made a direct reply to a remark of Jenny's. Jenny was excited and exalted. She talked more than usual. Still Peter remained affable, except that once he raised an eyebrow of fellowly condescension at me.

At eight-thirty, as usual, Jenny got up to go. She was still quietly excited. I didn't realize how much, but tried to let her down gently with some pedagogical admonition.

"Yes, Mr. Gates," she said, her eyes loving even upon me. "Good night, Mr. Gates."

In the door she said, "Good night, Peter Carr."

The whole name. I hadn't toned her down a bit.

Peter stood up and said, "Good night, Jenny. Sleep well."

She hesitated, looking at him with her lips a little apart. She didn't say anything more, though, but bobbed her head quickly at him, and, clutching her books, went out, closing the door very quietly. Through the window, I saw her in the moonlight, running across the snowy quad. She was making wild little excursions to the side, and sometimes skipping.

That was all there was to it. The only external difference was that Peter had never before used her name or told her to sleep well. Peter and I worked at his punctuation for half an hour, and then, from the door, I watched him cross the quad in that slow, limber gait, and, when he was gone into shadows on the other side, went back to work of my own.

I don't think it was more than fifteen minutes before he returned. He didn't seem upset, only a little more self-consciously haughty.

"Would you please get the matron for me, Mr. Gates?" he asked.

"The matron? Why, what's the matter?" I knew, all right.

"That girl," he said, "is in my bedroom."

"Jenny?"

He nodded. "I thought I'd better report it, to avoid misunderstanding."

"Can't you put her out?"

"It would be better to have someone in authority, I think."

I was as stiff as he was. "If you prefer," I said.

It was early still, and the older girls at the dormitory would be up. There wasn't a chance of Jenny being brought in by the matron without the whole school guessing. I was afraid we would lose all we hoped of Jenny under their flogging. An unsuccessful amorous advance was the funniest thing they could think of, and their humor was more durable than delicate.

I got up. "I'll go over with you," I said.

"It would be better to call the matron."

"We won't need the matron," I said angrily. "I won't have the whole damned school laughing at her."

"The girl is in my bed," he said quietly. "I doubt if she has anything on, and she refuses to come out."

I stared at him while I considered what they would do with that. He thought I doubted him. "It is so," he said.

It was, too. I went over without calling the matron. Jenny's books were on the living-room table, and she had the bedroom door locked now. I talked to her, but she wouldn't come out, or make any answer to my arguments except, "No, no," as if she were crying. Peter Carr sat down across the room and watched me pleading like a fool with "No, no" through a locked door. Finally I told her I would have to call the matron. She knew what that meant, but she told me, wildly, to go ahead and call her. I looked at my watch. It was just after ten o'clock. I told her what time it was, and that I'd give her till eleven, and then I'd have to call the matron, if she wasn't already looking for her. She didn't answer me.

I sat down with one of Peter's handsome leather books, and pretended to read. I figured that an hour, if it didn't bring her out, would at least make it late enough to give her a chance of getting in without being seen.

At half past there had been no sound from the room, except perhaps a sound of smothered crying so quiet

I might have imagined it. I got up and threw the book onto the table and signaled Peter to come outside. I wrote out an excuse for Jenny, and left it on the table. At the bedroom door I told her about the excuse, and that I would give her a half hour with nobody there. She didn't answer, and we went outside. Peter was satirically agreeable to everything I tried.

I intended to walk out the main road toward the mountains, which were snow-covered, and looked immense and impending in the moonlight, but from the porch I saw somebody among the shadows of the trees. When I went toward his tree he moved back to another, and when he crossed an open patch of moonlight, not furtively, but slowly, I recognized Jim Blood's squat, long-armed figure. I kept my voice down when I called to him.

"Is that you, Jim Blood?"

I had to repeat the question before he said, "Yeah," gruffly. I played the face-saving ignorance which is always the first move of badgered authority.

"What are you doing, wandering around after lights out?" I wanted to know. "Get back to the dormitory before I have to report you."

It didn't take. He stood there in the shadow without saying anything.

"You get on over to the dorm," I ordered. "Or do I have to call Mr. Reilly and take you back? Move along now."

I walked toward him. Then he retreated. I stopped and watched him go out from under the trees and across the road in the moonlight, stopping to look back two or three times. He disappeared in the shadow of the office building. I knew he hadn't gone any farther, but I was glad to let it go at that.

Jenny made us go most of the way. Even when the matron came, she wouldn't open the door. We had to break it open. She was still in bed. She stared at us sullenly, and wasn't crying now, if she had been. Her uniform and shoes and coarse cotton stockings were in a little heap on the floor. I thought she was even going to make the matron pull her out and dress her, for she made no answer, but just kept staring when the matron, who was a big and quick-tempered woman, ordered her, from the doorway, to get up. But when the matron started for her, she jumped out of bed with no attention to my being there. Peter Carr wasn't. He was on the porch, with his back turned, smoking a cigarette. Jenny was screaming at the matron, "Don't you touch me; don't you touch me." The matron said she didn't intend to, to hurry up and get her clothes on, and came out to wait with me in the living-room.

Jenny didn't take long. She came out with her hair down loose on her shoulders, and didn't look at us or pick up her books, but after a moment's pause went across the room in a stiff walk, unlike hers, and across the porch. She wouldn't detour, and Peter had to move aside to let her down the steps. The matron followed her, and I went as far as the porch.

At the foot of the steps, she stopped and turned on Peter. The moon was behind her, but the light from the door was on her face, and it was wild with fury and contempt. She spoke very quietly though. "Woman-man," she said. She said it in Piute. It's an insult in any language, but in Piute it has specific moral and physiological connotations for which we have no equally concentrated counterpart.

If he understood, he didn't show it.

She looked at him a moment, waiting, and then smiled, and said it again, even more quietly, and went on back to the dormitory, walking well ahead of the matron.

We couldn't hush the story, because she chose to tell it herself. She made woman-man a name which stuck to Peter Carr. They had all chosen, after a short time, to consider him something of a sissy, and now their judgment was confirmed in a delightfully literal way. Jenny was clever. She came out of it with a kind of spicy glory, which may have been why she made us come and get her, and even Jim Blood seemed now to accept her estimate of Peter as a fact, which put Peter safely beneath his attentions.

Their cold avoidance, however, bothered Peter no more than the previous light heckling. I was half inclined, then, before I saw that reason also, to agree with them myself. Jenny was a beautiful girl, and not one to make such an offer lightly. At any rate that ended our worry about the others, excepting Jenny. Poor Jenny, we'd lost her as much as if the school had picked on her. She didn't go loose, but she didn't get over it either. Pride in her revenge wasn't enough. She became savage and brittle, until the whole school was afraid of her, and the next fall she didn't come back.

It was June again, the heat and summer quiet returned, before Peter Carr's culture was considered complete, and his gods revealed. The car arrived for him one afternoon, a dust-colored Rolls-Royce driven by a chauffeur in livery. In the back seat was a big-breasted, middle-aged woman in a wide-brimmed hat and a dress with a big flower pattern. Cuyler came out of the office to meet her, with an affectionate arm around Peter Carr's shoulders. He sent one of the boys for me. It would take a Rolls-Royce to put that much unguarded expression on a small Piute.

The woman, Varney was her name, was pleased at the progress dear Peter had made. It was clear, she said, in the letters he had written her. She thanked me. She repeated Cuyler's line about my being unusual. She also repeated, several times, in varying forms, an enlightening perception of her own to the effect that Peter was a remarkable character, so intelligent, so sensitive, and how fortunate it was that they had been able to find a man like myself, able to cultivate that character and intelligence, in a place which would not damage his fundamental Indian nature, with its gift for simple, deep, she said bone-deep, realities with which the white man has largely lost touch. She looked at Peter often, with terrifying affection, while she reconstructed him. I was ashamed for him, as for a shy child being talked about to his face. But when I finally looked at him, he was obviously even kindled by this exposure. He was smiling, and not sardonically. He was back in his world, with the people who amounted to something.

Mrs. Varney thanked me again, with details, and then went into the office. Cuyler held the door open for her, and for Peter after her. Then he closed it.

The chauffeur, understanding that I was disposed of, got out of the car and lit a cigarette. He spit twice before he spoke.

"Damned Indian doll," he said. "You'd think he owned creation."

I asked if Peter Carr had lived in Boston.

"Who, him? Oh, I get you; the way he talks, eh?"

I nodded.

"Naw. Born on a ranch in New Mexico, and never been off it before. It's a dude ranch, you know, high-class place, thousand bucks a summer. Mostly women from back east. He heard it from them, that's all.

"His clothes," he went on, "they're Mrs. Varney's idea. Mustn't forget his great heritage," he lisped. "The sap," he said violently. "He don't even know he's nothing but a toy."

He sat down on the running board and looked at me speculatively. "She's a widow," he said. "They're getting married this summer."

"Oh," I said.

"Won't that be a nice package to drive around," he said. "Opening doors for that coffee-colored fake. Kee-rist.

"Hell," he said, leaning over and spitting again, "a fellow's gotta live!"

"Yes," I said, "sure," and went back to my papers.

The Buck in the Hills

I LEFT THE peak about two o'clock, drank the very cold, shale-tasting water coming from under last winter's snow in the notch, went on down, and then south through the marshy meadow, already in shadow from the col, the grass yellowing and the sod stiffening from the fall nights, so that I could walk straight across and feel only the first solidity and then a slight give which didn't spring back. It was strange in the meadows, walking in the shadow, but with the sky still bright blue, as in the middle of the afternoon, and the sunlight, when I stopped to look back at the peak, just beginning to look late. It was chilly in the shadow too, but I didn't hurry. The peak was sacred to me, the climb was pilgrimage, and five years is a long time. I had been very happy all day, climbing with the sun on my neck and shoulders, and I was very lonely happy now. I took my time, and looked at everything, and remembered a lot, and would have yodelled sometimes, but the quiet was better.

I climbed over the big rock barrier, which a million winters had cracked into terraces, saw the dry, shriveled clumps of leaves and single dead stems in the cracks, and remembered times I had come up there in the sum-

mer, which is spring at that height, and seen it pouring
with green, like cascades, and lighted by flowers. I remembered the dark girl who knew all the flowers, and
who, when I bet her she couldn't find more than thirty
kinds, found more than fifty. I remembered how we had
eaten our pocket lunch dry, in a niche on the east side
of the peak, out of the strong wind we could hear
among the rocks and more heavily in the notch below.
We couldn't see it then, but the image was new in our
minds of the big basin to the west, with its rolling of
dark green to pale blue, heavily timbered hills, and the
wide, dark-blue flat of Tahoe, rough with wind and
jointed exactly into all the bays and coves, and the
little lakes at different heights around it, also fitted like
single pieces into a relief puzzle. In front of us, way
down, squared with fields and pencilled by the straight
roads, was the chain of ranching valleys, and then the
lesser, burned mountains rolling to the east, and in the
far northeast just a sky-colored sliver of Pyramid Lake
showing through the last pass. I remembered that the
clouds that day had gone all around the horizon in a
narrow band, flat underneath, all at exactly the same
level, with clear sky between them and the mountains,
and with their tops standing up in little, firm bosses
and domes, and not a single cloud in the field of sky
above them, so that we sat high up in the center of a
great circle of distant cloud. This seemed to mean
something, and gave our thoughts, and the big arch of
world we looked at, a different quality that made us
uneasy but happy too, the way I was now.

I went on through the sparse trees and the rocks over
two ridges, and could see from them, and from the

little valley between, the rock castle at the end of the high col to the west, where I had eaten at noon another time, when I was alone, and then stayed for two hours to watch a hawk using the wind over the hollow to the west of me, feeling myself lift magnificently when he swooped up toward me on the current up the col, and then balanced and turned above.

I was feeling like that when I got back to the little, grassy lake where I'd left my pack. The pack was still there all right, under the bench nailed between two of the three trees on the hump at the farther side. Beyond the three trees, which were stunted and twisted by wind, I could see the wall of the col, very dark now, with a thin gold sky above it. Besides the bench, there was a pine-bough bed and a rock fireplace in the shelter of the trees. I hadn't made them, just found them there, but in the dusk the place gave me the hawk lift again. I had the night here alone, and another day in the mountains. That was a lot. And I had already stacked my firewood; brought it down that morning from the east slope.

I went around to the camp side and stood looking at the lake, thinking about swimming before I made a fire and ate. It was cold, and the water would be cold too. The lake was really just a pool of snow water, with no outlet, and no regular inflow, shallow enough so the dead grasses showed up through at the edges. But I like that kind of clean, cold feeling, and it had been warm climbing in the middle of the day. I peeled off, and stood liking the cold on my body, and the frozen, pebbly earth under my feet, and then, when I went nearer the edge, the wiry grass. It was very still in the valley, and the water reflected, exactly and without break, the mountains and the last of that thin, yellow light. I got that lift again. This time I would take it out. I ran splashing till I was thigh deep, and then rolled under. The water was even colder than I had expected, and hardened my whole body at once. For a minute or two I swam rapidly in circles in the small center that was deep enough. Then I was all right, and could roll easily, and even float looking up. The first stars were showing above the ridge in the east. I let go a couple of bars of high, operatic-sounding something. It came back at me from under the col, sounding much better, sweet and clear and high. God, I was happy. This was the way I liked it, alone, and clean cold, and a lot of time ahead. I rolled over to dive and start one more fast turn, when I heard the yodel that wasn't an echo.

I stood up, feeling the cold rim of the water around my chest, and even in the dusk could see the shape of the man coming over the hump and down toward the lake. When he was part way down, I could tell by the walk, a little pigeon-toed and easy, giving at the knees all the time, that it was Tom Williams. He had his pack on, and his rifle over one shoulder, with a thumb in the sling, the way Tom always carried it. The remainder of ecstasy went out of me. I'd rather have Tom than almost anyone I know for outside company, but I didn't want anybody now. And Tom meant Chet McKenny, and I didn't want Chet now or any other time. Chet was a big-boned, tall Scotchman, probably ten years older than either Tom or I, with gray in his stiff hair. He had a kind of stubborn originality that wouldn't use a joke somebody else had told, but he couldn't make a good one, so he was laughing all the time over bad jokes of his own. But that wasn't what I disliked, though it got tiresome. What I didn't like about McKenny was deeper than stupidity. You saw it when you saw that his eyes were still watching you when he laughed; you were always on guard against McKenny.

The three of us had come up in Tom's car, and they'd left me at the summit meadows. They were going on over to the flat to start a deer hunt. I was supposed to have today and tomorrow and then be back out at the meadows by sunset to wait for them.

Tom came down to where I'd dropped my clothes, and unslung his rifle and pack and put them down.

"Cold?" he asked. He didn't have to speak loudly.

"Plenty," I said.

I kept looking for Chet to come over the rise too.

Tom peeled off and came in, but slowly, and then just lying out and letting himself sink under. He came up slowly too, as if the water weren't cold at all, and just stood there, not even rubbing himself. There was something wrong.

"Where's Chet?" I asked. It would even be pleasant, with a fire after supper, to have Tom to talk to, if he was alone.

"That bastard," Tom said. Then he let himself down into the water again, and came up a few feet farther off, his thin, blond hair streaming down and the springy, blond mat on his big chest holding a few drops.

"He won't be here, anyway," he said, "so you don't have to worry."

He began to swim hard, and I took another turn,

to get the blood stirring again. Then we walked up
out of the water. Tom didn't say anything more, and I
didn't either. I knew it would come. Tom doesn't often
talk much, except about engines, but this was different. It was working in him, hard. He went up to his
pack, and I could see the muscles in his heavy white
shoulders working while he hunted in it. He got out a
towel and threw it to me. Then he went back down to
the water, and I saw he had a cake of soap in his hand.
But he didn't bathe. I stood there wiping off and watching him, and he just bent over in the shallows and
washed his hands. He washed them hard, three or four
times, rinsing them between. That was queer for Tom.
He was an auto mechanic, ran a little shop of his own,
and he'd long ago given up hoping to have his hands
really clean. Often on trips like this he'd go two or
three days without washing them at all.

He still didn't say anything, though, when he came
up; just took the towel from me and began to wipe himself slowly.

It felt good to be in the warm flannel shirt and cords
again, and shod heavily. Maybe that's even the best feeling, the cold that makes you feel thin and single, with
no waste matter, but beginning to get warm. I lit a
cigarette with stiff fingers, and saw against the match
flame how dark it was getting. The cigarette tasted very
good too. I was all set to be happy again, if Tom was
right.

Tom didn't talk while he was dressing, or while we
went up to the camp, or while he was cooking and
watching the coffee and I was putting some new boughs
and the sleeping bags on the bed. The bed was a good
one, wide enough for three, and in a pit a foot deep. I

went down to the lake to get two cans of beer out of the water. They're a lot of weight to carry in a pack, and I'd thought maybe I was pampering myself when I'd put them in, one for each evening. Now I was glad I'd brought them. When I came back up with them, he was just letting the things cook, and standing away from the fire, looking at the stars over the valley and in the little lake.

"This is a swell place," he said in an easier voice. "Gee, I haven't been in here for years. I'd forgot what a swell place it was."

Then I knew it was going to be all right, once he got around to telling me, and I had to sing a little while I put the beers between roots and took the eggs and beans off the fire; not loudly, but just about like the crackling of the fire.

When he came back and sat down on the bench, the light on his face with its fine mouth and big, broken nose and blue eyes, and its hard weather lines, he looked at me because I was singing, and I could see he was still thinking, but not feeling the same way about it.

When we'd started to eat, I asked, "How did the hunting go?"

"Don't you worry," Tom said. "I didn't get anything. I didn't even get a shot. I didn't see a thing."

He looked closed up again, as he had when he came into the water. He finished his beans, staring into the fire. Then he said suddenly, "That McKenny is a first-rate bastard."

"What's he done now?" I asked.

Tom looked right at me for a moment, as if he'd start, but then he said, "Oh, hell, let it go."

He got up and went down to the edge of the lake

slowly, and after a moment I saw his match flare, and then, every now and then, the fire point of his cigarette moving.

I'd never seen Tom let anything eat in him like that before. He made up his mind very .hard about what was wrong and what was right, especially about people, but he did it carefully, and he was usually gentle about it, even afterwards. It was the first time I'd heard him speak out like that. Whatever had happened, it must have been pretty bad.

Well, I was sure now that McKenny wasn't coming. I stopped thinking about it, put more wood on the fire, and lay on my back where the light wouldn't be in my eyes. Then I could see the silhouette of the col, where it walled out the stars, and the big peak glimmering in the starlight in the north. The size of the place, and the cold quiet, came back on me, and I was happy again.

I'd forgotten about Chet when Tom came back up and sat down on the bench. He stared at the ground for a moment. Then he looked across at me.

"You always thought so, didn't you?"

"Thought what?"

"That Chet McKenny was a first-rate bastard?"

I didn't like to say so.

"All right," Tom said. "I guess he is, at that."

He didn't say anything more, so I sat up.

"Have a beer?"

"No, thanks."

I had to get him started.

"Did Chet get anything?" I asked.

Tom looked at me hard.

"Yeah, he got one, all right, a good big buck, better

than two twenty, I'd guess. Ten points." He looked down.

Then he looked up again, and said suddenly, and loudly for that place, "You know what that bastard did? He—" but stopped.

"He what?"

"No," Tom said. "I'll tell you the way it was. Maybe I'm wrong.

"I worked down south, toward the lake meadows. I didn't see a thing all day; not even a doe; not even a fresh track or droppings. I figured it had been worked over and got disgusted and went back to the flat in the afternoon to get some sleep. I was washing up at the brook, and when I stood up and turned around, there was this big buck, a mule, on the edge of the trees across the flat. Even from there I could tell he was a big one, and I cussed, because there was my rifle up against a tree thirty yards from me, and the buck had spotted me. You know, his head was up and right at me, and those big ears up too. He was trying the wind. I figured if I moved he'd be back in those trees before I could take a step. So I held it. After a while he let his head down, way low, and began to go along the edge of the flat toward the pass. Then I saw there was something the matter with him. He wasn't using his left front leg; just bucking along on the other one, in little jumps. He was tired out, too, stopping every few jumps and taking the wind again, and then letting his head drop that way, like he couldn't hold it up. I figured somebody'd made a bad shot. I started for the gun. He saw me then, but he was so far gone he didn't even care, just kept hopping and resting. Then I didn't

know whether I wanted him or not. Only I might as
well, if his leg was really busted.

"I was standing there on the edge of the flat, wondering, when I heard this yell. It was Mac, coming down
through the trees. He yelled at me to head the buck
off. Your lousy shot then, I thought.

"When I went right out at the buck, it tried to
hurry. I yelled at Mac did he want me to finish it,
and he yelled at me, hell no, it was his buck. The buck
stood there with his head up when we yelled; he didn't
try to do anything.

"I don't know. It made me mad. But it was Mac's
buck. I started to work around so as not to hurry it any
more than I had to. Mac was working along in the
timber to get right above him. When I got around in
front, we worked in closer, and then the buck saw us
both, and just stopped and stood there. He was shivering all over, and didn't have any fight left in him. I
could see now that he'd been hit in the leg, right up
against the body. The blood was mostly dried on black,
but there was a little fresh blood coming out all the
time too. The bad leg was all banged up from being
dragged on things too, and he was soaked with sweat
on the hind quarters and under the throat, and making
cotton at the muzzle."

Tom stopped.

Then he said, "It's funny the way they look at you
like that. I don't know. There wasn't anything, no
fight, no panic, no hope, no nothing. He just looked at
you. But you couldn't move. They got such big eyes.
I don't know."

Tom kicked at a stone with his boot.

"Well, anyway, I couldn't move. But Mac could. He came up close behind. He had his cap on the back of his head and he was grinning. He said wasn't it a nice one. Ten points, he said.

"When he talked, the buck got going again, that same way. It was headed across the meadow toward the camp. I got ready to finish it, but Mac yelled at me to mind my own damn business and let it go or he'd damn well lather hell out of me. You know the way he does, grinning, but mad as the devil. I asked him what he thought he was doing, but he said that was his business, and to mind my own.

"The buck was going so slow you could pass it walking; had to wait on it. And it stopped two or three times. Mac could have killed it a long time before it got to the flat; I was sure of that. I began to think he wanted to take it in alive, or something. But it wasn't that."

Tom stopped talking and sat there.

"No?" I said.

"No," Tom said. "When the buck stopped, near where we'd had the fire, Mac said that was good enough, like he was pleased, and unslung his rifle and took mine too, and stood them up against a tree. Then he told me to hold the buck's head."

After a moment Tom went on again.

"I don't know why I did it. I just did. I never felt that way before. I guess I thought he was going to operate, as near as I thought anything. He just said to hold it, and I did, like I was in a daze. The buck kind of backed a little, and then, when I had hold of his antlers, he stood still; didn't make a move. Holding onto the antlers, I could feel him shivering all over, you know, like putting your hand on a telephone pole. Mac had his skinning knife out.

" 'Hold his head up,' he said.

"He was kind of leaning over and looking at the bullet hole when he said it, and I did.

"Then all of a sudden he leaned down on the buck's neck with one hand, and slit its throat wide open with the knife in the other. Leaning on it that way, he put all his weight on the buck's one leg, and the buck fell over front, and I didn't get out of the way fast enough. It knocked me onto my knees too, and the blood came out all over my hands and arms. It kept coming, in big spurts; there was an awful lot of it. I don't know."

Tom got out a cigarette and lit it. I didn't have anything to say. The story made a difference though, as if it were a lot darker all at once, and we were farther away from other people than before, and there were things alive in the rocks, watching us. I noticed there was a wind coming up too, but didn't think about it, just heard it in the trees as if it had been going all the time.

"It's funny," Tom said. "When the buck got pushed down, it stretched way out; you know. Its muzzle was right in my face, and it blew. It made a little spray of blood, but it had a sweet-smelling breath, you know, like a cow's. And then all that blood came out, hot."

Finally he asked me, "You know what Mac said?"

"No."

"Well, he laughed like hell when the buck pushed me over, and then he said, 'I never take more than one shot,' and then he laughed again.

"I was mad enough, I guess. I told him it was a hell of

a shot, and he said two inches to the right would've killed him, and pointed at the hole, and laughed again and said hell, it was perfect. The bullet had busted the joint all to pieces. There was splinters sticking out where they'd worked through."

I was looking at Tom now.

"You mean he meant to?" I asked.

"That's right," Tom said. "He thought he was real clever. He boasted about it. Said he'd spotted the buck way up in that little meadow under the castle rocks; what's its name? The buck was on the north edge of the meadow, and up wind of him, what wind there was. He said he figured it all out, that it was eight miles back to camp, and the buck was a big one. He couldn't see carrying it all that way, so he just laid down there on the edge of the timber, to make his shot good, and waited till the buck was broadside to him, and then busted that foreleg. Said he'd never made a better shot, that it was a hundred and fifty yards if it was an inch, and uphill. He was set up about that shot."

"Well," I said, letting out my breath.

"Yes," Tom said.

"He told me all about how he drove it, too," he said angrily. "How it kept trying to run at first, and falling over so he had to laugh, and then how it tried to turn on him, but couldn't stand it when he got close, and what a hell of a time he had driving it out of a couple of manzanita thickets where it tried to hole up. Then he figured that if he stayed off it, it would keep going steadier, and it did.

"So, I guess you were right," Tom said, making it a question.

"I didn't think he was that bad," I said. "You have to keep it up a long time to do a thing like that."

"He was still going strong," Tom said. "Only excited and talking a lot.

"Like I am now," he added.

I didn't want to ask. I figured anything he'd done wasn't enough. But I still looked at Tom.

"No," he said. "You don't have to worry. I didn't touch him.

"I don't know," he said doubtfully. "I wanted you to know the way it was, first."

"He had it coming to him," I said. But I was scared, so I nearly laughed when Tom told me.

"I told him if he'd been saving himself so careful, he could damned well carry his buck home, and I left him there."

"I'd like to have seen his face," I said.

"I didn't even look at him," Tom said. "I just put my things into the car and got out.

"He knew better than to say anything, too."

"Well," I said finally, "I wouldn't say you were too hard on him."

"No," Tom said. "But he'll try to bring that buck out."

"Sure," I agreed, "he wouldn't let it go if it was killing him."

Tom heeled his cigarette out carefully and said, "You wouldn't care to go up the mountain again tomorrow, would you?"

"Sure I would," I told him. "Now *you* quit worrying. He had it coming to him."

Tom said he was going to take another swim, and we

undressed by the fire, and went down together, and came back up wet. It felt very cold then, and the wind was stronger. But we piled more wood onto the fire, so it threw shadows of the three trees way up the hump, and when we'd dried off it felt so good we didn't get dressed, but just put on our shorts and stayed close to the fire.

"I'll have that beer now," Tom said. He was cheerful.

In the morning the wind was down, but it was snowing. We couldn't even see the mountain. I felt worse about the buck than I had when Tom told me, and kept thinking about it. We packed up and went back down trail, single file and not talking. Snow makes a hush that's even harder to talk in than the clear silence. There was something listening behind each tree and rock we passed, and something waiting among the taller trees down slope, blue through the falling snow. They wouldn't stop us, but they didn't like us, either. The snow was their ally.

Why Don't You Look
Where You're Going?

WHITE AS a sainted leviathan, but too huge for even God to have imagined it, the liner played eastward easily. It swam at a much greater speed than appeared, for it was alone in open ocean, and there were only the waves to pass.

Everyone on board was comfortable, even satisfied. The sea was a light summer one, still blue, although the sun was far gone toward the mountain range of fog on the horizon astern. Its swelling, and the rippling of the swells, could not give the slightest motion to the vessel, whose long hulk glanced through it as through warm and even air. The sense of well-being in the passengers was made firm by the knowledge that their fate was somebody else's responsibility for the next three days. There was nothing an ordinary mortal could do about a ship like this; it was as far out of his realm as the mechanics of heaven. He could talk about it, as he might about one of the farther galaxies, in order to experience the almost extinct pleasure of awe, but he could not do anything about it, and what was even more comfortable, he could not be expected to do anything about it.

Even the crew shared this un-Olympian calm, for the liner was a self-sufficient creature who, once put upon her course, pursued it independently, with gently rhythmic joy. The wheel took care of itself, the fuel sped upon quick wires, the warm and supple steel joints rose and fell, self-oiled to perfect limberness. More like a white Utopian city than any the earth will ever bear, she parted the subservient waters and proceeded.

A school of flying fish, which looked like dragonflies from the upper deck, broke water for an instant and fled back, no more than a brief proof of the pace of the liner.

The tall man in the gray topcoat stopped his circumambulation and peered toward the smoke of dusk rising out of the ocean. The woman in white flannel paused impatiently beyond him.

"What's that?" he asked.

"What?"

"There, ahead. No, a little more to the right. Like a log or something. See?"

"No."

"Well, look. There." He leaned over the rail and pointed.

"No. Oh, yes. Seaweed, I suppose."

"No, that wouldn't show; not so far. It sticks up."

The man's gesture drew other passengers to the rail. A boy in a white jacket was moving through them, clinking a musical triangle, and intoning, "First call to dinner; first call to dinner," but they were impressed by the pointing finger, and remained at the rail.

"What is it?" asked the stout, moustached man in linen knickers.

"I don't know," said the tall man, not looking around because his discovery was so small on the darkening sea.

"There's something, though," he added, and pointed again.

The other passengers also leaned over and peered hopefully. Those too far along to have heard the tall man's explanation looked at the sea vaguely, then at the people who were nearer the tall man, then at the sea again.

"He says there's something," the fat man informed them.

Then, "Oh, yes, I see it now." He pointed also. "There. See it? Still too far away to tell what it is, though." He appeared to think for a moment, and produced an original idea.

"We ought to pass it pretty close," he said, protruding his lower lip and puckering his mouth as a sign that he was considering carefully. "Pretty close, I should say, as we're going now."

The passengers exclaimed gratefully, and were able to look intelligent when they returned to peering. They felt better. Anybody could see by their backs that they felt better; much more decisive. As landsmen they were grateful for the discovery. Other walkers, coming to the side of the vessel, asked questions, and were almost told what the fat man had said. But there was never any citation of authority, or any admission of the pioneering of the tall man. The reputation for discovery was not easy to resign.

The latecomers remained until the entire rail was lined, and the number of the gathering excited each individual in it; the expected event attained mythological proportions.

This scene was re-enacted on the other three decks, although the watchers were fewer because the decks

were closed and all the watching had to be done from
port-holes. Children jumped up and down behind their
parents, inquiring in exasperated crescendos. Occasionally a beleaguered father or mother offered an unsatisfactory explanation, or held a child up to see that
there was only water. The entire starboard wall of the
gliding city was crowded with curious people, and their
curiosity was toughened by their desire to be first in
stating the nature of the discovery. Since the discovery
had already been made, it was now accounted common
property, and recognition of the object seemed more
important. The first idle speculation died, as meriting
scorn; most of the watchers were quiet and intent.

The young man with the fine blond hair left the rail
and returned almost at once with a victorious air and
a pair of binoculars. These he fixed to his eyes, turned
upon the focal point, and began to manipulate with
nimble fingers. At once others whose cabins were close
also got binoculars. They appeared determined, as if
to say the original inspiration was not what mattered
here, but the use made of it. Those who either had no
binoculars or had to go too far to get them, divided
their attention between the ocean off the starboard bow
and the blond young man, who had taken on the shining aspect of the clairvoyant. They watched his face
minutely for signs of recognition, and were affected by
his slightest movement. He bore their worship grandly,
almost with an air of not suspecting it.

"What is it?" they asked.

"I can't make it out yet." He continued to adjust the
binoculars.

When he ceased fingering and held the glasses

steadily, they asked again, "What is it?" and "Can you see it now?"

"Yes," he said, "I think I can." But he withheld the information, as one who will not be pressed into a hasty, and therefore possibly erroneous, conclusion. He fingered the binoculars just the perfect trifle more. Even the tall man in the gray coat abandoned his scrutiny and turned a tanned and bony face, drawn by staring, toward the blond young man.

The object was now close enough so that its location could be clearly marked by everyone at the moments when it appeared on the crest of a billow and balanced before beginning the long, gentle descent into the concealing trough. It might have been a great, triangular fin, if it had been much closer.

"Whatever it is, it had better look out. We're going right for it."

The fat man's suggestion that it might be a portion of the superstructure of a derelict caused a pleasant worry.

"I've heard," said a man with spectacles, and a checkered cap over a big nose, "I've heard they're often heavy enough below water to sink a good large boat." He spoke with quiet joy.

The tall man, who had been thinking about the fat man's suggestion, snorted.

"What part?" he challenged.

But, although the fat man was not insensible of the challenge, it was neglected because the blond young man had become signally rigid behind his binoculars.

He overplayed his pause, however, and a square, masculine, young woman said factually and loudly,

"It's a boat," and held her glasses a moment longer before lowering them to accept adulation in person.

"Yes," admitted the young man. "I was just going to say it's a boat." He added, "That thing that sticks up is a sail, a kind of triangular sail," and felt that this remark justified his lowering his glasses also, and looking around.

By now the boat was near enough so that the pace of the liner made it appear to draw nearer very rapidly. Since it was known to be a boat, and everyone could see it lay directly in the path of the liner, the guesses about what a small boat could be doing in mid-ocean gave way to irritation because it was doing nothing to save itself.

"We'd make matchwood of it," stated the fat man angrily.

"It would go to the bottom," declared the young man violently, "to the bottom, like a plummet."

The masculine young lady disagreed. "Not to the bottom; it would reach a level of suspension much sooner. The water is over three thousand feet deep here."

The other passengers rebuked her heartlessness with silence.

"Well, I do wish he'd wake up. I wish he'd get out of the way," complained the matron whose twin six-year-olds were extending her by their attempts to see over and under the rail. The passengers warmed to her humanity, and understanding that the young woman was quelled, all leaned over the rail and stared anxiously ahead.

High overhead the whistle of the liner hissed and

squealed abortively, and then settled into a long, mournful, gigantic moo.

Immediately a man appeared in the small boat. The liner was so close upon him that the passengers could see him look up startled. He became very active. He leaned over, stood up, disappeared behind the box-like cabin, and reappeared almost at once. He was working rapidly with his hands, glancing up frequently without stopping his work. The passengers knew he was frightened. Then the triangular sail swung slowly across the box-like cabin, slatted idly, two, three, four times, and slowly filled out like a breathing chest. The man, energetic as a jumping-jack, worked at the rail for an instant, then threw himself aft, slipped the noose from the tiller, and projected himself, chest and shoulders, against the bar. The sail flapped limp again, but only once, and suddenly drew a deep breath. The little boat heeled over until it was nearly awash, slithered along at a dog-walk during the ascent of one billow, then perfectly bit in and skittered off toward safety.

Four times the height of his sail above him, the bow of the liner passed over the tiny man in his cockpit, and left him valiantly awash, bobbing under four, three-hundred-foot tiers of fascinated eyes. They could see that he had no hat, that he wore a black beard, and that his pants were held up by a knotted rope. He braced the tiller with a knee, raised both fists over his head, and shook them at the liner. The passengers were immensely relieved. The women laughed, and the men leaned far over the rail to shout at him between cupped hands. They saw that he was shouting also; his mouth was wide open and his teeth showed in his beard. Everyone became silent and listened. But there was such a rush of white water back from the stem, and the wind wuthered so in the railing, that the man appeared to be trying to free his jaw from a cramp, making no sound. He addressed them continuously and energetically, but not until the liner had nearly drawn its whole length by did a wind flaw bring up his voice with an item of his lecture. The passengers aft repeated it with glee; indeed they wriggled with glee at it, their bodies and their faces.

"He said, 'Why don't you look where you're going?' "

Everyone was charmed.

They leaned over farther and farther to watch the little boat as it diminished. Why don't you look where you're going? That was good. That was conceit for you; a man who didn't count himself less than he was worth. "Everybody's out of step but Johnny," sang the young man with the blond hair. He sang it at the man in the little boat, who was obviously too far away to hear, but everybody else appreciated it; they leaned back and looked at the young man with many kinds of grins and smiles to appreciate it, and quickly leaned over the rail again to watch.

The stern of the little boat said to them, *"The Flying Dutchman—Rockport—Me."* They became silent, and watched the puppet of a bearded man sit to his tiller and labor earnestly to navigate the wake of the liner. A great many of them unconsciously went farther and farther aft, to keep the "Flying Dutchman" in sight. The stern of the liner was crowded, and all the faces were serious and fixed.

When the little man was far enough astern to feel

secure, and had his boat properly angled into the heave of the wake, he underwent a change of heart. The watchers could just see him, yet everybody recognized that he was standing up again and waving. Every face brightened spontaneously, and the afterdeck blossomed windily with hands, handkerchiefs, hats and caps.

The fat man bellowed astoundingly through the trumpet of his hands, "Good luck, sailor!"

" 'Why don't you look where you're going?' " he repeated gruffly. " 'Why don't you look where you're going?' That's good."

The masculine young lady stood with her hands on the rail and peered wistfully under the Andes of the cloud bank, where the tiny, black triangle of sail was only now and then visible, getting less so.

The Indian Well

IN THIS dead land, like a vast relief model, the only allegiance was to sun. Even night was not strong enough to resist; earth stretched gratefully under it, but had no hope that day would not return. Such living things as hoarded a little juice at their cores were secret about it, and only the most ephemeral existences, the air at dawn and sunset, the amethyst shadows in the mountains, had any freedom. The Indian Well alone, of lesser creations, was in constant revolt. Sooner or later all minor, breathing rebels came to its stone basin under the spring in the cliff, and from its overflow grew a meadow delta and two columns of willows and aspens holding a tiny front against the valley. The pictograph of a starving, ancient journey, cut in rock above the basin, a sun-warped shack on the south wing of the canyon, and an abandoned mine above it, were the last minute and practically contemporary tokens of man's participation in the cycles of the well's resistance, each of which was an epitome of centuries, and perhaps of the wars of the universe.

The day before Jim Suttler came up in the early spring to take his part in one cycle was a busy day. The sun was merely lucid after four days of broken showers and one rain of an hour with a little cold wind behind it, and under the separate cloud shadows sliding down the mountain and into the valley, the canyon was alive. A rattler emerged partially from a hole in the mound on which the cabin stood, and having gorged in the darkness, rested with his head on a stone. A road-runner, stepping long and always about to sprint, came down the morning side of the mound, and his eye, quick to perceive the difference between the live and the inanimate of the same color, discovered the coffin-shaped head on the stone. At once he broke into a reaching sprint, his neck and tail stretched level, his beak agape with expectation. But his shadow arrived a step before him. The rattler recoiled, his head scarred by the sharp beak but his eye intact. The road-runner said nothing, but peered warily into the hole without stretching his neck, then walked off stiffly, leaning forward again as if about to run. When he had gone twenty feet he turned, balanced for an instant, and charged back, checking abruptly just short of the hole. The snake remained withdrawn. The road-runner paraded briefly before the hole, talking to himself, and then ran angrily up to the spring, where he drank at the overflow, sipping and stretching his neck, lifting his feet one at a time, ready to go into immediate action. The road-runner lived a dangerous and exciting life.

In the upper canyon the cliff swallows, making short harp notes, dipped and shot between the new mud under the aspens and their high community on the forehead of the cliff. Electrical bluebirds appeared to dart the length of the canyon at each low flight, but turned up tilting half way down. Lizards made similar unexpected flights and stops on the rocks, and when they stopped did rapid push-ups, like men exercising on a floor. They were variably pugnacious and timid.

Two of them arrived simultaneously upon a rock below the road-runner. One of them immediately skittered to a rock two feet off, and they faced each other, exercising. A small hawk coming down over the mountain, but shadowless under a cloud, saw the lizards. Having overfled the difficult target, he dropped to the canyon mouth swiftly and banked back into the wind. His trajectory was cleared of swallows but one of them, fluttering hastily up, dropped a pellet of mud between the lizards. The one who had retreated disappeared. The other flattened for an instant, then sprang and charged. The road-runner was on him as he struck the pellet, and galloped down the canyon in great, tense strides on his toes, the lizard lashing the air from his beak. The hawk stooped at the road-runner, thought better of it, and rose against the wind to the head of the canyon, where he turned back and coasted out over the desert, his shadow a little behind him and farther and farther below.

The swallows became the voice of the canyon again, but in moments when they were all silent the lovely smaller sounds emerged, their own feathering, the liquid overflow, the snapping and clicking of insects, a touch of wind in the new aspens. Under these lay still more delicate tones, erasing, in the most silent seconds, the difference between eye and ear, a white cloud shadow passing under the water of the well, a dark cloud shadow on the cliff, the aspen patterns on the stones. Deepest was the permanent background of the rocks, the lost on the canyon floor, and those yet strong, the thinking cliffs. When the swallows began again it was impossible to understand the cliffs, who could afford to wait.

At noon a red and white range cow with one new calf, shining and curled, came slowly up from the desert, stopping often to let the calf rest. At each stop the calf would try vigorously to feed, but the cow would go on. When they reached the well the cow drank slowly for a long time; then she continued to wrinkle the water with her muzzle, drinking a little and blowing, as if she found it hard to leave. The calf worked under her with spasmodic nudgings. When she was done playing with the water, she nosed and licked him out from under her and up to the well. He shied from the surprising coolness and she put him back. When he stayed, she drank again. He put his nose into the water also, and bucked up as if bitten. She continued to pretend, and he returned, got water up his nostrils and took three jumps away. The cow was content and moved off toward the canyon wall, tonguing grass tufts from among the rocks. Against the cliff she rubbed gently and continuously with a mild voluptuous look, occasionally lapping her nose with a serpent tongue. The loose winter shag came off in tufts on the rock. The calf lost her, became panicked and made desperate noises which stopped prematurely, and when he discovered her, complicated her toilet. Finally she led him down to the meadow where, moving slowly, they both fed until he was full and went to sleep in a ball in the sun. At sunset they returned to the well, where the cow drank again and gave him a second lesson. After this they went back into the brush and northward into the dusk. The cow's size and relative immunity to sudden death left an aftermath of peace, rendered gently humorous by the calf.

Also at sunset, there was a resurgence of life among the swallows. The thin golden air at the cliff tops, in which there were now no clouds so that the eastern mountains and the valley were flooded with unbroken light, was full of their cries and quick maneuvers among a dancing myriad of insects. The direct sun gave them, when they perched in rows upon the cliff, a dramatic significance like that of men upon an immensely higher promontory. As dusk rose out of the canyon, while the eastern peaks were still lighted, the swallows gradually became silent creatures with slightly altered flight, until, at twilight, the air was full of velvet, swooping bats.

In the night jack-rabbits multiplied spontaneously out of the brush of the valley, drank in the rivulet, their noses and great ears continuously searching the dark, electrical air, and played in fits and starts on the meadow, the many young hopping like rubber, or made thumping love among the aspens and the willows.

A coyote came down canyon on his belly and lay in the brush with his nose between his paws. He took a young rabbit in a quiet spring and snap, and went into the brush again to eat it. At the slight rending of his meal the meadow cleared of leaping shadows and lay empty in the starlight. The rabbits, however, encouraged by newcomers, returned soon, and the coyote killed again and went off heavily, the jack's great hind legs dragging.

In the dry-wash below the meadow an old coyote, without family, profited by the second panic, which came over him. He ate what his loose teeth could tear, leaving the open remnant in the sand, drank at the basin and, carefully circling the meadow, disappeared into the dry wilderness.

Shortly before dawn, when the stars had lost luster and there was no sound in the canyon but the rivulet and the faint, separate clickings of mice in the gravel, nine antelope in loose file, with three silently flagging fawns, came on trigger toe up the meadow and drank at the well, heads often up, muzzles dripping, broad ears turning. In the meadow they grazed and the fawns nursed. When there was as much gray as darkness in the air, and new wind in the canyon, they departed, the file weaving into the brush, merging into the desert, to nothing, and the swallows resumed the talkative day shift.

Jim Suttler and his burro came up into the meadow a little after noon, very slowly, though there was only a spring-fever warmth. Suttler walked pigeon-toed, like an old climber, but carefully and stiffly, not with the loose walk natural to such a long-legged man. He stopped in the middle of the meadow, took off his old black sombrero, and stared up at the veil of water shining over the edge of the basin.

"We're none too early, Jenny," he said to the burro.

The burro had felt water for miles, but could show no excitement. She stood with her head down and her four legs spread unnaturally, as if to postpone a collapse. Her pack reared higher than Suttler's head, and was hung with casks, pails, canteens, a pick, two shovels, a crowbar and a rifle in a sheath. Suttler had the cautious uncertainty of his trade. His other burro had died two days before in the mountains east of Beatty, and Jenny and he bore its load.

Suttler shifted his old six shooter from his rump to his thigh, and studied the well, the meadow, the cabin and the mouth of the mine as if he might choose not to stay. He was not a cinema prospector. If he looked like one of the probably mistaken conceptions of Christ, with his red beard and red hair to his shoulders, it was because he had been long away from barbers and without spare water for shaving. He was unlike Christ in some other ways also.

"It's kinda run down," he told Jenny, "but we'll take it."

He put his sombrero back on, let his pack fall slowly to the ground, showing the sweat patch in his bleached brown shirt, and began to unload Jenny carefully, like a collector handling rare vases, and put everything into one neat pile.

"Now," he said, "we'll have a drink." His tongue and lips were so swollen that the words were unclear, but he spoke casually, like a club-man sealing a minor deal. One learns to do business slowly with deserts and mountains. He picked up a bucket and started for the well. At the upper edge of the meadow he looked back. Jenny was still standing with her head down and her legs apart. He did not particularly notice her extreme thinness for he had seen it coming on gradually. He was thinner himself, and tall, and so round-shouldered that when he stood his straightest he seemed to be peering ahead with his chin out.

"Come on, you old fool," he said. "It's off you now."

Jenny came, stumbling in the rocks above the

meadow, and stopping often as if to decide why this annoyance recurred. When she became interested, Suttler would not let her get to the basin, but for ten minutes gave her water from his cupped hands, a few licks at a time. Then he drove her off and she stood in the shade of the canyon wall watching him. He began on his thirst in the same way, a gulp at a time, resting between gulps. After ten gulps he sat on a rock by the spring and looked at the little meadow and the big desert, and might have been considering the courses of the water through his body, but noticed also the antelope tracks in the mud.

After a time he drank another half dozen gulps, gave Jenny half a pailful, and drove her down to the meadow, where he spread a dirty blanket in the striped sun and shadow under the willows. He sat on the edge of the blanket, rolled a cigarette and smoked it while he watched Jenny. When she began to graze with her rump to the canyon, he flicked his cigarette onto the grass, rolled over with his back to the sun and slept until it became chilly after sunset. Then he woke, ate a can of beans, threw the can into the willows and led Jenny up to the well, where they drank together from the basin for a long time. While she resumed her grazing, he took another blanket and his rifle from the pile, removed his heel-worn boots, stood his rifle against a fork, and, rolling up in both blankets, slept again.

In the night many rabbits played in the meadow in spite of the strong sweat and tobacco smell of Jim Suttler lying under the willows, but the antelope, when they came in the dead dark before dawn, were nervous, drank less, and did not graze but minced quickly back across the meadow and began to run at the head of the dry wash. Jenny slept with her head hanging, and did not hear them come or go.

Suttler woke lazy and still red-eyed, and spent the morning drinking at the well, eating and dozing on his blanket. In the afternoon, slowly, a few things at a time, he carried his pile to the cabin. He had a bachelor's obsession with order, though he did not mind dirt, and puttered until sundown making a brush bed and arranging his gear. Much of this time, however, was spent studying the records, on the cabin walls, of the recent human life of the well. He had to be careful, because among the still legible names and dates, after Frank Davis, 1893, Willard Harbinger, 1893, London, England, John Mason, June 13, 1887, Bucksport, Maine, Matthew Kenling, from Glasgow, 1891, Penelope and Martin Reave, God Guide Us, 1885, was written Frank Hayward, 1492, feeling my age. There were other wits too. John Barr had written, Giv it back to the injuns, and Kenneth Thatcher, two years later, had written under that, Pity the noble redskin, while another man, whose second name was Evans, had written what was already a familiar libel, since it was not strictly true: Fifty miles from water, a hundred miles from wood, a million miles from God, three feet from hell. Someone unnamed had felt differently, saying, God is kind. We may make it now. Shot an antelope here July 10, 188— and the last number blurred. Arthur Smith, 1881, had recorded, Here berried my beloved wife Semantha, age 22, and my soul. God let me keep the child. J.M. said cryptically, Good luck, John, and Bill said, Ralph, if you come this way, am trying to get to Los Angeles. B.Westover said he had recovered from his wound there in 1884, and Galt said, enigmatically and without date,

Bart and Miller burned to death in the Yellow Jacket.
I don't care now. There were poets too, of both parties.
What could still be read of Byron Cotter's verses, writ-
ten in 1902, said,

　. . . here alone
　Each shining dawn I greet,
　The Lord's wind on my forehead
　And where he set his feet
　One mark of heel remaining
　Each day filled up anew,
　To keep my soul from burning,
　With clear, celestial dew.
　Here in His Grace abiding
　The mortal years and few
　I shall . . . but you can't tell what he intended, while
J.A. had printed,

　My brother came out in '49
　I came in '51
　At first we thought we liked it fine
　But now, by God, we're done.

Suttler studied these records without smiling, like
someone reading a funny paper, and finally, with a
heavy blue pencil, registered, Jim and Jenny Suttler,
damn dried out, March—and paused, but had no way of
discovering the day—1940.

In the evening he sat on the steps watching the swallows in the golden upper canyon turn bats in the dusk,
and thought about the antelope. He had seen the new
tracks also, and it alarmed him a little that the antelope
could have passed twice in the dark without waking
him.

Before false dawn he was lying in the willows with his

carbine at ready. Rabbits ran from the meadow when
he came down, and after that there was no movement.
He wanted to smoke. When he did see them at the
lower edge of the meadow, he was startled, yet made
no quick movement, but slowly pivoted to cover them.
They made poor targets in that light and backed by
the pale desert, appearing and disappearing before his
eyes. He couldn't keep any one of them steadily visible,
and decided to wait until they made contrast against the
meadow. But his presence was strong. One of the antelope advanced onto the green, but then threw its head
up, spun, and ran back past the flank of the herd, which
swung after him. Suttler rose quickly and raised the
rifle, but let it down without firing. He could hear the
light rattle of their flight in the wash, but had only a
belief that he could see them. He had few cartridges,
and the report and ponderous echo under the cliffs
would scare them off for weeks.

His energies, however, were awakened by the frus-
trated hunt. While there was still more light than heat
in the canyon, he climbed to the abandoned mine
tunnel at the top of the alluvial wing of the cliff. He
looked at the broken rock in the dump, kicked up its
pack with a boot toe, and went into the tunnel, peering
closely at its sides, in places black with old smoke
smudges. At the back he struck two matches and looked
at the jagged dead end and the fragments on the floor,
then returned to the shallow beginning of a side tunnel.
At the second match here he knelt quickly, scrutinized
a portion of the rock, and when the match went out at
once lit another. He lit six matches, and pulled at the
rock with his hand. It was firm.

"The poor chump," he said aloud.

He got a loose rock from the tunnel and hammered at the projection with it. It came finally, and he carried it into the sun on the dump.

"Yessir," he said aloud, after a minute.

He knocked his sample into three pieces and examined each minutely.

"Yessir, yessir," he said with malicious glee, and, grinning at the tunnel, "The poor chump."

Then he looked again at the dump, like the mound before a gigantic gopher hole. "Still, that's a lot of digging," he said.

He put sample chips into his shirt pocket, keeping a small, black, heavy one that had fallen neatly from a hole like a borer's, to play with in his hand. After trouble he found the claim pile on the side hill south of the tunnel, its top rocks tumbled into the shale. Under the remaining rocks he found what he wanted, a ragged piece of yellowed paper between two boards. The writing was in pencil, and not diplomatic. "I hereby clame this whole damn side hill as far as I can shoot north and south and as far as I can dig in. I am a good shot. Keep off. John Barr, April 11, 1897."

Jim Suttler grinned. "Tough guy, eh?" he said.

He made a small ceremony of burning the paper upon a stone from the cairn. The black tinsel of ash blew off and broke into flakes.

"O.K., John Barr?" he asked.

"O.K., Suttler," he answered himself.

In blue pencil, on soiled paper from his pocket, he slowly printed, "Becus of the lamented desease of the late clament, John Barr, I now clame these diggins for myself and partner Jenny. I can shoot too." And wrote rather than printed, "James T. Suttler, March—" and paused.

"Make it an even month," he said, and wrote, "11, 1940." Underneath he wrote, "Jenny Suttler, her mark," and drew a skull with long ears.

"There," he said, and folded the paper, put it between the two boards, and rebuilt the cairn into a neat pyramid above it.

In high spirit he was driven to cleanliness. With scissors, soap and razor he climbed to the spring. Jenny was there, drinking.

"When you're done," he said, and when she lifted her head, pulled her ears and scratched her.

"Maybe we've got something here, Jenny," he said.

Jenny observed him soberly and returned to the meadow.

"She doesn't believe me," he said, and began to perfect himself. He sheared off his red tresses in long hanks, then cut closer, and went over yet a third time, until there remained a brush, of varying density, of stiff red bristles, through which his scalp shone whitely. He sheared the beard likewise, then knelt to the well for mirror and shaved painfully. He also shaved his neck and about his ears. He arose younger and less impressive, with jaws as pale as his scalp, so that his sunburn was a red domino. He burned tresses and beard ceremoniously upon a sage bush, and announced, "It is spring."

He began to empty the pockets of his shirt and breeches onto a flat stone, yelling, "In the spring a young man's fancy," to a kind of tune, and paused, struck by the facts.

"Oh yeah?" he said. "Fat chance."

"Fat," he repeated with obscene consideration. "Oh, well," he said, and finished piling upon the rock notebooks, pencils stubs, cartridges, tobacco, knife, stump pipe, matches, chalk, samples, and three wrinkled photographs. One of the photographs he observed at length before weighting it down with a .45 cartridge. It showed a round, blonde girl with a big smile on a stupid face, in a patterned calico house dress, in front of a blossoming rhododendron bush.

He added to this deposit his belt and holster with the big .45.

Then he stripped himself, washed and rinsed his garments in the spring, and spread them upon stones and brush, and carefully arranged four flat stones into a platform beside the trough. Standing there he scooped water over himself, gasping, made it a lather, and at last, face and copper bristles also foaming, gropingly entered the basin, and submerged, flooding the water over in a thin and soapy sheet. His head emerged at once. "My God," he whispered. He remained under, however, till he was soapless, and goose pimpled as a file, when he climbed out cautiously onto the rock platform and performed a dance of small, revolving patterns with a great deal of up and down.

At one point in his dance he observed the pictograph journey upon the cliff, and danced nearer to examine it.

"Ignorant," he pronounced. "Like a little kid," he said.

He was intrigued, however, by more recent records, names smoked and cut upon the lower rock. One of these, in script, like a gigantic handwriting deeply cut, said ALVAREZ BLANCO DE TOLEDO, Anno Di 1624. A very neat, upright cross was chiseled beneath it.

Suttler grinned. "Oh, yeah?" he asked, with his head upon one side. "Nuts," he said, looking at it squarely.

But it inspired him, and with his jack-knife he began scraping beneath the possibly Spanish inscription. His knife, however, made scratches, not incisions. He completed a bad Jim and Jenny and quit, saying, "I should kill myself over a phony wop."

Thereafter, for weeks, while the canyon became increasingly like a furnace in the daytime and the rocks stayed warm at night, he drove his tunnel farther into the mountain and piled the dump farther into the gully, making, at one side of the entrance, a heap of ore to be worked, and occasionally adding a peculiarly heavy pebble to the others in his small leather bag with a draw string. He and Jenny thrived upon this fixed and well-watered life. The hollows disappeared from his face and he became less stringy, while Jenny grew round, her battleship-gray pelt even lustrous and its black markings distinct and ornamental. The burro found time from her grazing to come to the cabin door in the evenings and attend solemnly to Suttler playing with his samples and explaining their future.

"Then, old lady," Suttler said, "you will carry only small children, one at a time, for never more than half an hour. You will have a bedroom with French windows and a mattress, and I will paint your feet gold.

"The children," he said, "will probably be red-headed, but maybe blonde. Anyway, they will be beautiful.

"After we've had a holiday, of course," he added. "For

one hundred and thirty-three nights," he said dreamily. "Also," he said, "just one hundred and thirty-three quarts. I'm no drunken bum.

"For you, though," he said, "for one hundred and thirty-three nights a quiet hotel with other old ladies. I should drag my own mother in the gutter." He pulled her head down by the ears and kissed her loudly upon the nose. They were very happy together.

Nor did they greatly alter most of the life of the canyon. The antelope did not return, it is true, the rabbits were fewer and less playful because he sometimes snared them for meat, the little, clean mice and desert rats avoided the cabin they had used, and the road-runner did not come in daylight after Suttler, for fun, narrowly missed him with a piece of ore from the tunnel mouth. Suttler's violence was disproportionate perhaps, when he used his .45 to blow apart a creamy rat who did invade the cabin, but the loss was insignificant to the pattern of the well, and more than compensated when he one day caught the rattler extended at the foot of the dump in a drunken stupor from rare young rabbit, and before it could recoil held it aloft by the tail and snapped its head off, leaving the heavy body to turn slowly for a long time among the rocks. The dominant voices went undisturbed, save when he sang badly at his work or said beautiful things to Jenny in a loud voice.

There were, however, two more noticeable changes, one of which, at least, was important to Suttler himself. The first was the execution of the range cow's calf in the late fall, when he began to suggest a bull. Suttler felt a little guilty about this because the calf might have belonged to somebody, because the cow remained near the meadow bawling for two nights, and because the calf had come to meet the gun with more curiosity than challenge. But when he had the flayed carcass hung in the mine tunnel in a wet canvas, the sensation of providence overcame any qualms.

The other change was more serious. It occurred at the beginning of such winter as the well had, when there was sometimes a light rime on the rocks at dawn, and the aspens held only a few yellow leaves. Suttler thought often of leaving. The nights were cold, the fresh meat was eaten, his hopes had diminished as he still found only occasional nuggets, and his dreams of women, if less violent, were more nostalgic. The canyon held him with a feeling he would have called lonesome but at home, yet he probably would have gone except for this second change.

In the higher mountains to the west, where there was already snow, and at dawn a green winter sky, hunger stirred a buried memory in a cougar. He had twice killed antelope at the well, and felt there had been time enough again. He came down from the dwarfed trees and crossed the narrow valley under the stars, sometimes stopping abruptly to stare intently about, like a house-cat in a strange room. After each stop he would at once resume a quick, noiseless trot. From the top of the mountain above the spring he came down very slowly on his belly, but there was nothing at the well. He relaxed, and leaning on the rim of the basin, drank, listening between laps. His nose was clean with fasting, and he knew of the man in the cabin and Jenny in the meadow, but they were strange, not what he remembered about the place. But neither had his past made him fearful. It was only habitual hunting caution which made him go down into the willows carefully, and lie there head up, watching Jenny, but still waiting for antelope, which he had killed before near dawn. The strange smells were confusing and therefore irritating. After an hour he rose and went silently to the cabin, from which the strangest smell came strongly, a carnivorous smell which did not arouse appetite, but made him bristle nervously. The tobacco in it was like pins in his nostrils. He circled the cabin, stopping frequently. At the open door the scent was violent. He stood with his front paws up on the step, moving his head in serpent motions, the end of his heavy tail furling and unfurling constantly. In a dream Suttler turned over without waking, and muttered. The cougar crouched, his eyes intent, his ruff lifting. Then he swung away from the door, growling a little, and after one pause, crept back down to the meadow again and lay in the willows, but where he could watch the cabin also.

When the sky was alarmingly pale and the antelope had not come, he crawled a few feet at a time, behind the willows, to a point nearer Jenny. There he crouched, working his hind legs slowly under him until he was set, and sprang, raced the three or four jumps to the drowsy burro, and struck. The beginning of her mortal scream was severed, but having made an imperfect leap, and from no height, the cat did not at once break her neck, but drove her to earth, where her small hooves churned futilely in the sod, and chewed and worried until she lay still.

Jim Suttler was nearly awakened by the fragment of scream, but heard nothing after it, and sank again.

The cat wrestled Jenny's body into the willows, fed with uncertain relish, drank long at the well, and went slowly over the crest, stopping often to look back. In spite of the light and the beginning talk of the swallows, the old coyote also fed and was gone before Suttler woke.

When Suttler found Jenny, many double columns of regimented ants were already at work, streaming in and out of the interior and mounting like bridge workers upon the ribs. Suttler stood and looked down. He desired to hold the small muzzle in the hollow of his hand, feeling that this familiar gesture would get through to Jenny, but couldn't bring himself to it because of what had happened to that side of her head. He squatted and lifted one hoof on its stiff leg and held that. Ants emerged hurriedly from the fetlock, their lines of communication broken. Two of them made disorganized excursions on the back of his hand. He rose, shook them off, and stood staring again. He didn't say anything because he spoke easily only when cheerful or excited, but a determination was beginning in him. He followed the drag to the spot torn by the small hoofs. Among the willows again, he found the tracks of both the cougar and the coyote, and the cat's tracks again at the well and by the cabin doorstep. He left Jenny in the willows with a canvas over her during the day, and did not eat.

At sunset he sat on the doorstep, cleaning his rifle and oiling it until he could spring the lever almost without sound. He filled the clip, pressed it home, and sat with the gun across his knees until dark, when he put on his sheepskin, stuffed a scarf into the pocket, and went down to Jenny. He removed the canvas from her, rolled it up and held it under his arm.

"I'm sorry, old woman," he said. "Just tonight."

There was a little cold wind in the willows. It rattled the upper branches lightly.

Suttler selected a spot thirty yards down wind, from which he could see Jenny, spread the canvas and lay down upon it, facing toward her. After an hour he was afraid of falling asleep and sat up against a willow clump. He sat there all night. A little after midnight the old coyote came into the dry-wash below him. At the top of the wash he sat down, and when the mingled scents gave him a clear picture of the strategy, let his tongue loll out, looked at the stars for a moment with his mouth silently open, rose and trotted back into the desert.

At the beginning of daylight the younger coyote trotted in from the north, and turned up toward the spring, but saw Jenny. He sat down and looked at her for a long time. Then he moved to the west and sat down again. In the wind was only winter, and the water, and faintly the acrid bat dung in the cliffs. He completed the circle, but not widely enough, walking slowly through the willows, down the edge of the meadow and in again not ten yards in front of the following muzzle of the carbine. Like Jenny, he felt his danger too late. The heavy slug caught him at the base of the skull in the middle of the first jump, so that it was amazingly accelerated for a fraction of a second. The coyote began it alive, and ended it quite dead, but with a tense muscular movement conceived which resulted in a grotesque final leap and twist of the hindquarters alone, leaving them propped high against a willow clump while the head was half buried in the sand, red welling up along the lips of the distended jaws. The cottony underpelt of the tail and rump stirred gleefully in the wind.

When Suttler kicked the body and it did not move, he suddenly dropped his gun, grasped it by the upright hind legs, and hurled it out into the sage-brush. His face appeared slightly insane with fury for that instant. Then he picked up his gun and went back to the cabin, where he ate, and drank half of one of his last three bottles of whiskey.

In the middle of the morning he came down with his pick and shovel, dragged Jenny's much lightened body down into the dry-wash, and dug in the rock and sand for two hours. When she was covered, he erected a small cairn of stone, like the claim post, above her.

"If it takes a year," he said, and licked the salt sweat on his lips.

That day he finished the half bottle and drank all of a second one, and became very drunk, so that he fell asleep during his vigil in the willows, sprawled wide on the dry turf and snoring. He was not disturbed. There was a difference in his smell after that day which prevented even the rabbits from coming into the meadow. He waited five nights in the willows. Then he transferred his watch to a niche in the cliff, across from and just below the spring.

All winter, while the day wind blew long veils of dust across the desert, regularly repeated, like waves or the smoke of line artillery fire, and the rocks shrank under the cold glitter of night, he did not miss a watch. He learned to go to sleep at sundown, wake within a few minutes of midnight, go up to his post, and become at once clear headed and watchful. He talked to himself in the mine and the cabin, but never in the niche. His supplies ran low, and he ate less, but would not risk a startling shot. He rationed his tobacco, and when it was gone worked up to a vomiting sickness every three days for nine days, but did not miss a night in the niche. All winter he did not remove his clothes, bathe, shave, cut his hair or sing. He worked the dead mine only to be busy, and became thin again, with sunken eyes which yet were not the eyes he had come with the spring before. It was April, his food almost gone, when he got his chance.

There was a half moon that night, which made the canyon walls black, and occasionally gleamed on wrinkles of the overflow. The cat came down so quietly that Suttler did not see him until he was beside the basin. The animal was suspicious. He took the wind, and twice started to drink, and didn't, but crouched. On Suttler's face there was a set grin which exposed his teeth.

"Not even a drink, you bastard," he thought.

The cat drank a little though, and dropped again, softly, trying to get the scent from the meadow. Suttler drew slowly upon his soul in the trigger. When it gave, the report was magnified impressively in the canyon. The cougar sprang straight into the air and screamed outrageously. The back of Suttler's neck was cold and his hands trembled, but he shucked the lever and fired again. This shot ricocheted from the basin and whined away thinly. The first, however, had struck near enough. the cat began to scramble rapidly on the loose stone, at first without voice, then screaming repeatedly. It doubled upon itself snarling and chewing in a small furious circle, fell and began to throw itself in short, leaping spasms upon the stones, struck across the rim of the tank and lay half in the water, its head and shoulders raised in one corner and resting against the cliff. Suttler could hear it breathing hoarsely and snarling very faintly. The soprano chorus of swallows gradually became silent.

Suttler had risen to fire again, but lowered the carbine and advanced, stopping at every step to peer intently and listen for the hoarse breathing, which continued. Even when he was within five feet of the tank the cougar did not move, except to gasp so that the water again splashed from the basin. Suttler was calmed by the certainty of accomplishment. He drew the heavy revolver from his holster, aimed carefully at the rattling head, and fired again. The canyon boomed, and the east responded faintly and a little behind, but Suttler did not hear them, for the cat thrashed heavily in the tank, splashing him as with a bucket, and then lay still on its side over the edge, its muzzle and forepaws hanging. The water was settling quietly in the tank, but Suttler stirred it again, shooting five more times with great deliberation into the heavy body, which did not move except at the impact of the slugs.

The rest of the night, even after the moon was gone, he worked fiercely, slitting and tearing with his knife. In the morning, under the swallows, he dragged the marbled carcass, still bleeding a little in places, onto the rocks on the side away from the spring, and dropped it. Dragging the ragged hide by the neck, he went unsteadily down the canyon to the cabin, where he slept like a drunkard, although his whiskey had been gone for two months.

In the afternoon, with dreaming eyes, he bore the pelt to Jenny's grave, took down the stones with his hands, shoveled the earth from her, covered her with the skin, and again with earth and the cairn.

He looked at this monument. "There," he said.

That night, for the first time since her death, he slept through.

In the morning, at the well, he repeated his cleansing ritual of a year before, save that they were rags he stretched to dry, even to the dance upon the rock platform while drying. Squatting naked and clean, shaven and clipped, he looked for a long time at the grinning countenance, now very dirty, of the plump girl in front of the blossoming rhododendrons, and in the resumption of his dance he made singing noises accompanied by the words, "Spring, spring, beautiful spring." He was a starved but revived and volatile spirit.

An hour later he went south, his boot soles held on by canvas strips, and did not once look back.

The disturbed life of the spring resumed. In the second night the rabbits loved in the willows, and at the end of a week the rats played in the cabin again. The old coyote and a vulture cleaned the cougar, and his bones fell apart in the shale. The road-runner came up one day, tentatively, and in front of the tunnel snatched up a horned toad and ran with it around the corner, but no farther. After a month the antelope returned. The well brimmed, and in the gentle sunlight the new aspen leaves made a tiny music of shadows.

The Fish Who

Could Close His Eyes

UNTIL Hamlet, the purple fish, appeared in the aquarium, Tad Manson probably lived the happiest life at the marine institute. He did just odd jobs about which there was no hurry and nothing which had to be carried home and worried about. He fed the fish in the aquarium, watered the scattered trees and plants on the grounds, collected quarters from the men who came to fish on the long pier, and sometimes helped to get squid, crabs, eels, anemones, all sorts of living creatures from the tide pools, or drove the old Dodge truck over to the village on the point and picked up everybody's groceries and mail. Collecting the quarters he didn't like. He dreaded going from man to man along the rail, always being received with silent, hostile looks and made to explain the whole thing over again, although most of the men had fished there before, and knew all about it. Anyway, there was a big sign on the entrance gate which told everything. But nothing else about his work interrupted his dreaming, which was active, constant and always upon the verge of the final discovery which would lift him into unity with everything. Since dreaming was his real work, that made a good life for Tad Manson.

He had to pay closer attention to what he was doing

when he drove the old Dodge, but even that did not distract him seriously. The motor made a noise to which he could sing as loudly and experimentally as he chose, in imitation of operatic tenors and baritones, and such freedom was good for the dream.

Nothing else about the way he lived interrupted Tad's dream either. Except when he went over to the village in the evenings or on Sunday to visit the redheaded girl with the wonderful voice, he wore only blue jeans and a blue shirt with the sleeves cut out. There was nothing to hamper his body. He was able to forget it entirely, except as an instrument of exaltation. He had to put on shoes and socks, creased trousers and a white shirt with sleeves when he went to see the redheaded girl, but then the thought of the redheaded girl herself uplifted him so that he scarcely felt the difference. He ate out of cans and bottles and didn't think about it, and he had a cabin of his own, near the edge of the cliff. He could always hear and smell the ocean in his cabin, and he never had any visitors, so the dream went on unbroken while he read or thought in the evening. It must have gone on even in his sleep, for no matter when he went to bed, he always woke up with the same shining and beating of wings inside him, and the racing expectation of something he could not quite define.

Even the redheaded girl was really just a part of the dream. When the time came to leave her late at night in the whisper of faraway surf and the smell of eucalyptus trees, it would seem to him that both of them, because of their longing to stay together, had fallen out of the crystal globe of the dream, and would never be able to get back into it. They would have to stand there forever, the only real creatures left in space, holding each other's hands and trying to think of a way to say good night which wouldn't annihilate them. But when they really had said good night, and Tad came down onto the beach alone, he always discovered that his sorrow and loneliness were quickly transformed into profound exaltation. Even when the tide was in and he had to carry his shoes and socks and wade through the surge, he would soon be celebrating the oneness of the sea, himself and the redheaded girl. He celebrated by singing with the surf the way he sang with the old Dodge. And when he was singing his loudest and saddest, he would nearly believe that he could wade out into the sea and be absorbed by it without the least damage to the essence which was Tad Manson, and that the redheaded girl could do the same thing. Then they could be together forever, not only as part of the sea, but also as part of the stars, the space between stars, the wind and light of day, the grass on the headlands, the brush in the canyons, and even the singing of insects. He would celebrate all these things in his song. There was almost nothing which his dream could not include sooner or later.

There was one thing, however, for he regarded them all as one thing; he could never include the men from whom he had to collect quarters, or the scientists who lived in the little houses all alike on the hills and came down the winding, dusty road to the laboratory every morning with inturned eyes, unvarying pace and a way of saying good morning which showed they really didn't know it was good, or even that it was morning. The scientists in particular evaded him, because they were there all the time. To such men, who could see only the motions of his arms and legs, Tad appeared amazingly lazy. They became suspicious when they looked out of their big windows in the laboratories at five o'clock and saw Tad, who had moved very slowly and not very often all day, wearing his swimming trunks and running like an antelope down to the beach. They couldn't see that his inner tempo hadn't changed a bit during this outward transformation. They didn't understand that he was going at the big secret as hard as they were, only all at once, from the top down. If they had understood, it wouldn't have improved their opinion of him. They had no use for the top-down approach. All this Tad sensed when they looked at him with their enumerating and carefully remembering eyes, and the look made him uneasy. He was always afraid, in their presence, that the dream would be interrupted by an accident like the one when Dr. Skene, the director of the institute, found him watering the century plant.

The century plant wasn't supposed to be watered. Tad was watering it only because he had found a trap-door spider trying to work a caterpillar down into his silken cistern, and feeling the secret touched upon by this incident, had squatted there, right between the laboratories and the aquarium and forgotten both time and place. Time and place were ephemeral existences to him, anyway, capable of amazing disappearances and changes of pace. He didn't know it was the century plant he was watering. He just felt vaguely that it was better to keep the water on something, and the century plant was the nearest thing. Neither did he know how long Dr. Skene had been standing there behind him before he spoke.

"Young man," said Dr. Skene's voice, "do you know what that plant is that you are bathing so assiduously?"

Tad stood up and turned around. "Huh?" he asked.

The director was not like the other scientists. His life, which included many visits to foreign places and speeches before important meetings, made him different. He had a neat Vandyke beard, was always elegantly dressed, and wore a hat and carried a cane. His eyes were outward-looking and quick. Also, it seemed to Tad that he always spoke as he was speaking now, very gently, very quietly, but not with a simple intention. There was only one other man among the scientists who sometimes spoke like that, Dr. Litter, the collector, but Dr. Litter always sounded like what he meant, so he didn't confuse Tad as much as Dr. Skene did. Tad listened more to voices than to words. He was so startled by Dr. Skene's voice sinuously entering his sunlit nowhere that he almost splashed the water on Dr. Skene's spats when he stood up.

Dr. Skene didn't flinch. He continued to smile, pointed at the century plant with his cane, and repeated his question.

"Oh," Tad said, and resumed his body and his spot on earth between the laboratories and the aquarium. He watched a gull coast low over the water tower and out to sea, but the director, although insignificant compared to such an escape, remained undeniable. Tad turned the water onto some salt bushes which didn't

need it either. Dr. Skene asked him the same question
about salt bushes, and Tad turned the hose so the water
splashed on bare ground.

"Perhaps you'd better turn the water off," Dr. Skene
said gently. He waited while Tad turned the water off.
He waited until Tad came back and stood in front of
him again. He even waited a long time after that. Then
he asked softly, "When were you born?"

"What?"

"The day and the year of your birth?"

"Oh," Tad said, but understanding now that Dr.
Skene was joking, said nothing more.

"When were you born?" Dr. Skene insisted. "Think
hard."

Tad looked down at his bare toes in the dust and
told him.

"And how long have you been watering the plants
on the grounds of this institution?"

Dr. Skene knew better than Tad did, but Tad made a
guess for him. Humiliation was the most intolerable
thing in life to Tad, but also he felt that if Dr. Skene
were allowed to finish his fun, he would probably move
on without any major disruption, and allow the dream
to heal quickly. Dr. Skene corrected the guess and then
stood there looking at Tad with pity. Finally he shook
his Shakespearian head.

"Young man," he said, "it is most fortunate, for you,
that you probably have a long time yet to live."

Tad didn't look up or say anything.

"Now, my young friend," Dr. Skene continued, "you
are to go at once, while you are thinking of it, to Mr.
Gregg. You remember Mr. Gregg, the superintendent
of grounds?"

Tad nodded.

"Good. Very good. You are to go at once to Mr. Gregg. Tell him exactly what you have been doing. Tell him that you have been watering a nearly matured century plant for . . ." Dr. Skene drew back his cuff and looked intently at his wrist watch. "For thirty-seven minutes. Then tell him that I would appreciate it if he would put you at some work upon which the future appearance of the institution is less dependent. Do you understand?"

Tad nodded.

"Repeat my instructions," Dr. Skene ordered softly.

Fortunately Tad could almost repeat them.

"You are improving," Dr. Skene said, "but keep repeating them until you find Mr. Gregg. Now, trot along."

The heat in Tad's face had subsided a little by the time he found Mr. Gregg in the storage shed, ticketing large flasks of preservatives for the laboratories. "Jim," he said.

Mr. Gregg removed the homemade cigarette from the corner of his mouth and squinted up. "Now what haav yuh been do-ing?" he asked.

Mr. Gregg was a big, dark Scot with a look of constant anger which really came from frowning against the sea-light. He had been a sailor. He appeared far more formidable than Dr. Skene, but actually he was much easier to talk to. Tad told him almost everything about watering the century plant. Mr. Gregg put his cigarette back into his mouth and regarded Tad with eyes narrowed against the smoke.

"So what will I do now?" Tad asked, after a minute.

"What wud yuh do?" Mr. Gregg asked in four distinct explosions. "Git on with yourrr wut-terring," he said patiently.

"Unly," he continued, turning back to his ticketing, "dawn't do ut wherrr Dawcturrr Skin cahn see yuh. In fahct," he added wearily, "dawn't do ut wherrr an-y of us cahn see yuh. Take yourrr hose oup bahk o' the lawst cawtuges. Therrr's a settin' o' new shoots oup therrr. Therrr's also near ahs mony bugs ahs yuh could norrr-mally wunt.

"Uh dawn't knaw why Uh keep yuh awn," he mut-tered in farewell. "You'rrr oonderrrminin' the hul ins-tit-ooshun. Get a-long noo."

So Tad, already partially healed by the pleasure he took in Jim Gregg's accent, coiled his hose into the old, wooden wheelbarrow, and pushed it up onto the last hill overlooking the colony. There, with the water running steadily into the pools, the tall, yellow grass swaying in the sun, with the insects clacking and sing-ing all through it, and the unbroken dome of the Pacific sparkling in the west, the dream readily resumed its enormous and shining unity.

It took Hamlet, the purple fish, to change all that as Dr. Skene could never have changed it.

The part of his work Tad liked best was feeding the fish in the aquarium. Early in the morning, when it was usually foggy, he went down to the beach with a scoop, a screen and several buckets on a pushcart. With his pants rolled up to his knees, he followed the reced-ing waves as the sandpipers followed them, and dug big shovelfuls of sand. He shook the sand through the screen, and left the sand-crabs wriggling and scuttling on the wire, heavy little creatures, shaped like scarabs, with gray-mottled shells and orange underparts. Then he poured the sand-crabs into the buckets. When the buckets were full, he pushed the cart back up to the aquarium. He left the cart by the high back stoop, and carried the buckets up onto the runway behind the tanks. There, tank by tank, he fed the silent inhabitants, dropping the sand-crabs in little showers onto the water and watching them nose over and row frantically for the bottom. Often big shadows darted out of the lower gloom and the sand-crabs disappeared in mid-water. Sometimes, especially in the tank where the big Spotted Moray eels lived, only half a sand-crab would disappear, and the rest, just drifting a little because of its shape, but not wriggling, would float on down to the sand floor. Usually Tad hurried through his feeding of the last few tanks, just pouring the sand-crabs from the buckets, and ran downstairs into the audience part of the aquarium to see what happened. This watching from downstairs was an important exercise of the dream. After Tad had stood there awhile in the midst of the glass-faced cubicles of water full of light and shadow, sand, seaweed, rock and painted coral, with hovering fish seeming to push back the walls of space, and other creatures, giant slugs, anemones, creeping shells, sharks, rays, seeming to push back even the walls of time, he could slowly imagine away the glass and partitions. Then he became the undrownable, observing essence, at one with the meaning of the sea. He was not deeply concerned about individuals in the aquarium, any more than he was outside in the sun. What was lost to the sand-crabs was in the same instant made up in the voracious Morays, balancing upward in the water as gracefully as lily stems, their fanged mouths gulping and their hard, hawklike little eyes staring steadily. Until Hamlet came, they were all merely parts of the one indestructible dream.

Tad wasn't sure just when Hamlet had come. He went into the aquarium for a moment's worship one morning, and there, where he had last seen a school of sardines, was Hamlet, by himself, since you couldn't quite count such half-forms as the three abalones, the sea-lettuce and the spiny urchin. Hamlet was a gross fish, like a carp or a sheepshead, with suety lips, but a lovely black-purple back, which faded down through lavender and pink into a creamy belly. In a way he was a comical, clownish-looking fish, yet to Tad he became Hamlet in that first glimpse. Tad didn't intend the name as a comment on the shape of the fish, either. For a reason which Tad was long in realizing, although he must have been moved by it at once, Hamlet appeared to be a pathetic, even a tragic fish, and the christening was the result of spontaneous pity.

Hamlet was balancing in mid-water and staring about him in panic. His eyes moved independently of each other, like the ears of a horse, so that he could look front and back or up and down at the same time. He would do this, and then he would look at the surface with both eyes and at the bottom with both eyes. His suety mouth remained a little open, as if gasping. Once, while Hamlet was looking up, someone leaned over the tank from above. Hamlet, perceiving the shadow, as of a shark or barracuda crossing his water, lashed off in the only open direction and flattened his fat mouth against the glass. Tad put out a hand to steer him off, but Hamlet misunderstood. He swerved, dove into the gloom of a back corner, and hung there, head down, thumping his mouth again while he tried to get under the ledge he understood to be the cause of the gloom. Tad had to laugh, but at the same time he felt his own mouth. Hamlet was clearly a very new prisoner. His dashing and digging brought home, so strongly that Tad could feel it like fear in his own stomach, a faith in space suddenly betrayed by incomprehensible limits.

This first meeting with Hamlet troubled Tad all day. He kept imagining Hamlet in his native water. He even worked up the courage to ask Dr. Litter, the collector, what kind of fish Hamlet was and where he came from. It didn't help any. The name was long and Latin and the place was just as strange, probably Mexican or South American. Tad asked what Hamlet liked to eat, and Dr. Litter stared through his thick glasses and said, "Oh, any damned thing. What are you fussing about that damned fish for? It has no more guts than a carp, and it's no better to eat, either."

This remark turned Tad's sympathy for Hamlet into violent partisanship. He was angry that Dr. Litter should suggest that he was interested in Hamlet as something to eat, and he was wounded by the accusation of cowardice. It reminded him of the way he felt when he had to collect the quarters. After work he went back to the aquarium to see how Hamlet was getting along, but he couldn't get a good look. Every time he approached the glass, Hamlet tried to leap out of the tank. He kept trying, and Tad was afraid he would succeed, and hurt himself on the boardwalk behind the tanks; so he went away.

The next day Hamlet dove for the corners as before, but then he subsided, as if the strength had gone out of him. He appeared very tired, able to work up energy only in the first flash of terror. Tad wondered if he had been dodging moon shadows from the skylight all night. He took care to drop Hamlet's sand-crabs near the suety mouth. Hamlet didn't seem to care. He paid no attention to the sand-crabs. Tad came back three times during the day. The first time he went in downstairs, but Hamlet tried to jump out of the tank again, so the other two visits were made above. Hamlet tried to burrow. Tad reached into the tank and touched him, and Hamlet lunged across and tried to dig into the other back corner. There was nothing to do but leave him alone again.

The third day seemed better, though. Tad thought Hamlet must have slept or gone into suspended animation or whatever it is fish do to rest. He was still shy of shadows, but he was much quicker, and he seemed to understand his cell. Instead of bruising his mouth against the glass, he slithered quickly along it at the first touch, in a manner that could have been fun. But this improvement didn't last. The moon shadows must have worked again that night, or else Hamlet's first slight uplift of familiarity had subsided into the beginning of prison melancholy. The fourth morning he swam idly out of Tad's shadow, banked without touching the glass, and lay still an inch off the bottom. He rose slowly at the first sand-crab Tad dropped in, but spit out half of it and hung there, fanning slowly, and let the other sand-crabs reach bottom. Still, he tried to burrow when Tad touched him. That habit had to be broken. Tad touched him again, and he swam into the other corner. Tad touched him a third time, and he just turned around and remained in the same corner, tail down, eyes up, regarding Tad unhappily. The profound sorrow of the gaze pierced Tad as if with intimations of innumerable ancient and nameless wrongs. He drew his arm slowly out of the tank. He thought about Hamlet all day, and when he found the sand-crabs untouched at each return, he began to speak to him consolingly. But pity didn't seem to be what Hamlet wanted either.

For three days there appeared to be little change. Hamlet still wouldn't eat. Tad tried other things. He left his watering several times to read the thermometer in Hamlet's tank. It remained steadily at ocean temperature. Perhaps that was wrong for Hamlet's home waters, but Tad didn't know what to do about it. He cleaned the drain, although it wasn't too clogged. He examined the tube which kept the fresh water flowing into the tank, and the tube which kept letting out into the water a stream of air bubbles of different sizes, like little pale green and white balloons, but they were both all right. He tried to tempt Hamlet with bits of fresh fish with the skin on, so they shone. Hamlet lipped one which struck him on the nose, but blew it out, and wouldn't try any more. Tad put into the tank some seaweeds and grasses which appeared to him probably medicinal, but Hamlet didn't want them either.

Later that day, while he was again watering the settings on the hill, it came to Tad for the first time that it might not be enough for a fish that his food and water were good, that it might not satisfy a fish to imagine away walls and glass when he had beaten his mouth against them. Tad was excited by this discovery of a new and secret bond. Hamlet was lonesome; he was homesick. His trouble was not of the flesh, but of the dream. Hamlet's dream was failing him, and he was heartbroken.

It required a difficult bending of his pride, but Tad told Dr. Litter that Hamlet wasn't eating, though he said nothing about why.

"How do you know?" Dr. Litter asked.

Tad admitted that he had been kind of watching the new fish.

"Are you nursemaiding the brute now?" Dr. Litter inquired. "What do you mean, watching him? Do you sleep with him? Do you feed him with a spoon?"

Tad looked at his bare toes on the gray-painted concrete floor and said nothing.

"What do you mean, watching him?" Dr. Litter repeated more loudly. "What do you mean? Twenty-four hours a day?"

Tad had to admit that he just went in to look once in a while.

"I see. And how long, in your matured judgment, hasn't this pig of a fish been eating?"

"About a week, I guess," Tad said.

"About a week, you guess," Dr. Litter said. "Boloney," he exploded. "He'd be belly up by now. Long before now."

"I counted the sand-crabs," Tad insisted. "He doesn't touch them."

"My God," said Dr. Litter. "That hog eats his own

weight every day, just to keep going. He's lazy as hell, that's all. Lazy."

"He doesn't look right, though," Tad murmured. "I thought maybe if we'd change . . ."

"Oh, you did, did you?" said Dr. Litter. "Now listen," he said. His eyes, glaring through the glasses were enormous. "If that fish dies," he said, "you know where to throw it, don't you? Not where you threw the last one, anyway. That infernal stink behind the garage."

"But," Tad began again.

"Get out," the collector roared. "Go on, get out. You're wasting my time. That fish doesn't matter; it's unimportant; it doesn't signify. There are probably ten billion just exactly like it, and nobody wants any of them for anything. Do you understand? Scientifically, gustatorially and aesthetically, God made this one mistake, that's all. Feed it paté de foie gras if you want to, and put it to bed in a feather puff, but don't come bothering me about that damned fish again."

"Yes, sir," Tad said. That was a kind of permission, anyway, even if it didn't help much about what to do.

He was nearly out of the laboratory when Dr. Litter called, "Listen." Tad stopped and waited. There was no use trying to explain to Dr. Litter that Hamlet was heartbroken, not with the way Dr. Litter seemed to feel about him.

"I look at those fish, all of them. Understand?"

Tad nodded.

"I look at all of them every damned day."

Tad nodded.

"I even look at that bloated parody on the lower forms of being."

Tad nodded again.

"So if there's anything needs to be done about those fish, *any* of them," Dr. Litter concluded triumphantly, "*I'll* tell *you*."

"Yes, sir," Tad said.

So there wasn't even a kind of permission after all. In fact, if anything were to be done for Hamlet, it would have to be done secretly, in a kind of criminal way. And it would have to be lucky, too. For the first time, Tad was disturbed when he considered how little he knew about fish, about any one fish. That night he forgot to pray before he went to bed, and then he lay awake for a long time and plotted unhappily. This was significant. Prayer was the great exercise of the day to Tad, the time of intense concentration, when understanding seemed closest upon him and the final unity most vibrant. Even when he came in at four o'clock in the morning from seeing the redheaded girl, he never forgot to pray.

The next morning, Hamlet was still tail down in his corner. He didn't move a fin or an eye as the sand-crabs came swimming down and began to scuttle and dig on the bottom. He winced away when one of the sand-crabs came to rest upon his nose and scurried quickly off it, but that was all. Tad felt a little panic. He fed the remaining tanks quickly, and ran downstairs and peered at Hamlet through the glass. Then he saw the difference in Hamlet, and it was so impressive that he couldn't understand why he hadn't seen it before. Hamlet had eyelids. No fish had eyelids, but just the same, Hamlet had them, great, heavy, gray-purple lids, and they were drooping half over his eyes. He looked terribly human

for a fish, old and sad human. Also, the lavender of his
flanks was turning gray and hairy, and he had long,
loose wrinkles instead of being full and tight. While
Tad was looking at him, Hamlet listed to one side,
opened his suety mouth a little wider, as if in the gasp
accompanying an unbearable thought, and rolled his
eyes up until only pale, sightless crescents showed beneath the lids. Then he righted himself with a feeble
flip of his tail, and hung as before.

Tad went into the aquarium a dozen times that day,
and each time Hamlet was still balancing there in the
corner, gazing listlessly from under the weeping lids. It
got so that Tad couldn't look away from Hamlet's eyes,
and that night he had a dream about the aquarium. The
aquarium enlarged about him, as in his waking exercise.
Its partitions and glass fronts dissolved into watery
waverings, and there, in the universal, blue-green
gloom, shoals of unrecognizable fish melted slowly away
from around their eyes, and the eyes grew until they
were as large as plates. Staring with empty concentration, they began to move, passing each other at different distances and upon different planes, clustering,
scattering, changing the rhythm of their dance. Gradually they approached one another, overlapped, formed
a single, upright circle, and began to revolve, like targets on a shooting-gallery wheel. At their center, a
fixed hub, but slowly expanding, appeared the head of
Hamlet, gazing listlessly from under the weeping lids.
All the eyes began to grow, as if drawing nearer, and
their wheeling was accelerated. Tad felt the whole
terror and weight of the sea pressing upon him. He
couldn't utter a sound into its density, or move against

its burden. Suffocation and fear were about to extinguish him when suddenly Hamlet's eyes, enormous by now, filled with tears. Abruptly all motion ceased. The lidless eyes became fast in a deep and limitless constellation with no more form than the Milky Way, and the waters were breathable. Then the lids of Hamlet's eyes began to move up and down very slowly, drowsily, like those of a man who has borne a fearful shock and wishes to faint, but can't. Never had Tad felt drawn from him such an agony of pity as went out toward those eyes. In the end, all the eyes were lidded and painfully blinking, and there was no longer anything to fear from them.

It seemed to Tad that he made up his mind at breakfast the next morning, but possibly it had been made up for him during the dream. The homesick Hamlet must be freed. In time his yearning, his compass of desire, would draw him home. Still, nothing too extreme could be risked while he was as weak as he was now. It was going to be very hard, almost impossible, after that last talk, but Tad would have to talk to Dr. Litter again. All day he fed his courage, and after work, when everybody was waiting in the hall of the main building for the mail, he asked Dr. Litter if the plankton and other food content was the same in the aquarium tanks as in the ocean. Jim Gregg, with short, gruff jokes, was giving out the mail. Dr. Litter held three letters in his hand, and one of them, at least, must have promised something other than facts or inquiries about fishes, tides and temperature, for he was much softened. He turned upon Tad a large and hazy stare, almost benevolent.

"Such curiosity," he said, as gently as Dr. Skene. "My

boy, you will make a scientist some day. If," he added, looking dreamily out through the glass door, "you ever get to know your hands from your feet." After a moment he looked at Tad again. "Where the devil did you think we got the water?" he asked kindly.

"Well," Tad said, "that new fish . . ."

"Oh," said Dr. Litter, and studied him. "Son," he said finally, placing a gentle hand upon Tad's shoulder, "try to forget her. She'll never make you happy. She's cold, unbelievably cold, and much too slick for one so young. She has no more heart than a fish." He patted Tad's shoulder and moved off toward the door, chuckling and beginning to open a letter. He paused at the door. "What's even worse," he said, "she's been off the deep end all her life, all her life." He shook his head regretfully and went out. Tad could tell by his back that he was laughing to himself. Apparently everybody else had learned about Tad and Hamlet, too. There were many small, suppressed sounds behind him. Even the young and pretty librarian, who was very kind, made half a giggle. Tad could feel how much bigger the grins were than the sounds. He could feel how the heat on the back of his neck must be giving him away too.

Just the same, he waited there until Dr. Litter was out of sight, and then, without once looking around, went out the same way and around to the aquarium to look at Hamlet. Besides his main worry, he was now a little troubled also by the suggestion that Hamlet might be a female after all.

One look at Hamlet, however, reassured him in this matter. That countenance, aged, bold-nosed, furrowed and now even faintly whiskered, was as masculine as the face of a tired bull. The name had not been wrong all this time. Dr. Litter had just called Hamlet she so he could make his long joke. In the more important concern, the look was not at all reassuring. Hamlet's eyes were entirely closed now, and he was lying on the bottom. Only because his gills were still pumping, though faintly and at irregular intervals, was Tad convinced he wasn't already dead.

Tad turned off the light in his cabin early that evening. Then he sat by the window and watched the other cabins, across the commons, where the tennis court was, and up on the hills. It was after eleven o'clock when the last light winked off. Then it was very dark all over the institute, because there was a fog in, and not even the stars showed. Tad put his flashlight in his pocket and went cautiously over to the aquarium. It was clear that Dr. Litter didn't like Hamlet, but it wasn't anywhere near as certain that he would approve a kidnapping from his aquarium, no matter what he thought of the victim. Tad unlocked the back door as quietly as he could, tiptoed in, and closed the door behind him.

It was very dark inside, but he worked his way up the stairs and along the boardwalk by hand, saving his flashlight until he had to use it, for fear of its glow in the skylight. The aquarium seemed eerily crowded, and full of wet sounds Tad had never noticed in daylight, gurglings and chucklings, ripplings and drippings and sudden small splashes. In a tank on the far side, little fish kept jumping, probably the anchovies, who were naturally jumpy. Tad stepped on a wet sponge. It felt alive under his bare foot, when his mind was full of sea creatures. He tripped on a hose and barked his shins against jars and metal containers. Once he bumped his head against the corks of a net dangling from the rafters, and ducked quickly before he realized what it was. Still he kept his count of the tanks, and stopped beside Hamlet's. He wanted to be perfectly sure it was Hamlet's, though, because the Spotted Morays had the next tank beyond. He turned his flashlight into the tank. Only a faint, diffused glow reached below the surface, but it was enough to show Hamlet, huge, motionless and alone in his corner.

Tad considered a pail, but he knew there was none big enough for Hamlet. He snapped on his light again and found a rusty wash boiler under the work bench on the back wall. He rinsed it with water from the salt-water hose. He was shocked by the roar the stream of water made against the empty tin, and turned it off quickly and swished the little water he had around inside the boiler. Then he filled the boiler with water from Hamlet's tank, using a tin can for a dipper. It was very heavy when there was enough water in it to cover Hamlet. He talked to Hamlet constantly, in a reassuring tone, while he netted him, drew him up, and submerged him again in the boiler. Hamlet moved little against the net, and Tad could see, when he had him in the boiler, that the big eyes were still closed. Hamlet nearly filled the boiler, and his tail had to be bent a little to fit its length. Hamlet did not object. Tad had been afraid he would put up a noisy fight. Now that he had offered almost no resistance, the thing that had been bothering Tad all day, surged up with a full, accusing power, augmented by night. Had he waited too long? Was Hamlet too nearly gone, too far spent with his longing, to survive a return to the sea? At the moment, subdued by his own caution, and remembering the first effect of his dream, Tad saw the sea as black, endless and unrelievedly hostile. He put together the whole web of the marine appetites he knew about, and almost decided to return Hamlet to his tank. But that was certain death, and a slow, miserable death too. Even the lightning of the barracuda was better, if it had to come. And there was a chance Hamlet would escape it; there was a chance that in the clean, open waters, and feeling the pull of home beginning to work in him, he would revive.

It was a slow, straining, sweaty job getting Hamlet and his boiler down from the loft and outside. There Tad put them on the wheelbarrow and trundled them out onto the pier, locking the land-end gate behind them. The pier was very long, but it seemed even longer than it was, in the dark and with the loud noise of the wheelbarrow rattling over the cross-boards. Near the end, where the piles stood in thirty or forty feet of water, there was another gate. Then they were in the holy place where the little weather house stood, secreting its charts and instruments, and where the boats of the collecting yacht hung in their davits, like great, pale fish themselves in the darkness and fog. Tad was worried about the next task. He locked the end-gate behind them too, and talked softly to Hamlet while he thought about it. The floor of the pier was still twenty or thirty feet above the water here, and the only way down, besides jumping off, was a rusty ladder on one of the end piles.

When he had the method clear in his mind, he carried the boiler over to the head of the ladder and set it down. He descended the ladder until his shoulders were level with the floor of the pier, and drew the boiler slowly and carefully onto his right shoulder. Then he began to labor down. He had to stop on each rung, get the boiler balanced, and grab quickly with his left hand for the next rung below. The boiler became heavier and heavier, and its edge began to cut into his shoulder painfully. He made a face at the pain, and then kept his face that way. Even in the fog and the cool stirring of the night air above the cool waves, he began to sweat again, and feared that his left hand would slip from the rungs or his right lose hold of the handle of the boiler. But he kept reminding himself that it was all for Hamlet, and discovered a great, enjoyable patience, which made him gloat, sometimes even aloud, over each accomplished rung.

When the rippling crests of the rollers washed coldly about his ankles, there came the problem of how to get Hamlet into the water without dumping him. Hamlet was too sick to be dumped. There was only one answer. Tad continued to descend the ladder, the rungs now slippery with seaweed and occasionally sharp with a barnacle, until the crests of the waves came to his chin and their passing ebb nearly sucked him off the ladder. Then the boiler floated free, though he had to bend way down with it, and finally descend two more rungs, to keep it afloat in the troughs. Here, with the boiler rising above him on each roller, so that he was periodically submerged and almost floated himself, he managed finally to press the boiler under, so that Hamlet

had only to float from his narrowest waters into freedom. He felt Hamlet bump against the tin four times
during this submersion, and cursed himself, quietly but
wildly, for this clumsiness. It seemed to him now that
Hamlet was as fragile as fine-blown glass, and that his
chances would be shattered by the slightest injury. He
also muttered again and again, breathing it like a rote
prayer, "Take it easy, old fellow, take it easy."

When, at last, he had turned the boiler over and
lifted it empty from the sea, he climbed quickly three
or four rungs up the ladder, and felt in his hip pocket
for the flashlight. He wanted to see how Hamlet had
taken the change. This first moment seemed to him to
hold the token of all success or failure. The flashlight
wasn't in his pocket, and he remembered that he'd left
it in the wheelbarrow after unlocking the end-gate. He
went up another two rungs, and strained his eyes down
toward the oily, gliding darkness below him. It remained impenetrable. He listened intently, but there
were no meaningful sounds either, but only the low,
wet chuckling of each roller as it passed about the piles.

The next morning, while Tad, feeling half saint and
half murderer, was clearing a pool about the base of a
eucalyptus on the commons, Dr. Litter stopped beside
him. Dr. Litter was happy. He was wearing the brown
work-clothes, covered with stains and fish scales, in
which he went to sea, and Dr. Litter was always happy
when he went to sea.

"So you threw that pink pig out after all," he said
cheerfully.

Tad straightened up slowly and nodded. That would
do as Dr. Litter's way of putting it.

"And right you were, too," said Dr. Litter. "Quite right. I took a look at him last evening. He was dying of a fungus. He was blind from the fungus. That's why he wouldn't eat. Tank's probably infected. Better drain it and give it a good scrubbing before you fill it again."

"Yes, sir," Tad said. He was falling apart inside. The saint part was falling out fast.

Dr. Litter looked out at the blue, sparkling sea. "Ought to be going out with me this morning," he said. "This is the kind of day to go out."

"If we get far enough south," he said, "I'll pick you up another of those purple hogs to cuddle, a sound one, with reciprocations." He chuckled and went on down the path across the commons, his back still jiggling a little as he enjoyed himself.

Tad stood there for a long time, staring out at the bland, happy, heartless sea in the morning freshness. Nothing moved inside him to its dancing. Finally he turned back and bent over and began to hoe at the pool for the eucalyptus again. After a little while, he was hoeing faster and harder than he had ever hoed in his life before.

The Portable Phonograph

THE RED SUNSET, with narrow, black cloud strips like threats across it, lay on the curved horizon of the prairie. The air was still and cold, and in it settled the mute darkness and greater cold of night. High in the air there was wind, for through the veil of the dusk the clouds could be seen gliding rapidly south and changing shapes. A sensation of torment, of two-sided, unpredictable nature, arose from the stillness of the earth air beneath the violence of the upper air. Out of the sunset, through the dead, matted grass and isolated weed stalks of the prairie, crept the narrow and deeply rutted remains of a road. In the road, in places, there were crusts of shallow, brittle ice. There were little islands of an old oiled pavement in the road too, but most of it was mud, now frozen rigid. The frozen mud still bore the toothed impress of great tanks, and a wanderer on the neighboring undulations might have stumbled, in this light, into large, partially filled-in and weed-grown cavities, their banks channeled and beginning to spread into badlands. These pits were such as might have been made by falling meteors, but they were not. They were the scars of gigantic bombs, their rawness already made a little natural by rain, seed and time. Along the road there were rakish remnants of fence. There was also, just visible, one portion of tangled and multiple barbed wire still erect, behind which was a shelving ditch with small caves, now very quiet and empty, at intervals in its back wall. Otherwise there was no structure or remnant of a structure visible over the dome of the darkling earth, but only, in sheltered hollows, the darker shadows of young trees trying again.

Under the wuthering arch of the high wind a V of wild geese fled south. The rush of their pinions sounded briefly, and the faint, plaintive notes of their expeditionary talk. Then they left a still greater vacancy. There was the smell and expectation of snow, as there is likely to be when the wild geese fly south. From the remote distance, toward the red sky, came faintly the protracted howl and quick yap-yap of a prairie wolf.

North of the road, perhaps a hundred yards, lay the parallel and deeply intrenched course of a small creek, lined with leafless alders and willows. The creek was already silent under ice. Into the bank above it was dug a sort of cell, with a single opening, like the mouth of a mine tunnel. Within the cell there was a little red of fire, which showed dully through the opening, like a reflection or a deception of the imagination. The light came from the chary burning of four blocks of poorly aged peat, which gave off a petty warmth and much acrid smoke. But the precious remnants of wood, old fence posts and timbers from the long-deserted dugouts, had to be saved for the real cold, for the time when a man's breath blew white, the moisture in his nostrils stiffened at once when he stepped out, and the expansive blizzards paraded for days over the vast open, swirling and settling and thickening, till the dawn of the cleared day when the sky was a thin blue-green and the terrible cold, in which a man could not live for three hours unwarmed, lay over the uniformly drifted swell of the plain.

Around the smoldering peat four men were seated cross-legged. Behind them, traversed by their shadows, was the earth bench, with two old and dirty army blankets, where the owner of the cell slept. In a niche in the opposite wall were a few tin utensils which caught the glint of the coals. The host was rewrapping in a piece of daubed burlap, four fine, leather-bound books. He worked slowly and very carefully, and at last tied the bundle securely with a piece of grass-woven cord. The other three looked intently upon the process, as if a great significance lay in it. As the host tied the cord, he spoke. He was an old man, his long, matted beard and hair gray to nearly white. The shadows made his brows and cheekbones appear gnarled, his eyes and cheeks deeply sunken. His big hands, rough with frost and swollen by rheumatism, were awkward but gentle at their task. He was like a prehistoric priest performing a fateful ceremonial rite. Also his voice had in it a suitable quality of deep, reverent despair, yet perhaps, at the moment, a sharpness of selfish satisfaction.

"When I perceived what was happening," he said, "I told myself, 'It is the end. I cannot take much; I will take these.'

"Perhaps I was impractical," he continued. "But for myself, I do not regret, and what do we know of those who will come after us? We are the doddering remnant of a race of mechanical fools. I have saved what I love;

the soul of what was good in us here; perhaps the new ones will make a strong enough beginning not to fall behind when they become clever."

He rose with slow pain and placed the wrapped volumes in the niche with his utensils. The others watched him with the same ritualistic gaze.

"Shakespeare, the Bible, *Moby Dick, The Divine Comedy*," one of them said softly. "You might have done worse; much worse."

"You will have a little soul left until you die," said another harshly. "That is more than is true of us. My brain becomes thick, like my hands." He held the big, battered hands, with their black nails, in the glow to be seen.

"I want paper to write on," he said. "And there is none."

The fourth man said nothing. He sat in the shadow farthest from the fire, and sometimes his body jerked in its rags from the cold. Although he was still young, he was sick, and coughed often. Writing implied a greater future than he now felt able to consider.

The old man seated himself laboriously, and reached out, groaning at the movement, to put another block of peat on the fire. With bowed heads and averted eyes, his three guests acknowledged his magnanimity.

"We thank you, Doctor Jenkins, for the reading," said the man who had named the books.

They seemed then to be waiting for something. Doctor Jenkins understood, but was loath to comply. In an ordinary moment he would have said nothing. But the words of *The Tempest*, which he had been reading, and the religious attention of the three, made this an unusual occasion.

"You wish to hear the phonograph," he said grudgingly.

The two middle-aged men stared into the fire, unable to formulate and expose the enormity of their desire.

The young man, however, said anxiously, between suppressed coughs, "Oh, please," like an excited child.

The old man rose again in his difficult way, and went to the back of the cell. He returned and placed tenderly upon the packed floor, where the firelight might fall upon it, an old, portable phonograph in a black case. He smoothed the top with his hand, and then opened it. The lovely green-felt-covered disk became visible.

"I have been using thorns as needles," he said. "But tonight, because we have a musician among us"—he bent his head to the young man, almost invisible in the shadow—"I will use a steel needle. There are only three left."

The two middle-aged men stared at him in speechless adoration. The one with the big hands, who wanted to write, moved his lips, but the whisper was not audible.

"Oh, don't," cried the young man, as if he were hurt. "The thorns will do beautifully."

"No," the old man said. "I have become accustomed to the thorns, but they are not really good. For you, my young friend, we will have good music tonight.

"After all," he added generously, and beginning to wind the phonograph, which creaked, "they can't last forever."

"No, nor we," the man who needed to write said harshly. "The needle, by all means."

"Oh, thanks," said the young man. "Thanks," he said

again, in a low, excited voice, and then stifled his coughing with a bowed head.

"The records, though," said the old man when he
had finished winding, "are a different matter. Already
they are very worn. I do not play them more than once
a week. One, once a week, that is what I allow myself.

"More than a week I cannot stand it; not to hear
them," he apologized.

"No, how could you?" cried the young man. "And
with them here like this."

"A man can stand anything," said the man who
wanted to write, in his harsh, antagonistic voice.

"Please, the music," said the young man.

"Only the one," said the old man. "In the long run
we will remember more that way."

He had a dozen records with luxuriant gold and red
seals. Even in that light the others could see that the
threads of the records were becoming worn. Slowly he
read out the titles, and the tremendous, dead names of
the composers and the artists and the orchestras. The
three worked upon the names in their minds, carefully.
It was difficult to select from such a wealth what they
would at once most like to remember. Finally the man
who wanted to write named Gershwin's "New York."

"Oh, no," cried the sick young man, and then could
say nothing more because he had to cough. The others
understood him, and the harsh man withdrew his selection and waited for the musician to choose.

The musician begged Doctor Jenkins to read the titles
again, very slowly, so that he could remember the
sounds. While they were read, he lay back against the
wall, his eyes closed, his thin, horny hand pulling at his

light beard, and listened to the voices and the orchestras and the single instruments in his mind.

When the reading was done he spoke despairingly. "I have forgotten," he complained. "I cannot hear them clearly.

"There are things missing," he explained.

"I know," said Doctor Jenkins. "I thought that I knew all of Shelley by heart. I should have brought Shelley."

"That's more soul than we can use," said the harsh man. "*Moby Dick* is better.

"By God, we can understand that," he emphasized.

The doctor nodded.

"Still," said the man who had admired the books, "we need the absolute if we are to keep a grasp on anything.

"Anything but these sticks and peat clods and rabbit snares," he said bitterly.

"Shelley desired an ultimate absolute," said the harsh man. "It's too much," he said. "It's no good; no earthly good."

The musician selected a Debussy nocturne. The others considered and approved. They rose to their knees to watch the doctor prepare for the playing, so that they appeared to be actually in an attitude of worship. The peat glow showed the thinness of their bearded faces, and the deep lines in them, and revealed the condition of their garments. The other two continued to kneel as the old man carefully lowered the needle onto the spinning disk, but the musician suddenly drew back against the wall again, with his knees up, and buried his face in his hands.

At the first notes of the piano the listeners were startled. They stared at each other. Even the musician lifted his head in amazement, but then quickly bowed it again, strainingly, as if he were suffering from a pain he might not be able to endure. They were all listening deeply, without movement. The wet, blue-green notes tinkled forth from the old machine, and were individual, delectable presences in the cell. The individual, delectable presences swept into a sudden tide of unbearably beautiful dissonance, and then continued fully the swelling and ebbing of that tide, the dissonant inpourings, and the resolutions, and the diminishments, and the little, quiet wavelets of interlude lapping between. Every sound was piercing and singularly sweet. In all the men except the musician, there occurred rapid sequences of tragically heightened recollection. He heard nothing but what was there. At the final, whispering disappearance, but moving quietly, so that the others would not hear him and look at him, he let his head fall back in agony, as if it were drawn there by the hair, and clenched the fingers of one hand over his teeth. He sat that way while the others were silent, and until they began to breathe again normally. His drawn-up legs were trembling violently.

Quickly Doctor Jenkins lifted the needle off, to save it, and not to spoil the recollection with scraping. When he had stopped the whirling of the sacred disk, he courteously left the phonograph open and by the fire, in sight.

The others, however, understood. The musician rose last, but then abruptly, and went quickly out at the door without saying anything. The others stopped at the door and gave their thanks in low voices. The doctor nodded magnificently.

"Come again," he invited, "in a week. We will have the 'New York.'"

When the two had gone together, out toward the rimed road, he stood in the entrance, peering and listening. At first there was only the resonant boom of the wind overhead, and then, far over the dome of the dead, dark plain, the wolf cry lamenting. In the rifts of clouds the doctor saw four stars flying. It impressed the doctor that one of them had just been obscured by the beginning of a flying cloud at the very moment he heard what he had been listening for, a sound of suppressed coughing. It was not near by, however. He believed that down against the pale alders he could see the moving shadow.

With nervous hands he lowered the piece of canvas which served as his door, and pegged it at the bottom. Then quickly and quietly, looking at the piece of canvas frequently, he slipped the records into the case, snapped the lid shut, and carried the phonograph to his couch. There, pausing often to stare at the canvas and listen, he dug earth from the wall and disclosed a piece of board. Behind this there was a deep hole in the wall, into which he put the phonograph. After a moment's consideration, he went over and reached down his bundle of books and inserted it also. Then, guardedly, he once more sealed up the hole with the board and the earth. He also changed his blankets, and the grass-stuffed sack which served as a pillow, so that he could lie facing the entrance. After carefully placing two more blocks of peat on the fire, he stood for a long time watching the stretched canvas, but it seemed to billow naturally with the first gusts of a lowering wind. At last he prayed, and got in under his blankets, and closed his smoke-smarting eyes. On the inside of the bed, next the wall, he could feel with his hand, the comfortable piece of lead pipe.

The Watchful Gods

BUCK WOKE when the first gray light stole in at the window over his bed. His mind grabbed back after a last, small, elusive dream, like a hand trying to catch a lizard by the tail. He felt happy and excited, and almost as if he hadn't been asleep at all, so he believed that the dream might have been a good dream about Janet Haley, in which case he wanted to keep it. It skittered out from under his memory, however, and vanished completely.

He turned his head on the pillow and looked up through the window at where the big, brown hill should have been, with the grove of white-stemmed eucalyptus trees high and faraway on top of it. The hill wasn't there at all, though, and only a little of the eucalyptus grove showed in each of two places, up on the right shoulder of the hill. The fog drifted among the gently bowing, dark plumes, and across them, changing the shapes of the two openings, and everywhere else there was only fog moving across fog or turning slowly within fog. Still higher, above where the top of the hill would have been, it was all one pale, pearly color, and motionless, so that it might have been, except for the visibly moving fog below, just the clear sky of so early in the morning that there was no blue in it yet.

The black edge of the eucalyptus grove in the fog reminded Buck of the Japanese prints his mother liked so
much, the ones that showed just the fuzzy, black edges
of mountains standing up out of a gray mist that covered the rest of the paper, and was soft and pleasant because the paper was rice paper, and soft and pleasant
itself. The Japanese mountains reminded him of others
that he liked better himself, the craggy, storms and
light-covered highlands in the engravings in his father's
big, green edition of the works of Sir Walter Scott. It
was easy, looking up at where the hill ought to be, and
seeing only the black plumes of the eucalyptus, to imagine a much higher mountain with black crags and cliffs.
Because this was an old exercise for Buck in the summer mornings, when there was usually fog over the hill,
and because the fog always started in him the same
searching and heroic sadness the engravings started, he
began to arrange the characters for another version of
The Lady of the Lake, which was his favorite theme,
next after the Tristram story. He didn't even get into
the action this time, however. He established Janet
Haley as the lady of the lake at once, and passed over
the details of her age and costume to settle first the
always-perplexing problem of whether he himself should
be the successful lowland prince, attractive in his lone
daring, or the dour, short-spoken highland chieftain,
whose long history of wrongs to be avenged and of
rigorous, hungry living fitted in so much better with
the engravings and with the fog outside the window.

It was at this point that he recognized what his eyes
were looking at. They were looking at the wooden gun
with a red-painted stock, and an old window-latch for

a combination trigger and hammer, which his father had given him on his sixth birthday. The wooden gun was supported by two nails fixed in the redwood wall beyond the foot of his bed. It wasn't fastened diagonally and permanently, as an ornament, but lay free across the nails, ready to be taken down and used at any time.

At once, when he recognized the wooden gun, Buck remembered what day it was, and understood, though with a slight leavening of guilt at his disloyalty, that it wasn't because of Janet Haley that he was awake so early and so expectantly. It was because this was his twelfth birthday, and when, at the proper time, he went out through the living room and into the dining room, he might find, lying across his chair, with HAPPY BIRTH-DAY, BUCK on the tag tied to the trigger guard, the real twenty-two rifle that always rested on the bottom pegs of the gun-rack in his father's study. There would be other presents on the chair too, of course, probably all in different-shaped boxes wrapped in paper with different-colored pictures, but for the moment he thought of them as all of one lightness and inconsequence, unless there were among them the small, very heavy boxes that meant ammunition for the twenty-two. The thing was to see the twenty-two, which couldn't very well be wrapped, lying there across the chair in the middle of the nearly invisible other presents, with the morning light shining in a long, ruler-straight line on the oily barrel.

At the thought of the twenty-two, and of how short the time must be now, the small, contained excitement which he had misunderstood a moment before, rose up in him quickly, and swelled to such dimensions that it

threatened to burst into a thousand glittering fragments. In this great column of joy he saw, like motes
turning in a shaft of light, many of the minute, shining
activities of the world which always created the same
kind of excitement in him: gulls playing in the wind
over the surf, with the morning sunlight dazzling on
their breasts and underwings, the jewel-like sparkling
of the far-out Pacific on a clear, breezy afternoon, the
serpents of light that went slithering up across the wild
wheat on the hills, and the tiny, multiple flashings of
minnows in the waters of the marsh that was cut off
from the ocean by the long, flying curve of empty beach
between the cliff, where his house stood, and the village
over on South Point, where Janet Haley lived. Behind
these quick visions, just glimpsed in passing because
they were all allied, because they all had their small,
brilliant parts in the glad meaning of life, he perceived
quieter things: the grains of beach sand, which contained even more light, for their size, than a flight of
gulls, drops of the radiant mist that hung over the
breakers when there was a shore wind blowing, even
the tiny, conical shells, light as paper, abandoned by
their inhabitants in a dark tangle of sea-weed on the
beach, the empty, leopard-spotted half-shell of an egg
no bigger than a fingernail lying under a black sweet-
bush on the canyon wall, and the delicately grooved
armor of a beetle, half sunk in red earth, with the beetle
all eaten out of it by the enterprising ants. Even such
inanimate things as these, or such cast-off husks of life,
had the glad spirit of sparkle in them, the sprites that
were Buck's innumerable friends, and so could not be
dead. The great, swelling happiness that rose from any

considerable gathering of the sprites, when quickened by the union of warm sunlight and cool sea-wind on Buck's naked body, could make him strut and sing loudly, if the surf was heavy enough to hide his voice, and then suddenly break into a wild run or a leaping, circling dance that he kept up until the excitement burst and suddenly sent him sprinting down the slope of the beach, to dive with a shout over the first wave and under the second. Such ecstasy, which was to Buck the very proof of being alive and goal of living, invariably swept all being up into one golden, weightless suspension, leaving no important difference between the living and the dead, or the great and the small, or the past and the present and the future. And this ecstasy could be approximated in memory.

This time, however, Buck had seen, in the same vision, the village over on South Point, with its miniature red roofs going up like stairs among the trees, from the seaward rocks, with the white border of surf among them, almost to the top of the mountain. It was inevitable, then, that all the winking sprites who were the companions of his daily solitude, should give way almost at once to the more fortunate sprites who inhabited the regions immediately surrounding Janet Haley, or, even better, dwelt in the very parts of her. For a moment he gazed upon Janet Haley as when he had first seen her, almost two months before.

Janet—he hadn't known her name then, of course—was sitting across the center tennis court from him, with her father beside her, as Buck's father was beside him. Two big, enviable men, somewhere between seventeen and twenty-five, were playing on the court. They were

playing very well, dancing on their toes, with their elbows up and their rackets ready before them, each in
the center of his base-line, darting from there first to
the right and then to the left to hit swift, low shots,
now down the line, now across to the farther corner,
every shot making that convincing, firm pop on the
strings of the racket, and the points continuing, one
little explosion after another, with the light rushing of
feet between, to sometimes as many as ten or twelve
pops. The brown faces and necks and arms and legs of
the men were shining like armor from their sweating,
and they were panting audibly, and grinning all the
time, showing their white teeth, and sometimes shouting suddenly when a point was all at once ended by a
quick, hard shot in an unexpected direction. Until
Janet Haley, with her father behind her, had come in
and sat down across the court, Buck had been watching,
with his fists closed, every whispering passage of the
ball, every move of each player in turn as he received
it, thinking himself hard into first one of them and then
the other, so that he was able to make every stroke for
both of them, and to feel himself getting bigger and
swifter and more powerful all the time. A kind of golden
haze, made up of millions of the sprites of joy, and just
a trifle brighter than the sunlight itself, hung over the
court where such magnificent action was going on. Because there was a fascinating point in play at the time,
with the shorter, stockier man making one nearly impossible get after another, Buck didn't really see Janet
and her father come in, but only in one corner of his
mind, and through one corner of his eye, knew that
somebody had come in and sat down on the gray bench

opposite. But finally one of the stocky man's lobs was too short, and the taller, black-haired man moved in with two or three long, confident strides and leapt into the air and smashed the ball away into the corner farthest from the stocky man. The spell was broken then, and Buck was not only able to look away, but almost had to, in order to rest from the excitement and be ready to participate in the next point. So he looked across the court to see who had come in, and saw Janet Haley. She wasn't returning his look, but only watching the stocky man go back to the fence to pick up the ball, but immediately the golden haze from all over the court flowed together and was concentrated about her, so that her father sat nearly invisible in a separate and shadowy realm beside her. It was as if, suddenly, all the splendor had drained out of the sweating, brown, young men and entered her, although she was just sitting there, very upright, with her feet together so the pale blue ankle socks touched, and her racket across her lap on the starched, white skirt, with her hands folded over each other on the throat of it.

After that, Buck looked across at her frequently, sometimes even when the ball was in play, so that her face was turning rhythmically from side to side to follow its flight. Always he found her within that swarming, radiant nimbus, so that her father not only never emerged from the shadow of inconsequence that must lie, like a dimness of life, a half-being, upon any mortal in the immediate neighborhood of an immortal, but seemed even to recede in time also, toward becoming only the memory of a mortal. Buck looked at Janet more and more and at the magnificent young men less and less, until he was looking at Janet so continuously that he became unaware of looking at her at all, and found himself, without even knowing how he had got into it, engaged in playing a strangely sensible but unorthodox, and therefore difficult, Tristram, who was gently but masterfully in love with a Janet Haley—Isolt of Brittainy, and seeking to escape from the dangerous toils of an Isolt of Ireland who was a good deal like Alice Gladding, who had sat in the row beside him, but two seats ahead, during the last school year, and been an orthodox Isolt of Ireland for eight months and a half out of the nine. Time and place were reversed, so that the brown, young men could be seen only dimly, like spirits in a mist, moving soundlessly and without meaning, far behind the distinct, audible and contemporary figures of the tragedy.

It was while the taller young man was walking slowly out to the side of the court to pick up a ball that the ages were again transposed. Tristram, in royal-blue velvet, sewn with golden lions, stood by the fair Isolt on the beach of Brittainy. The sun was setting ominously in a mountain range of fog across the sea and over invisible Cornwall, where the dark Isolt sat with her mind coiled against them like a serpent. Tristram's eyes gazed, sad with this knowledge, down into the blue eyes of Isolt of Brittainy, and the blue eyes, in return, gave up to him a whole and trusting love. Despite the evils he foresaw, Buck-Tristram was about to make his final and irrevocable vow, when Buck-not-Tristram saw that the blue eyes of Janet Haley were actually gazing across the center court into his own. For a moment the confusion of time and place and degree of acquaintance

caused a panic in Buck compared with which the be-
wilderment of Tristram was a happy clarity. He was
shocked by the discovery of Janet Haley's eyes looking
into his own. He was unable to look away or to think
or to breathe, and he was aware of no other part of
Janet Haley but her eyes. So it was Janet who looked
away first, and let him return to the present entirely
and with a rush. He became abysmally conscious of
how long and intently he must have been staring. The
distance across the tennis court became greater than
that to the sands of Brittainy in exactly the proportion
that the embarrassed Janet Haley, seeing him for the
first time in her life, could not be expected to share
the feelings of Janet-Isolt. Buck experienced a ferocious
shame that had in it not the least remnant of the pleas-
urable sorrows of Tristram. Despite this shame, however, he continued to stare, and finally, with the pair
of practically invisible young men still hurling themselves about the court between, Janet Haley's blue
eyes, though not straight on, but a little sideways, looked
into his once more. They looked away again at once,
but only shyly, and the determined unconsciousness
with which Janet Haley was then following the foolish
ball, could not wholly deceive even Buck. The flush
which arose along her very white throat and then
bloomed upon her equally white and only faintly freckled cheeks, could not be mistaken for an affect of sun,
either on her skin or in his eyes. It was at this moment,
naturally, that Buck, as if himself newly possessed of
immortal particularity of vision, recognized the most
fortunate sprites of all, those which lived always touching her, twinkling in her blue eyes, gleaming upon the

delicate lower lip which at that instant she moistened
with just the tip of an uneasy tongue, and shining in
joyous, stirring thousands in the thick, red-gold hair
which hung down almost to her waist behind, and was
bound away from her face by a ribbon of pale blue
silk.

Janet Haley, just as he had beheld her at that moment, always returned as the reigning goddess, the center, if not the veritable source, of Buck's moments of
ecstatic union. Yet now above all times, when he was
so close, perhaps, to possessing the twenty-two, he must
conceal every token of celebration. There was another
force in the world besides the tiny gods of light, a force
with none of their bright affection or infinitely divided
smallness. Rather, this force moved, when it moved at
all, as one, though it was capable of spreading its influence almost without limit, of reaching with its shadowing malice and jealousy into every act and every revealed hope of one's life, as the fog out there was now
reaching into every canyon of the brown hills. Buck
did not exactly confuse them, of course, for the presence
and power of the fog god could only be felt, single, oppressive and attentive, as the sprites, in sufficient numbers, were light and uplifting, but the fog god seemed
to him akin to many of the manifestations of the God
in the thin, blue book of Old Testament stories, the
one with all the colored pictures in it, that was lying
over there on his bureau now, under the small, black
New Testament.

If compelled to discuss God, Buck would have spoken
in the standard Protestant-go-to-Sunday-school terms
used in his presence by adults who also wished to veil

their reservations. He would have spoken as if there were one God, continuous through the Old Testament and the New. Often, even when thinking about the matter by himself, and feeling the immediate force of the fog god upon the side of evil and a vaguely conceived death, and of the little, twinkling gods upon the side of good and life, he would nonetheless place this God that was still only a word with a capital letter, vastly above and beyond them, as a kind of single, ultimate, unimaginable head-God, to Whom all the rest were subordinate. He could not, however, establish any direct contact with such a God. All the quick fluctuations of his internal life moved in accord with the dictates of the deputies, joy producing at once that all-embracing, the universe-is-one adoration of the sprites, and worry, or mischance, or the dark stroke of conscience, in particular the stroke of conscience, at once bringing the single, shadowing, malicious force very near to him, and making it terribly perceptive. Indeed, if Buck had been able to explain really what he felt, he must have confessed that for him the Jehova of the Old Testament and the God of Jesus were two quite different head Gods, the former akin to the fog god and the latter a fit master of the sprites. He must also have confessed that the Jehova of the Old Testament was not by any means always the same Jehova, or that, if He was, He was dangerously and incalculably whimsical. Certainly there was not at all the same intention operating in the deity which chose, simply because they were devoted to Him, a ribald, drunken, fleshy outfit like Noah and his family, to save the creatures of the world, and in the deity which quietly and gently walked with the good

Ruth at sunset, and put her life all in order again. It was still a different God, for that matter, or God in a very different mood, Who amused Himself by giving Adam his beloved companion Eve, and then, just when everything should have been happiest, doomed them with the smiling little apple trick, as if their tranquil drama bored Him. No, when you came right down to it, the Jehovas of the Old Testament seemed almost as many and as various as their worshippers.

Even so, Buck found the activities of the Old Testament, dark and uncertain though they were, much more convincing than those of the New Testament, which stirred in him only an exalted and insubstantial urge to be pure, an urge which could be induced, actually, more quickly and more completely just by touching the little, black book and thinking about it in a vague and general way, than by reading in it. Indeed, this hunger for Godliness, which arose much more vigorously when he read one of the stories in his *Book of Saints and Friendly Beasts*, and lasted longer afterwards, too, was often lost when he really tried to read in the New Testament. It was so hard to believe some of the things that happened in it, and so hard to understand much that was said, that the willing, hopeful awe with which he usually opened the book, the eagerness of one in great need of an answer, was almost always transformed, after a page or two, into a discouraging perplexity and wish to escape. The fog god gained strength from the Jehova of the Old Testament. They were alike jealous, capricious, frequently angry and totally selfish, and they both existed as single and separate powers, somehow wholly believable, if not admirable. The God of the New Testament, on the contrary, became real only in the moments of ecstasy which arose from the union of the small, glad spirits of the outside world. He could not, therefore, be remembered and thought about. He had simply to be celebrated, as with trumpets and harps and gay, unquenchable dancing, during the brief time of His presence. The best that could be done beyond that was to keep the moments themselves, more in the flesh and the feelings than in the mind, as tokens of the one truly desirable state of the self, a state light as air, warm and single as sunlight, clean as a naked swim in the sea. And since even this representation of the bright god could not be long sustained, the dark god had a considerable advantage in their struggle for Buck's soul.

The nature of the fog god, however, gave Buck one useful power against him, quite apart from ecstasy. Since that deity chose to act upon the level of malice and deception, it was also permissible to deceive him in turn, as, for instance, David had deceived Jehova by pretending to renounce a Bathsheba of whom he was already weary. Buck had heard his father say something like that once, and it had immediately struck him as the explanation of his uneasiness about David's penance, besides, of course, the obvious fact that the penance had come too late to do any real good. It was possible, then, to oppose the fog god by oneself if only one concealed all outward signs, not only of the opposition, but also of any hopes or expectations which might arouse his envy. It followed, of course, that to reveal such hopes might well be fatal to them. This explosive excitement about the twenty-two was very dangerous.

Actually the excitement had not produced a single

movement of Buck's body or a single sound from his swelling breast. The contest between him and the fog god was an old one, and his defense, a kind of rabbit's immobility, had been mounted at once when he remembered the day and the twenty-two. He lay perfectly still now, stretched out naked—he never wore pajamas in the summer—and straight under the blankets. He felt like the stone effigy of some medieval knight on the lid of a sarcophagus. His feet were together and his arms down straight along his sides. His careful breathing scarcely moved the covers. He continued to stare at the wooden gun with a face completely expressionless, save for a slight narrowing of his eyes and the least possible, scornful down-curving of his mouth. This contempt was not directed at the wooden gun, however, but at the thought of the twenty-two. It was designed to convince the fog god that a twenty-two was about the last thing in the world that mattered to Buck.

Thus concealed from the enemy, he listened attentively for any sound in those regions of the house beyond the closed door of his bedroom. His father always got up early, somewhere between five o'clock and six-thirty, and got breakfast for everybody, and then, when he'd finished his own, sat there at the table drinking coffee and smoking cigarettes and reading, or working out a chess problem, or thinking and sometimes quickly scribbling a line or two. He liked to have the house to himself for an hour before he began his work. This morning he would certainly be up early. Everybody got up early on birthdays. But there wasn't a sound in the house yet. Buck listened for a long time, and heard only the far-away, fog-softened breaking and whispering of the surf. It must be very early then. Maybe there was as much as an hour to wait still.

At the thought of waiting another hour, Buck felt a strong impulse to rise and sneak out into his father's study, and see if the twenty-two was still there on the bottom pegs of the gun-rack. For more than two years now, such visits had been almost as important to him, although he didn't make them nearly so often, as his constant revisions, with himself in the leads, of the adventures of Tristram and Roderick Dhu and Robin Hood, of Robinson Crusoe or the Swiss Family Robinson, and sometimes, for greater variety in time and personality, of Theseus or Perseus or Kit Carson, or even of one of the saints with friendly beasts, in particular Saint Francis. He didn't use the saints very often, though, because it was almost impossible to work a heroine in with a saint in a manner that was at all satisfying and still keep the saint much of a saint. It had seemed diplomatic to stay out of the study entirely during the last couple of weeks, even as he had avoided heroes who used firearms, but he could imagine the twenty-two in there as clearly as ever, lying, lithe and real and full of its fatal promise, across its two pegs under the four bigger guns, the two shotguns, the Springfield and the old Winchester carbine with the brass-colored housing and butt-plate. He could see it as if he were in there now, feeling the rough, woolly, Navajo rug under his bare feet, and the austere presence of his father's big, flat desk behind him, with all the papers and books that mustn't be touched laid out on it, just where his father would want them. The shelves of books that went clear up to the raftered ceiling on both sides of the gun-rack were visible only in a general and collective sense, and even the four bigger guns, still more dreadful than desirable, were a little vague also, but the twenty-two was visible in every detail. It held the eye of his memory, as it did his real gaze when he went in there, as if it were a living thing, beautiful and unreasonably attractive, but not wholly to be trusted, a creature a little of the same nature as the big rattlesnake he had almost stepped on two or three weeks ago, when he was running down the canyon trail to his secret, and, for that matter, forbidden beach. At times, to be sure, the gleaming barrel and polished stock of the twenty-two were clearly inhabited by the little shining gods, but so were the eyes and the softly colored scales of a snake, if it was far enough away, and minding its own business. The major allegiance of both was clearly to the fog god.

Most things made by people, especially those used indoors, didn't interest Buck, since they were devoid of both the haunting power of the fog god and the ecstatic magic of the sprites. This had not always been so, for he could still remember, though not without shame, a time when he had held conversations with the one-eyed teddy-bear which was now hidden at the back of his closet shelf, and almost nightly had watched his bureau come to threatening life. But now there were only a few objects left in that category of the possessed, and those subject to limiting conditions. His mother's piano, when he thought clearly of the sound of her playing a particular composition on it, especially one of the short Chopin or Debussy pieces she played most often, or

Beethoven's *Moonlight Sonata*, seemed full of the little gods, though in a queer, sad way that enlarged one more slowly and enduringly, as the engravings in the green Scott did. His own violin, a good deal when he was playing it by himself, inventing melodies that had in them little pieces of things he'd heard on the phonograph, especially from the Symphony Pathetique, and a little even when it was just lying shining at him in its case, was infused with their vitality, and often the phonograph was too, and his sister Evelyn's oil paints, when they were spread out in a row in their silver tubes with labels of the colors that were inside, or when they were squirted around in little puddles of pure color on her big, leaf-shaped palette. The memory of their presence remained in some of the books in his room, and out in the living room too, the ones he could just look at and remember scenes and people moving in them. But that was about all; nothing else that people made had them, or even had any of the fog god. And things without either, just didn't matter. They were practically invisible and stirred nothing inside but an occasional memory which seemed to come out of another age or world. Nor were the gods in even such things as the violin and the books in the same way they were outdoors, either. There were practically only the sprites, though quiet sprites, in Evelyn's paints, but in the sad, big music, and so in the instruments which made it, there was a good deal of the dark god as well, and in the twenty-two the dark god was more active than latent, and the residence of any gods of sunlight and air was most precarious.

For this very reason, of course, because the darkly, mysteriously desirable twenty-two was its particular, most concentrated symbol and token, the fog god was unusually concerned about it. He was likely to sense at once any long thoughts or strong feelings about the twenty-two. Once it was possessed, once it was seen lying upon the chair and had been picked up and held with both hands as one's own, then the envious spirit would be helpless to act against the giving, and would even, to some extent, fall into the power of the possessor, though never to a degree to be traded upon. But until that had happened, the envy had most particularly to be fended off.

So, the instant Buck realized that he was imagining himself into the study and worshipping the twenty-two, he gave up the notion of such a venture, all the more dangerous because his father might be getting up at any minute anyway. Instead, he set about creating a sound humility within himself, by means of examining his conduct, both internal and external, during the critical period leading up to this twelfth birthday. He had long felt such documented humility to be the best defense against the fog god, whose natural contempt for such a poor, unprovoking spirit was bound to relax his attention.

2

The diplomacy of the last few weeks had been most difficult, for it had entailed a constant propitiation of two, separate powers, his parents, in particular his father, and the fog god, and this double propitiation had, moreover, to be carried on by exactly opposed methods, since it was necessary to convince the hostile spirit of his indifference to the twenty-two, while the very heart of his purpose was to demonstrate to his father that there was nothing in the world he wanted so much, and that he was now of a maturity to be trusted with it. For several days, just as many days, to be exact, as he had been carefully hinting to his father about the gun, he had also, in order to mislead the fog god, been practicing an attitude of body which was the upright and active counterpart of his present prone immobility and scorn. His mother had said, more than once, "My, but a boy grows up fast when he gets to be almost twelve," and he had caught his father smiling now and then when he passed through the room in this nonchalant but guarded manner, which approximated, he believed, the relaxed and confident advance of a skilled boxer from his corner, a boxer who revealed to his opponent nothing whatever of his feelings or intentions, but was nonetheless ready to move like a flash in reaction to any threat. His sister Evelyn, who was fifteen, and a junior in high school, and even had dates with a letter-man, was always looking at him and smiling in that infuriating, superior way she had, as if she could guess everything he was thinking and trying to do, and found it all pretty silly and childish. In the present review, however, Evelyn's smile didn't matter because, for all her thinking she was so important, she had no power either to give or to deny, or even to influence the decision. When his mother joked about him, though, and his father tried not to smile, Buck felt his defenses inadequate, and the independence of twelve dangerously diminished. Nevertheless, he had maintained his disguise stubbornly, and even, once he was alone, convinced himself that it had achieved the perfect balance, since it had misled the fog god, without in the least deceiving his parents.

He had the same feeling about the hints he had made. The hints were of two kinds. First, there were the occasional direct hints, such as saying, while he was cleaning the twenty-two after target practice, "How much oil should you leave on the barrel, Dad, to keep it from rusting?" or, at meal times, and as if coming out of a long reverie, "I guess a twenty-two would be pretty expensive for just a kid's birthday present," and, later, lest that be taken as suggesting that only a new rifle would be acceptable, "I don't think I'd like any other twenty-two as much as the one you have. I don't think they make them as well now as they used to. Do you?" Then there were the much more numerous indirect hints, the carefully enacted proofs, without a word about the gun, that he was now an alert and responsible being, such as shooting his bow and arrow, when his father could see him, with perfect correctness and with a clearly harmless background for the target, or emptying the garbage or bringing in the firewood for his mother without being asked to, or even offering to take his little brother, Arthur, who was only five, out hunting on the beach, and watching him all the time, and letting him carry the wooden gun with the window-latch trigger. That last he had felt to be a particularly fine stroke, since it exhibited not only his own trustworthiness, but also the shortcomings of a wooden gun for a twelve-year-old.

Now, however, after glancing over the record, he

strove only to find the flaws in this campaign, and thereby, as they accumulated, to convince himself that his chances of being given the twenty-two were few and shaky. When he had succeeded in creating something very near real apprehension, a sad, heavy premonition of loss in his middle, he went on to maintain that salutary condition by examining in detail certain less directly related instances of misconduct which might. nonetheless, be construed by his penetrating elders as departures from the necessary discretion. After minor successes with incidents somewhat spuriously sinful, he suddenly remembered the last time he had come back from his secret beach, and was invaded by a misgiving that was not in the least invented.

He had been foolish that day. He was playing on the secret beach, building a pueblo out of wet sand, with ladders made of small fragments of the driftwood that was always strewn in wave-rows along the foot of the great sandstone cliff. When he had completed the pueblo, even to making a shade place in its plaza out of four upright twigs, with supporting twigs laid across and thatched with bits of the black, small-leafed, seaweed, he stood up to survey it whole. He was pleased with its completeness and with the verisimilitude the sun gave it by casting shadows of the buildings and the ladders and the well-like khiva mouths.

Feeling the pleasure grow in him, he looked up from the pueblo and quickly all around, taking in the high, sun-warmed cliff, the one, shadowy ravine, opening several feet above the beach, the creamy surf and the glitter of the rollers beyond it, the long, black, whale-shaped rocks that closed off the beach to the south, and the great, brown blocks of stone, like the tumbled masonry of some anciently industrious giant, that closed it off to the north. He felt himself wonderfully alone and in possession within these four barriers, the sea and the cliff and the two walls of rock. Thus fortified, he looked still farther north, miles farther, at the great, sun-smitten headland, wreathed about the base with surf and faintly misted over with spindrift. He often thought of this point as the shore throne of Poseidon, for there was room in his flexible universe for a small, not altogether serious classical pantheon somewhere between the primitive sprites and fog spirit and the latter day Jehova and God. He saw Poseidon as enormous and statuesque, like a Michelangelo Moses or Blake's God, lying all relaxed and mighty among the tidal boulders, his flesh still shining with sea-wet, his beard moving against his shoulder in the sea-wind, and his great eyes fixed dreamily upon the sparkling distances of his domain. Suddenly enlarged by distance and the magnificent, drowsy god, his pleasure about the pueblo leapt up like a surf and spread violently into the great, shining joy that at once destroyed his identity and made him one with the redoubled glow of sun and cliff that hung over the beach and was the afternoon celebration of incalculable billions of the sprites.

The transportation was even more than commonly explosive, catching him quite off guard after his long, selfless preoccupation with the pueblo. He stretched up his arms to the sky and made a great shout that was to be the beginning of a very loud, operatic-sounding song of praise, but even this gesture was insufficient, and before he could phrase the first bar of the chant, he had to turn and sprint down the steep beach, shouting a brassy challenge, and launch himself, spread like a bird, out into the surf. Even then he would have been secure in the practice of his rites, if only he hadn't been thinking about the pueblo on the canyon trail, so that he had started to build it at once when he reached the beach, without even stopping to take off the old pair of blue jeans, cut off half way between his knees and his hips, that he wore for shorts. Usually he took the shorts off first thing, and threw them over onto the whale rock, for one of the important pleasures of his worship on the secret beach was going naked.

Almost nobody else ever came there, for the rocks that made both sheltering wings were all but impassable save at low tide, and the canyon trail was long and steep, and hot if the sun had been out any length of time. Moreover, nakedness was not only condoned, but actively approved by the presiding spirit in the cliff, a vague but warm, enormous and beneficent being, and by all the associated sprites, and even by the great, inconceivable, Master-God, Who, from somewhere clear above the blue sky and out of touch, presumably governed all that went on through these deputies. To be naked hastened, by the increased influence of all the sprites of sea, sun, wind and sand upon him, the ascension into ecstasy. It also preserved, later on, and no matter what he was doing, building pueblos, lying on his stomach peering into the shadowy and pastel wonderlands of the tide-pools, or playing seal in the surf, a steady, happy aliveness that was just comfortably below ecstasy, and sometimes seemed to him even better than ecstasy, because it felt like a state that might become permanent. It was possible, of course, that the fog god disapproved of such nakedness. It was even probable, for he disapproved, to begin with, of the exhilaration that came with it. But the fog god almost never visited the secret beach at the same time Buck did. It was not his temple, and when he did come, either by way of guilt in Buck or quite literally, in a low, gray cloud from the sea, he was an unmannerly intruder, and the warm spirit of the cliff and the gay sprites of the sun and spindrift simply withdrew and awaited his departure. It was inconceivable that he should really dispossess them.

It might be said, then, that it was just because Buck had not strictly observed the ritual forms of the secret beach, but had built the pueblo with his shorts on, that he found himself contemplating a really threatening sin. He had started home for lunch late, and scrambled right up the side of the ravine, through the black, aromatic brush, to save time, so that when he got home the shorts were not only wet, but also a little muddy from the canyon dust. His mother looked at them when he came into the kitchen, and he was sure she guessed, for her mouth set a little, the way it did when she was experiencing a disapproval too strong for mere passing rebuke. But she saved him from telling a useless lie by saying, "I was down on the beach nearly all morning, with Arthur and Connie. We looked for you."

She meant the long, safe beach between the beginning of the cliffs and the village point, where a good many people, sometimes even strangers, often came. So his lie, at least, might now be fitted into possible fact, and so be reduced to a half-lie.

"I was up the other side of the pier," he said, trusting that his mother had not departed from her custom of taking little Arthur, and Connie, who was only three, in the other direction, onto the widest, white-sand part of the beach. "I was looking for ink-fish in the tide-pools," he explained, and then added, because of the mud on his shorts, "And then I went up the ravine to get some rocks to make houses." If he had actually been just north of the pier, instead of way north on the secret beach, he would have meant the little ravine that came down past the house, which was permitted territory, just as the first rocks north of the pier were.

His mother looked at him again in that same tight, hurt way that hurt him too, because of her big worry about the secret beach, but all she said was, "Get into some dry pants. Lunch is all ready."

So the half-lie stood, for he had been north of the pier, of course, and he had climbed up into a canyon to get some stones, and he had even, after he came out of the surf, spent a few minutes kind of half-looking for ink fish in the pools of the whale rocks.

But now he suspected, looking back, that his mother had understood only too well the device of the half-truth, and had refrained from pressing him merely to keep him from telling a complete lie. He suspected also that some time during the day she had passed on her doubts to his father, though probably guardedly, for she feared his father's anger against him at least as much as he did, for at supper his father had told about a man from the village, a big, young man who was a strong swimmer, who had gone to the secret beach to dive for abalone and had never been seen again. His father had put the lesson of the story into an unmistakable remark at the end, too.

"Even if nothing had happened to him," he had said,

"a man who would swim alone in a place like that hasn't sense enough to be trusted with anything." The "anything," of course, translated specifically into "twenty-two."

Evelyn had understood then what Buck was just now seeing fully for the first time. While the father was telling the story, she had kept glancing up from her plate and across the table at Buck, with that infernal, superior smile of hers, and after the father's last remark, she had kept on smiling while she ate, in a way that was even worse, as if she were continuing to discover ever profounder implications. But at least she hadn't said anything out loud, and so forced the application of the parable. That was something; that was a good deal, from Evelyn.

No, that whole guarded response to the wet shorts had been no accident, and his parents' fear of the secret beach was great enough to make his disobedience serious. Most grown-ups feared the secret beach. They said it was dangerous because it was so steep it had a bad undertow, and even rip-tides, and because, when the tide was high, it was completely cut off and the waves broke clear up against the cliff. There was no more use trying to tell them why he felt safe there than there would have been trying to talk to them about God in terms of sprites and fog. Indeed, Buck could not himself have put into words, or into a clear thought, his feeling of the goodness of the sprites and the kind, warm guardianship of the spirit in the cliff. There was no way to oppose adult reason except in adult terms, something about watching to see the tide didn't catch him, and being able to get up into the mouth of the canyon in spite of waves, and such things, and he knew better than to try to argue with adults in adult terms, clear aside from the implication there would be, in this particular case, that he still cherished the secret beach, and that, probably, since he could argue from its natural features so glibly, he still went there. No, that had been a truly dangerous error, and beyond mitigation by anything but silence and time.

For a moment or two Buck, still lying there looking at the wooden gun, calculated the time since his mother had observed the wet shorts, and coming out at almost two weeks, decided that it was enough, perhaps, to mean that punishment would not now be forthcoming, at least not in any such drastic form as that of a chair with only boxes in colored papers on it. The very fact, however, that he had, in the presence of the dark god, switched over to the optimistic side in his self-searching, was evidence of how far he had come from having to pretend uneasiness and humility. It was perfectly certain, he understood, that if his father had intended physical punishment, it would have been administered at once. It was not nearly so certain, since he had made no promise, that he would not consider even a suspicion that Buck was still visiting the secret beach as reason enough to make him wait another year for the twenty-two.

Hoping not only further to soften the jealous god, but perhaps even to enlist the aid of some kindlier force, Buck examined the half-lie he had told his mother, and silently confessed that it was a complete lie in intention and, moreover, that he would probably have made it a complete lie in fact, if his mother had pressed her suspicion. Then he decided, as a kind of offering in propitiation, that if the twenty-two were on his chair at the end of this everlasting hour, he would give the wooden gun with the red stock and the window-latch trigger to Arthur. He even considered, in addition, pledging himself right now, never again to go alone to the secret beach, but this impulse he had to abandon, despite a feeling of weakness, of softness, almost of moral stinginess, for there was clearly nothing good to be gained by betraying the gods of life merely because his parents didn't understand. Finally he set himself to re-examine, in order to increase the weight of his father's judgment and strengthen his own humility, the one time the ocean had really almost trapped him at the secret beach.

It was a very windy day, and the Pacific was heaped up into dark, saw-toothed ranges against the horizon, ranges that foamed and chattered as they came rolling in. There were seven or eight ranks of surf instead of the usual three or four, and as each rank leaned and broke, it boomed up along the shore like a thumping upon hundreds of huge, empty barrels. The spray leapt high in the air above the whale rocks, and the white, inpouring smother flowed smoothly and rapidly over them, waist deep on Buck and deeper, and leapt again on the base of the cliff. The tumultuous back-wash was almost as strong as the surf. Buck was washed off the whale rocks four times, and then dragged back and forth by the deep water on the beach, being turned under and knocked against the rocks by the surf, and then hustled back down by the undertow and scoured along the sand when the water thinned away in its final, hissing rush. Even then he wasn't really afraid, but only a little worried and excited because he could no longer figure out how he was going to make his escape from this huge and active power of water. It kept crowding him so, with no time between waves, the backwash taking up all the time until the next giant wave came trembling and cracking in, high over him. That there would be a chance, however, that an escape finally would take place, he never doubted. It was not a dark afternoon. Whatever the storm was like out in the great central meadows of the Pacific, where it must have started, it was only wind here. The sunlight lay warm and orange on the cliff, even as it did on any quiet summer afternoon, and the benevolent deity of the place was in it.

Before the waves had trapped him, he had thought several times, looking north toward the ghost of the headland that showed through miles of spindrift, of the great, easy-going Poseidon sprawled there against his throne and drenched by the spray. His beard was flying like a flag and his eyes were narrowed against the wind, but on his full-lipped mouth there was a smile of profound pleasure for all the uproar of water and air. And Buck had seen for a long time, with the accustomed lift of the heart going even higher and bolder than usual, the running shoreward of the white crests that were the horses of the sea, and the dazzling of the sprites of spray and ripple, and even, occasionally, dark, graceful shadows rising within the waves as they prepared to break, and then, with a quick flip of the tail, shooting up through the green, translucent curves to escape the crash by vanishing into light. They were shadows that might very well have been mermaids. He had imagined several times, with particular delight, one singularly graceful and playful mermaid among them all so graceful and playful, a mermaid with a very white body and arms and small, not yet womanly breasts, and with blue eyes and streaming, red-gold hair, the very color of the mist of sun-sprites that hung all that afternoon over the beach. How, on such a day and in such a place and such company, could anything happen under the sign of the dark god?

And sure enough, the chance came. One of the back-waves finally thinned away to a sliding sheet of water before the next incoming wave could cover it. He struggled to his feet and it pulled at him only up to his knees, instead of up to his waist or shoulders, and seemed to glide out under him more smoothly and slowly than any before it. He stood there, bracing himself and feeling the sand sucked away from under his feet, until the back-wash was clear down around his shins, and then sprinted up the beach ahead of the next breaker, and scrambled, by toe-holds and finger-holds, up the sandstone wall toward the high mouth of the ravine. Before the slow, pursuing wave struck the cliff, he had climbed high enough so it could only shower him and drag at his legs. He hung on, and when it receded, roaring, to meet and check the next wave, he worked carefully up the rest of the way and drew himself into the mouth of the ravine and altogether out of reach.

He stood in the mouth of the ravine for a long time, resting and catching his breath in the very warm, sunny, windy center of the benevolent god of the cliff, who was also smiling about the lively escape. He watched the magnificent battle of the waves under him, and felt the cliffs tremble when they were struck. He beheld the sprites out on the deep sea in such numbers that he had to squint against them, and stood in a pale radiance they made around him in the ravine. He had never before, that he could remember, felt so strong and confident and happy, or so much alive. He experienced one unification after another with the whole dazzling, wonderful world, so that, at moments, he even felt he could launch himself out from the canyon mouth, like a gull, and play with the wind over the surf in great, imaginative curves and swoops, and slow, feathery risings. Because of these bird thoughts, he finally, despite the weariness of struggle and repeated ecstasy, climbed up the north wall of the ravine to his lookout, almost at the top, and squatted there until just a little before the sun went down, watching the new, vast regions of glitter the height opened toward the ocean horizon.

The recollection of this glad triumph completely destroyed the remorse which Buck, lying straight out in his bed, like the effigy of a dead knight, had desired. Rather it exalted him toward celebration with such rapidity that he just caught himself in time. He promptly gave up trying to think of the secret beach as a place of sin, and listened again to the house beyond his bedroom, and glanced up toward the place where the hill should have been in his window. But there was not a sound in the house yet, and there was only a very little more of the eucalyptus crown of the hill showing, with everywhere below it the moving fog and above it the unmoving fog like a colorless sky. He could only conclude that the seeming hours of agitated, far-flung activity since his waking were actually, in the sluggish time kept by the thin, gold watch on his father's bedside table, no more than as many minutes, if that long.

Having failed so dangerously to procure directly the desired moral depression, he set himself to win at least a trustworthy sorrow by fiction. He considered first an adventure for a Buck-Kit Carson, in which Janet Haley, he could dimly see in prospect, would be rescued, in the depths of red, labyrinthine canyons, from the justly embittered but too personally and indiscriminately vindictive Navajos, but abandoned the theme before the outline was even completed, sensing immediately the twin dangers of such a rifle as Carson must use and of the concluding triumph. He scanned a number of safely tragic themes from older sources, but could not be quickly or wholly enough convinced by them this morning. He also passed over the return of Buck-Ulysses, despite the temptations of the butchery-of-the-suitors scene, because he felt impatient about its incurable moral and temporal difficulties. How, for instance, could Ulysses return as a worthy lover after such dubiously prolonged and explained visits with such women as Circe and Calypso? And how, even if he managed to fuse a Janet who could not be, at the most, more than eighteen, with a Penelope who had been waiting twenty years, and was no girl when she started, how, even then, was he to make a reunion with a wife of such long standing very exciting? And if he made her not yet a wife, but only a faithful lover, how was he to justify shooting all those suitors?

Because these several rejections had suddenly pro-

duced one of those rare, realistic moments in which he
was forced to admit that he had never even spoken one
word to the real Janet Haley, and probably never
would, he settled at last into one of the few contemporary pieces in his repertoire, a piece which went back
hopefully, as if in search of a new and more promising
beginning, to the very center court where he had first
seen Janet. In this tale he was always himself, though
possessed of the physical attributes of a fine athlete of
perhaps seventeen or eighteen, with moments of the
worldly independence of twenty-one. In this form he
saved Janet, who had moments of a marriageable
eighteen, from the decadent intentions of a tennis
player of national ranking and of thirty or even more
sinister years, who was almost exclusively given, aside
from tennis and seduction, to alcohol, cheating at
poker, and miscalling his opponent's winning shots.
He managed this rescue with something like the visible
activities of the most inspired passages between the two
brown, young men on that memorable afternoon, and
with the third-set climax produced in point-by-point
detail, by defeating the licentious old expert in an ex-
hausting, five-set final before such a multitude as probably only the Rose Bowl could have seated, with Janet,
by an evil, pre-match agreement into which Buck had
somehow been trapped, as the real trophy. Janet sat in
the front row center of the center box, with her shadowy father somewhere near her, and twisted her hands
and prayed all through the six-hour feud, and covered
her eyes each time Buck fell or crashed into the barrier
while making a nearly impossible get, and flushed each
time Buck was insulted by the sneering veteran. That

turned out to be a good many times, since Buck lost the first two sets, though only at 9-7 and 15-13, and then went down 4-1 in the third before he pulled himself together and lifted his game to new heights by virtue of his cleaner living and more suitable youth, and by the greatness of his love, for which his opponent's mere ugly and perverse desire was no match. Even then the outcome was long in doubt, for the veteran had a great store of questionable resources with which to oppose the revival. Buck finally saved the crucial third set at 21-19 and four hours and twenty minutes.

He was about to undergo a similar harrowing in the fourth, which he expected to take at 12-10, when, at six all, he became aware that his father and mother had been moving around, and even speaking to each other, in the kitchen and dining room for some time, and that the smells of coffee and of bacon frying gave dependable evidence that the presents, whatever they might be, were already safe upon his chair. At this point the drenched and weary Buck on the center court, which was already in shadow, looked over at the prayerful Janet and received from her eyes, despite the watchfulness of both the vicious veteran and the shadowy father, who were, for financial reasons, allied, the first direct and passionate appeal she had made.

The effect was magical. Of a sudden Buck felt his weariness not at all, but bounded upon the green turf —the center court in the village was actually concrete, and Buck had never seen a turf court except in photographs and the movies, but turf was only fitting, as at Wimbledon or Forest Hills, for such important and masterful play—bounded upon the green turf like a hungry panther, volleying the hardest drives as he ran in, leaping at mid-court to put away terrific, untouchable smashes, serving booming ace after ace, and meeting his opponent's most desperate serves with crowding pick-up shots, almost contemptuous, and of deadly accuracy. The dismayed veteran had no further resources of any sort to oppose such an improbable renaissance. The grueling ten- and twelve-shot rallies fell away to explosive one- and two-shot points, the fourth set, in a matter of seconds, was gone at 8-6, and the final set, which had earlier promised the most desperate conflict of all, was put away at a stunning 6-0, with four love games and two games-fifteen. But then, just when the unforseen seemed complete, came the most astonishing move of all. The flushed and radiant Janet was just left sitting there in her front-row seat, with nothing in the way of reassurance from the new champion but the most perfunctory glance and wave of the racket, and the silver tournament trophy, huge and cumbersome as a coffee urn, likewise remained, unclaimed and desolate, on its table beside the referee's stand.

Buck jumped out of bed and stood, naked and skinny and nearly black all over from the sun of the secret beach, and propelled an unexplicit prayer upward toward, perhaps, the inconceivable head God beyond the blue. That is, he stood rigid and motionless for almost a minute, containing a tremendous upheaval of the spirit, half exaltation and half strenuous propitiation, which erased Janet, the center court, the despicable opponent, the conniving father, the wildly cheering multitude and the gigantic trophy all at once and in its first instant.

With the prayer stopped off just short of betraying incandescence, Buck quickly drew on, instead of the tight, blue-jean shorts, a pair of regular tan shorts which were distractingly long, coming clear down to his knees, so that he felt like the photographs of English explorers and army officers and tennis stars, who always looked as if something had slipped, but which did have nice, baggy pockets for carrying such things as, perhaps, twenty-two cartridges. With the shorts, he assumed the expressionless face and deceptive carriage of the prize fighter. Thus prepared, within and without, he opened the bedroom door, paused in the doorway for a final moment of token prayer, much more specific than any he had ventured before, and stalked slowly out into the living room.

This morning the living room was at once familiar and disturbingly unfamiliar. The gray sea-light shone softly, with an odd, exciting significance, upon everything in it, the piano, his violin case on top of the piano, his father's favorite, high-backed Spanish chair by the west window, and the gilt titles of the many familiar books, now become all containers of a single lore and meaning, quite strange and unsettling. Still cautiously erect and ready, but with a violent, breathless tumbling going on under his ribs, he passed among these reborn beings and entered the dining room.

3

The terrible tennis final must have taken longer than he had realized, for his father had already finished eating, and was sitting at his place with his book and cigarette and coffee. When Buck stopped on the other side of the table from him, he read a few words more, perhaps finishing a paragraph, and looked up. At first his gaze was that of a preoccupied, though kindly, stranger, one who was not really looking. Then his mind came gradually up out of what the book had been saying to him, or what he had been thinking about it, and he himself was present in his eyes and regarding Buck quizically. He made a little grin, and Buck gave him back almost exactly the same grin. Buck had the feeling he so often had when he and his father grinned at each other, a feeling that, save for the first gray at his father's temples, and the difference in time it indicated, he was practically grinning at his own image in a mirror which made it larger.

"How does it feel to be twelve?" his father asked.

"Not much different, I guess," Buck said, and the mirror likeness diminished, because his father was maintaining the grin more easily than he could.

"No," his father agreed. "It's too gradual."

"Maybe if I was fifteen, it would feel different," Buck said.

"No," his father said, and the meaning of the grin was in his eyes too, now. "It would still be too gradual. It's always too gradual, thank God." He grinned a little more, and continued. "If you live to be as old as Methuselah, it will still be too gradual. You'll never know the difference. The ancient believeth himself one with the babe he was. It's a comfortable arrangement."

This was a complicated thought, and even in his present expectancy, it distracted Buck. He couldn't quite get hold of what he had to know in order to begin straightening it out.

His father's grin became the teasing one to which Buck could not respond. "It is also an arrangement amazingly influential in even the most consequential matters," he said. "One could do worse than to regard it as the key to an understanding of all human activity. All by itself, for instance, it has been sufficient to convince the learned Mr. Toynbee—" he tapped the open book upon his knee "—that, because he himself has the habit of it, the frail and imitative offspring of a moribund European dogma is sufficiently dynamic to become the fusing faith of a new world."

Buck understood, after a few words, that this second statement was not intended to mean anything to him, so he let it pass in order not to lose his hold on the first. He believed he could get the first all straight in time, except for that "thank God." Why thank God because you never felt any older? His father was always putting in little things like that "thank God," things that changed the whole feeling of what he was saying, and charged his most casual remark with hidden meanings almost certainly more important than those which appeared at once.

Buck had intended to explain that he meant there would be a difference if he somehow, and suddenly, became fifteen on the day when he should have been twelve, but now he let that go too, in order to store the complications of Methuselah and thank God for a future turning over. It might not have been wise to explain about fifteen anyhow. His father had a dangerous way of thinking right into one's mind. He was just as likely as not to ask, "Why fifteen in particular?" and there was no dignified way of explaining to anyone as old as his father that fifteen had become a kind of goal in time, as the ecstatic union was a goal in feeling. Fifteen, for instance, might easily be the point of maturity at which one could really speak, without fear of being ridiculous, to a girl like Janet Haley. It would probably be an age at which one would be big enough and far enough along in school to go out for the real teams in football and basketball, and experienced enough to play tennis that men would have to respect. It would certainly be an age at which he could go alone to the secret beach, and at which his sister Evelyn would have to quit her superior smiling.

"Or did you mean if you were fifteen this morning, although you were only eleven and three hundred and sixty-four days last night?" his father asked.

There it was, the mirror thought, like the mirror grin. Still, there was a kind of pleasure, a slight touch of the little gods, in such an understanding.

"Yes," Buck said, really grinning again. He shifted his weight to one foot, stood with the other foot clenched across it, and glanced away from his father's eyes at the back of his own chair where it showed above the table. He couldn't see what was on the chair. Because of his father's manner, the joking he didn't understand, and this stringing the talk out, that he knew was mostly teasing, he was greatly reassured. Nonetheless, even if everything had gone well as far as his father was concerned, the shadowy god of mischance was still near, and the act of possession, the holding in the hands, was yet to be accomplished. Also, they had gone far enough about fifteen.

His father refused to take the hint. "And why fifteen in particular?" he asked.

The face in the mirror was there again, and it was now exactly Buck's own, feature for feature. He unfolded his feet and folded them the other way, and replied with an entirely false vagueness designed to cover his deliberate selection of the one most public reason, "Oh, I don't know. I ought to be big enough to play football by then."

Because the quizzical look and the grin remained, and because there was a little pause, with nothing said at all, during which he heard his mother come in behind him from the kitchen, he knew that his father understood perfectly that football wasn't the only reason or the most important. The big face in the mirror carried the inquisition no further, however. There was an undefined but profound and trustworthy agreement between him and his father on what could and what could not be discussed or joked about in front of the mother or Evelyn.

"Well," his father said, laying his book down and settling back with his thumbs in his belt, prepared to watch, "there may even be compensations at twelve."

That was very good of him. That was the double reassurance, the fresh seal upon their enduring covenant. The fresh seal was required every now and then, for often, especially when he was in the grim or faraway state before he began to write something new, the father would go for hours, and even for days, without appearing to know that Buck existed, or at least without remembering that he was alive and had feelings.

His mother was standing there smiling at him, in

quite a different way from the way the father smiled, a way that was like soft finger-tips moving out to touch his face, and made him afraid a hug was coming on. Right now, though, she was just wiping her hands on a dish towel with a border of bright blue and yellow stripes. Things like the bright stripes in the dish towel were almost painfully noticeable this morning. The gleaming in the diamond of his mother's engagement ring, although it came from the soft fog light in the windows, almost hurt his eyes, and the colors in it were too distinctly different. Also, he heard too distinctly the rubbing of the towel in her hands, and felt, in tiring detail, and then in an oppressive unity, so that the effect was of being for a moment with strangers, her presence before him and his father's behind him. It was like the strangeness that had been in the living room when he came through it. He was seeing and hearing and feeling everything too much. Probably that was just because he was excited, and maybe a little because he hadn't slept as long as usual, but he didn't like the feeling. It was as if he had carried across into the real world one of the most fully experienced scenes from a legend. The Tristram legend in particular, often developed that intensity, because the sadness of its final tragedy was in it from the start. Buck-Tristram would be looking at Isolt, for instance, standing outside her and seeing every least thing about her with the fierce clarity of expected loss, the blue light on her hair, the reflections of himself in her eyes, the burning color of every gem she wore, yet he wouldn't, as story-teller, just be making her say what she had to, but would actually be thinking it in her head and feeling it as if her breast were his. At the same time he would hear, as if he were there also, old Mark mumbling in another room, and would feel with him the dark, baffled rage against Tristram because Tristram made him feel like a coward and, in the weakness of his betrayed age, he could do nothing manly about it. Such painful omniscience belonged, really, only to the world of the tragic legends, in which it was mitigated by the pleasure of making things happen and making the people move and speak. The fear of death, either for one's self or for one very bitterly beloved, was what produced it, and when it happened really, among living people, like this, it brought a little of the fear of death and the shadows and stained-glass colors of the legends into the everyday world. Buck had come to think of the sensation as being dead but knowing. It was alarming in the dining room in the morning, and he wanted to get rid of it.

His mother stopped wiping her hands. She was anxious to see him get his presents. If he didn't begin, she would hug him yet. The melting promise of that indignity was growing in her eyes.

Arthur and Connie, still in their cotton pajamas that had been washed so often you could nearly see through them, were standing one at each side of her, half-protected by her skirt. Connie appeared to be busy with some long dream of her own and quite separated from the event, but Arthur was very much in this place and this moment and practically bursting with information. Buck turned away from the three of them and moved around the table. His mother said something, but he heard only her voice, and his whispered "Gee," was not a reply to her.

The twenty-two was there, lying across his chair in the middle of the unimportant packages in colored paper, and there was the tag tied to the trigger-guard, with "Happy Birthday, Buck, from Dad," on it in his father's bold, neat printing. Everything was as he had been seeing it for weeks, yet he was not pretending the awe in his "Gee," for the rifle, in its heavy, cold reality, lying there to be touched and picked up, was vital so far beyond his every imagination of it as to be a wholly new and unexpected creature. It had been oiled and polished until it really looked brand new anyway, and the long, tapered, blue-black barrel, set with its neat little sights, and shining full length with a thin line of window light, was beautifully and fatefully alive. The forbidden power, the one thing more, dwelt in the long tunnel of that barrel; that was the narrow repository of the secret of the fog god that made him fearful. The lovely, dark pattern in the grain of the polished stock, like ripple marks on the beach, was even more beautiful in itself, but the fascinated reluctance which was the chief ingredient of Buck's awe did not arise from the stock.

He came beside his chair and stared directly down at the twenty-two, but still did not touch it. He was no longer guarding his expression, however, and when he looked up, he found his father grinning a little at him again, but now not at all in the teasing, delaying way. Their understanding of that moment was the most complete of all their many understandings.

He became aware of his mother waiting attentively behind him for the decisive words or act. He could feel that she did not understand about the twenty-two, that she was afraid without being fascinated, that she could not, in any part of her, touch the desire that was in the dread. He was sorry she felt that way, but his concern for her had to remain small and outside the understanding between him and his father.

"It's yours, son," his father said, and the deterring spell was broken.

"Gee, thanks," Buck said, and picked up the twenty-two and held it in his hands, by the narrow throat of the stock in his right hand and by the grooved, walnut grip of the pump action in his left. He had held it in this manner a hundred times before, yet this was the first time. Through his hands, by the weight of the rifle, always so surprising compared to its size, and by its smooth, slippery feel, and also by its smell of cold metal and oil in his nostrils, possession was consummated. The need for deception and propitiation was at an end. The dark, stolen power of the twenty-two entered into him, adult and self-sufficient among the innumerable brighter, more familiar, less consequential spirits of his twelve years of worship.

"Golly," he said softly, turning the twenty-two on its side and gazing down at the paler, oil-streaked steel of the ejection chamber, where also each new, living bullet must rise into the barrel. This was the small, sufficient gate of the dark power.

"Golly," he said again. "Thanks, Dad."

"You're welcome, Buck," his father said gravely, and then went on in another of his own ways of speaking, the way that sounded as if he weren't speaking of anyone in particular, but just stating a general principle. "It has always seemed to me," he said, "that when a boy is old enough to own a gun, he is also old enough to know how to handle it, and should be allowed to take it out alone."

"All by himself?" Arthur cried. He was impressed.

His father nodded without looking away from Buck. "All by himself," he said. "How else would he know it's his?"

Which again was exactly what Buck had been feeling all the time. He smiled quickly at his father, and then looked down at the twenty-two again, and slowly caressed the stock with his hand. He didn't want to do this with the others watching, but he must show his father that this understanding was complete also, and he couldn't think of any words that would tell him.

"Breakfast," Connie said suddenly. "Want breakfast."

This seemed like a very good way out of the difficult silence, but then his mother spoke.

"Just a minute, darling," she said, and drew Connie's small head, with its curly, goiden hair, against her thigh with one hand. "How about a birthday kiss, twelve-year-old?" she asked, and the distance between them, the misunderstanding, even something more uncomfortable, as if he had hurt her feelings by caring so much for the twenty-two, was in her voice. He believed, unhappily, that he should be particularly kind to her at this moment, but that there was nothing he could say without weakening the power he had just won. So he didn't try to say anything, but only raised his face and allowed her to kiss him. The twenty-two lay crossways between them, and she took hold of his shoulders as she bent over it and kissed him, first on one cheek and then on the other. That wasn't at all the way she usually kissed him. It reminded him, especially because he was holding the twenty-two that way, of French generals kissing war heroes in the movies, after the medals had been pinned on. When she let go of his shoulders, he bent his head again at once to look down at the twenty-two, and closed his hands upon it very tightly. He had a feeling that her unseemly insistence might somehow have transformed the twenty-two, degraded it toward the nature of some foolish toy like the wooden gun with the red stock. It hadn't, though. The twenty-two lay there, beautiful and real as ever in his hands, steel-heavy and full of its sinister genius. Suddenly he was ashamed to be holding it so, between him and his mother, making so much of it while she was looking at him. The shame became resentment almost at once. Why can't she let me alone? he thought. Why can't she stop acting like I was a baby, or something? Or like I was going to murder somebody?

He heard Evelyn's voice coming from the living-room side of the table. "Aren't you even going to look at your other presents, Bucky?" she asked.

He didn't know when she had come into the dining room, but there she was, standing behind her chair and smiling at him as if she understood something he didn't, as if he were making a fool of himself in some way which she particularly, if silently, enjoyed. His resentment was at once turned against her, and considerably strengthened. No doubt she had entered just in time to see him being kissed. She never missed anything, the old nosey, not anything at all that would help to tease him. She knew he hated to be called Bucky, as if he were still Arthur's size. Even the mother had prac-

tically quit calling him Bucky. At the same time he felt
what he had learned only by repeated shameful, angry
experience, that it was no good trying to answer her. It
would only spoil everything even more than her just
being there spoiled it. The only thing to do with
Evelyn was just never to tell her anything. There were
some things, of course, like the secret beach, and singing
and dancing on it, and telling himself stories about
Janet Haley, that he couldn't tell anybody, but they
weren't really keeping secrets. It just happened that
way about them. You had to keep things secret from
Evelyn on purpose. The only thing to do with Evelyn
was just look right back at her, dead-pan, like the
fighter coming out of his corner, and not say anything.
Everything she got to know about, she spoiled.

What was more, on this particular morning she had
undoubtedly given him a present herself. It would also
spoil things to show ingratitude or indifference, even
to Evelyn. He wondered, for a wavering instant, if she
wasn't making fun of him because he had hurt her feelings by paying no attention to her present. And his
mother had given him a present also, maybe even two or
three presents, and Arthur had given him a present,
and so had Connie, although his mother must have
chosen the present for Connie, and maybe even for
Arthur. They would all be hurt because he wasn't
looking at their presents and being pleased about them,
and anything slighting he said to Evelyn would hurt
their feelings a lot more than hers. It would hurt the
mother's, anyway. Connie probably didn't even know
what she was giving him; all she was interested in was
her breakfast. And Arthur, small as he was, under-

stood as well as Buck did that the twenty-two was the most important present. It was the presence of the twenty-two which had nearly split him with silence. He must remember to give Arthur the wooden gun.

It was all very complicated and uncomfortable, making him feel hemmed in and pushed around, even though he already had the twenty-two. The importance of everything he said and did was enlarged this morning, and intensified. He was the person they all waited for and watched and listened to. He was the public figure, and it was up to him to get it all over with.

"Gee, yes," he exclaimed, answering Evelyn just as if she had asked an honest, interested question, and being much heartier than he had been about the twenty-two.

Carefully he stood the twenty-two up against the table beside his chair, and looked at the other presents, trying to make it appear that he just couldn't decide, in his excitement, which one to start on. Finally he picked up the cylinder wrapped in paper with little red and blue tennis rackets and bathing suits and sun shades all over it, because he saw Evelyn's name on the card, and wanted to get that over with first. The rest would be easier. He knew perfectly well, from the shape of the package, and then from its hardness through the paper and the tiny clink and soft, inside thud it made when he picked it up, what it was. It was a can of tennis balls. That was a good present, though, a fine present. It would have been really exciting, if the twenty-two hadn't come first. He began to unwrap it, and at the same time to prepare himself to make a natural-sounding, astonished thank-you. Evelyn came around the table to watch him, and his father leaned forward

to see better. Connie was saying something about breakfast again, and trying to climb into her high-chair, but
the other four were all there, close around him and
watching. The mother was helping Connie into her
high-chair, so she wouldn't fall and start squalling,
but she was helping only with her hands. Otherwise
she was watching the most of all.

"Gee," he exclaimed, as soon as enough of the can
showed. "Gee whiz, brand-new tennis balls. Gee, thanks
ever so much, Evelyn. I can sure use those."

"My, aren't we surprised," Evelyn said, as if she
were as old as the mother. He didn't even have to look
at her to know just how she was smiling. "You could
never have guessed what was in it, of course."

Still Buck fought resolutely against letting her spoil
things. It was up to him to get through all this so everybody would feel good about it, and the quicker the
better, so he could get by himself with the twenty-two.
Maybe Evelyn was just talking like that because she was
embarrassed too.

"Just the same," he said, "they're swell. Just what I
needed. Those old balls I been using are getting so light
they practically float." And to show he meant all this
pleasure, he even went so far as to open the can and
pour the three balls out, releasing their fresh, inky-
woolly, closed-in smell, and then to hold them up for the
father to look at, and to bounce one of them, although
he would much rather have kept them sealed in the can
until right before he was going to use them.

He went even further for his mother. She had given
him a pair of dark-blue bathing trunks with white
stripes down the sides and a white belt, and a white

sea-gull on one leg, and then, in a separate package, another big book about the knights of the round table, called *Sir Lancelot and His Knights Companion,* to go with the three books of the same set that he already had. They were very good presents too, and he religiously made them more important by giving each of them a particular thought about how he would enjoy it most. He thought of wearing the trunks over on the village beach, where lots of people went every afternoon, and where even Janet Haley might come, and he thought of lying on the couch in the corner of the sun porch, with his knees up and *Sir Lancelot* on them, and a couple of big pillows behind him. There would be nobody else out there, and he could hear the ocean all the time, and even look out at it once in a while, getting himself more into the story, feeling what Lancelot felt, which, for the moment, remained a good deal like what Tristram felt, and making additions of his own for Buck-Lancelot to say or do. He thought of the day as a foggy one, like this morning, or maybe even rainy, with the rain beating on the porch roof and sometimes blowing against the windows, and water from the roof running gurgling down the drainpipe, which was in that same corner, and gushing out onto the rocks. Fog or rain made reading much cosier and more satisfying, because there was nothing else you wanted to do in them, and because they made you feel so much more alone and inside the story. They were particularly well suited to the mood of King Arthur stories anyway. With each of these quick little visions, especially that of himself reading *Lancelot,* barefooted and burrowed into the pillows, Buck conjured up a small but real flight of ecstasy, and so was able to make his thank-yous sound better, and even to bring himself, after opening each present, to kiss his mother with some show of spontaneity.

With the last presents, it was easier. Connie's name was on a package that had another book in it, a book about how to play tennis, with lots of photographs of the big stars running and jumping on the courts, so it wasn't hard to be glad about, and besides, all he had to do was wave the book at Connie and say thanks, it was swell, and scratch the top of her head. It was all much easier to act when you were older than the person who gave the present. Everybody laughed this time too, because, when he tickled Connie in her curls, she pointed at the book and said, "Bucky got book," which was close enough to saying she'd never seen it before, but not so close that it needed explaining. There wasn't anything very hard, either, about thanking his father for the queer-looking package that turned out to have a cleaning rod and a can of gun oil in it, or about thanking Arthur for the little package shaped like two steps, and wrapped in old red Christmas tissue, which turned out, as he had guessed at first glance, to be three boxes of cartridges. He was so glad to have the cartridges, especially since they were all long-rifles, that he almost promised Arthur the wooden gun right there, but a moment of his old affection for it, which produced such memories as stalking tigers in the tall, pale wild wheat, and holding off a thin, yelling Confederate line from his entrenchment at the edge of the eucalyptus grove on top of the hill, and riding on a stick horse beside Kit Carson into the ominous, red-templed land of the Navajos, prevented the immediate gesture, and the moment was lost.

By the time he had closed the box of cartridges he

had opened to let Arthur look at them and touch them, his mother had gathered up the pile of wrappings and ribbons and tags from beside his chair, Connie was eating her cereal, and Evelyn had put bacon and eggs and toast on the table for the rest of them, and was filling the father's coffee cup again.

Buck wished to eat breakfast with the twenty-two across his lap, but he understood how much that notion lacked of manly restraint, and, again wearing the face of the watchful boxer, he walked over and stood it carefully in the corner. He consoled himself by leaving the opened box of cartridges beside his plate, and then, as an afterthought, because it would divert attention from his preoccupation, the tennis book also. The rest of his presents, he carefully arranged on the bench under the east window.

He made himself eat some of his breakfast, meanwhile, to keep from having to look at anybody, turning over, backward and forward, from picture to picture, the pages of the tennis book, and pretending to examine the leaping, white-clad figures against the black turf and crowd. He didn't want food. He was already filled with prevision, a kind of dark power of prophecy. Food was repugnant to him, as to one of the dedicated for the first time setting foot on the steps of the temple he has dreamed of during a lifetime and trudged hundreds of miles to pray in. When he had managed to swallow the last mouthful of fried egg and to break up his toast enough to conceal how much of it he hadn't eaten, he drank a sip or two of milk to make his mouth feel clean, wiped his lips hard, and looked at his father. His father, however, was deep in his book again, and didn't see the look or say anything to help. Buck returned to flipping the pages of the tennis book, and again thought about giving Arthur the wooden gun. The good moment having passed, the decision was now difficult. The old gun tugged at his affections like a long-time friend he was betraying. On the other hand, not to give Arthur the gun now would be almost like breaking an oath, besides being miserly. He tried to tell himself that there were many games he would still want to play with the wooden gun, because he couldn't use a real gun for games, but something small but adamant within him refused to break under this casuistry. Now, having accomplished the pilgrimage, having arrived at the threshold of the temple of the power and the fear, he would never again take the wooden gun off its pegs, unless it were, in a final act of traitorous condescension, to stand it in the corner or put it in the closet or under his bed to make room for the twenty-two on the pegs.

Throughout this brief trial, he kept looking back at his father, but still the father remained beyond reach in his book. Failing of intervention, Buck hit upon a logical, saving compromise, which had, for its instant, the brilliance of inspiration. He couldn't give Arthur the wooden gun right now, because if he did Arthur, beyond any question, would beg to go with him, and that would make an unpleasant scene. Fortunately it was not only Buck who wouldn't want him to go. The parents would never consent to letting Arthur go, all excited by the wooden gun, when there was a real gun around. He would wait until he returned to give Arthur the wooden gun.

Strengthened by this apparent decision, Buck looked

once more at his father, closed the tennis book, and said,
"Well," as a preliminary to the escape, and stood up.
Pushing his chair in carefully, he said, "If you'll excuse
me, I guess I'll give her a try."

He at once reinforced this declaration and covered
himself from the suddenly focused attention by slowly,
right before them all, drawing the first two of the closely
marshalled cartridges, the tiny troopers of the fog god in
their lead helmets and copper caps, out of the box, and
then shaking about half of them from the loosened end
into his hand, and slipping them into the right pocket
of his shorts.

"I want to go too," Arthur cried, letting his fork clatter
down on his plate. "Can I go too, Buck?"

So it was coming anyway. Buck closed the box, and
held it in his hand, and looked at his father.

"I don't really think," the mother began, but the
father, who was looking at Arthur, not Buck, said, "No,"
just that, and because of the way he was looking, Arthur
didn't say anything more.

The father slowly transferred his gaze to Buck and
nodded.

The excitement leapt up in Buck again. His hand was
on the barred gate and the gate was unlocked. But in
order not to expose himself before Evelyn, and also a
little because of Arthur's expression, he restrained himself once more.

"I better get these things out of the way, I guess," he
said, and gathered up the tennis book and the presents
from the window bench and carried them all into his
bedroom. While he was in there, putting the boxed
cartridges under the socks in his top bureau drawer, his

mother called, "Put on a warm sweater or jacket, Bucky. The fog's cold, and it's hanging on this morning."

"My lord, old softy women," Buck muttered, but when he went to the closet to put the tennis balls and cleaning rod and oil up on the shelf, where Arthur couldn't reach them, he took down his oldest sweat shirt, the red one that was washed and bleached to a streaky pink and had only the ghost of a mounted Red Ryder on the front of it and holes in both elbows. There were certain realms in which his mother's gentle indecision could not be depended upon. He put the sweat-shirt on, pushed the sleeves up above his elbows, and returned to the dining room, walking like the fighter coming out of his corner. It felt different this time, though, exactly the opposite of the way it had been before. It was against his mother and Evelyn and Arthur that the attentive dead-pan was turned now, not against the jealous god. Rather, he was allied with the jealous god; the jealous god, at last won over, or forced over, was awaiting him out there where his moving fog still covered the hills and filled the ravines. In this venture the fog god, for the first time, and however reluctantly, would be a kind of partner.

He picked up the twenty-two and looked at his father again. His father, grinning a very little, nodded.

Perhaps his mother was only dreamy from getting up so early, but she made him uneasy because she was staring at the gun with wide-open, half-seeing eyes. He felt almost that she was looking the gun away from him. Whatever she was day-dreaming about, it wasn't happy, either. As he was going past her, out of her gaze toward the kitchen, she woke up suddenly and looked at him again, making herself smile, and put a hand very lightly on his arm, almost as if she were afraid to touch him.

"Bucky, do be careful, won't you?" she said.

Again she was making everything wrong. She seemed to be trying to draw him to her, though she didn't, actually, not with her hand. It was as if she thought he was going a lot farther away than just out on the hill; as if she thought he might not come back. And calling him Bucky, though he had the twenty-two in his hand.

This time his father helped at once. "Buck will be all right, Mother," he said impatiently. "Stop fussing at him."

The mother took her hand off his arm, but she was still smiling at him that way. She still sounded just as wrong, too, although she said, "Of course he'll be all right. I'm just a nervous old hen." He still felt, as he went on toward the kitchen, that he was doing her a wrong, and that the whole hunt was going to be ruined because she couldn't understand.

"Don't forget your birthday dinner's at noon, Bucky," she called after him.

"And leave something for the other hunters, Bucky," Evelyn called, making fun of both him and the mother with her "Bucky."

But he was almost free now. He was pulling away from the hold of the mother's gentle, foolish concern, and away from Evelyn's superiority too. He could afford, though not altogether with an easy conscience about his mother, to be supremely contemptuous of them both, too contemptuous even to show it.

"Sure," he said casually, without turning his head, and went on only a little more quickly through the kitchen, padding softly on his bare feet, and went out onto the latticed porch, and closed first the door and then the screen door so carefully they scarcely made a sound.

4

The moment his feet touched the hard earth of the yard, however, he began to run. He carried the twenty-two balanced by the pump grip in his right hand and ran as hard as he could up the narrow dirt road that climbed around the base of the hill and vanished into the first ravine. He was running himself free of the hold they had on him down there in the house, of what he suspected Evelyn would be saying and his mother feeling. He was pulling straight all the little kinks and snarls they had made inside him, so that the threads could be drawn right out, leaving nothing at all attaching him to the house, nothing to hold him back.

The fog had lifted and thinned a good deal since he'd first looked out at it through his bedroom window. The whole big, rounded, lower part of the hill was revealed more distinctly in the darkened air than it ever was in sunlight, and even the eucalyptus grove on the summit was faintly but entirely visible. The eucalyptus, the laurel, the sweet grass, even the earth and stones, had strong, damp smells after the fog, and everything was so quiet that his own panting and the quick, rhythmic patting of his bare feet became disconcertingly loud. There was no wind at all; not even the wild wheat was moving. It was the interval of perfect balance between earth and ocean, when the land wind had died away to nothing, and the sea wind couldn't quite begin. The whole world of hills and ravines was waiting for the change, silent, motionless and attentive.

Buck stopped running as soon as he was around the big curve into the ravine, and out of sight from the house. Then, with only the fog above him and the brush-grown slopes of the ravine going up on each side, he could pretend that the family no longer had any hold in him at all. He turned his attention outward to the motionless world of the fog god, who was in his ascendency at this hour, and to the twenty-two that was a passport into that world as a new and considerable being. He cradled the twenty-two in his left arm, the way the mountain men had carried their guns, and climbed as swiftly and softly as an Indian, walking a little pigeon-toed, as they did, to keep a better grip on the path. Sternly he repressed each of the repeated little uprisings of excitement in himself that were too dangerously reminiscent of the ecstasies in sun and wind to be permitted their courses in this watchful silence.

Toward the top of the ravine, he turned off into a narrow branch trail that climbed more steeply and closed in upon him until dark brush often scraped lightly but sharply across his bare legs. Here he became Kit Carson, acting as scout for a cumbersome military expedition which was, at present, coming along slowly, far below and behind him, because he was hunting fresh meat for the noon halt. With the weight of the real twenty-two in his arm, he felt much more convincing as Carson than he had ever felt before, yet he felt himself drawn out of the part too often to follow it consistently, or shape the action to come, or select the rest of the cast, except, of course, for Janet Haley, who would be in it somewhere.

For one thing, the scraping brush kept distracting him. He liked the scraping, and the fine, white traceries it drew on his brown legs. It made his body feel awake and alive, a proper, mobile, alert explorer of the ravines and the hillsides under the low sky. It made him like the chill of the air and the drench that shook off the leaves onto his shorts and bare calves and feet. It made him feel careless and bold. But also, it kept drawing him back out of Kit Carson's mountains and Kit Carson's unmoved, familiar assurance with a rifle, into these real hills and the struggle against his childish delight about the twenty-two. Moreover, every time he was drawn back from Kit Carson's world into his own, he would remember that he was not just pretending to hunt something big, like an antelope or a deer, but was really hunting something much smaller, a ground-squirrel or a cottontail. Then he would be peeved because he had been dreaming, and would make his mind and his eyes and his feelings pay close attention to what he was doing, so that he caught the first movement of each small bird that started up near him and flitted away over the bushes. For a moment, as each flight began, he would think of shooting, and then, briefly, he would become the hunted, knowing exactly, as he stood still to watch, how much the bird wanted to go a safe distance and be hidden again to watch him, so that it was only the danger of breaking silence that kept him from calling out to reassure it.

The narrow, dramatic weight of the twenty-two in his

arm also, of itself, made everything more real, with
that intense reality of legend, so that legend, for once,
was thinner than actuality, and it was more exciting to
be himself than to be Kit Carson. He became constantly
himself the hunter and himself the hunted, and as he
climbed closer to the fog the bursts of happy excitement became fewer and fewer, until, at last, he was
feeling all the time, with oppressive reality, the kind of
tragic foreknowledge that was only enjoyably sad in the
legends. The dark spirit became present everywhere,
and became, also, allied with what drew him back
toward the house. It was secretly and maliciously grinning at him, with a kind of infinitely enlarged, demoniac
version of Evelyn's smile, because it had tricked him into
coming up here where it was all-powerful.

The twenty-two was not, after all, a sufficient token of
the fog power to protect him. He felt the presence of the
fog god directly with his body in the damp air, which
was chilling him even through the old red sweat shirt,
and on the damp earth and the black, shot-like pebbles
under his feet. The little drops the fog had left clung
at the points of leaves all around him and swelled and
suddenly let go, falling with a sound like faint, scattered rain. He listened to this pattering always with a
feeling that he was listening for something far more
important behind it, and the hunter in him made the
hunted fearful and cautious. Because of this slow transformation and the confusion made by the quality of
legend in reality, he was very quiet and widely attentive when he came up around the hill onto a wide,
sloping bench-land.

This region, covered with dark brush and cut across

by ravines reaching down toward the ocean, extended north as far as he could see and the fog hung low over it, like the curtain of an enormous stage, just beginning to rise. This vast reach, after the small hills so close about him, added intolerably to his sense of seeing and feeling too clearly. He believed also that he could feel his ears stretching up and twisting forward, straining their gristle into the cupped, tapered shape of a rabbit's ears, for the silence on the bench-land was so great that the sounds of his own movements, reassuring within the confines of the pass, dwindled almost to nothing, and seemed not to come from him. Yet the sounds his body made by itself were alarming. The faint whispering of the surf, diminished by distance and height and fog, was less important than the sigh of his own breathing and the portentous pounding of blood in his head. The most insistent sound of all was a faint, soprano tocsin, which he knew must be in his own ears, but which nevertheless seemed to be ringing in the air itself, intent upon warning every living creature of the coming of this armed deputy of darkness.

Buck had run many times, and often singing, too, along these same narrow paths through the brush, but now the bench-land was as unfamiliar and hostile as the great plateau of Tibet. He had never been on it before, and the path was strange and possibly misleading. Against his uneasiness, he clenched his hand upon the stock of the twenty-two and declared, in bold words in his mind, that he would conquer this unknown, that, with this new power he had, he would make the whole region his in one journey across it. The exultation which followed this challenge and hastened the drumming of his blood, concealed from him the fact that at the moment he had come onto the bench-land and gazed so far and so much too clearly north along it, the fog spirit had separated itself into innumerable tiny parts, the very counterparts of the sprites, each alive and malicious with the original nature, and that these innumerable parts had scattered at once into their thousands of hiding places around him. They were no longer fragments of his own hunted self in all the bushes, but clever, vindictive little enemies, concealed and cowering for the moment, because he had the potent twenty-two, but only awaiting the instant when he should lay it down or misuse it.

Although he believed that it was because of his glee of anticipated conquest, and would have said, inscrutably, to any dull adult question, that he was far enough from the house now so he could really begin to hunt, it was actually because of this new enemy surveillance that Buck stopped walking, and looked all around him, first in one sweeping survey of the distance, and then more particularly at each near bush and open patch, before he lowered the twenty-two and began to load it. He slid up the loading tube until the small, arched doorway at which the emissaries of death went in showed dark and open. Then, drawing nearly all the cartridges from his pocket, he inserted them one by one, until twelve of them were lying concealed in close file within, ready to sally forth at his least touch. He closed the tube upon them, returned the disappointed unchosen to his pocket, and, with ceremonious care and firmness, only increased by the shockingly loud double-click of the action, pumped the first cartridge into the barrel. Then, with the twenty-two cradled again in his left arm, now the very instant, living, impatient instrument of the fog god, he moved forward upon the strange plateau.

He moved firmly and proudly, but also slowly, taking great care to be quiet, and watching every opening in the brush before him and beside him, for the first suitable token of life, the first moving target—he did not think of it more particularly—upon which to test his prowess. He felt exceedingly alert, but also exceedingly alone. He was too completely occupied with the task he had set his eyes, however, and too accustomed to feeling himself accompanied by swarms of the friendly little beings of light and wind, to know that he was alone. He knew only that he was so tense that any discernible movement, however distant or trivial, halted him if it didn't occur exactly where he was looking. Sometimes, if a movement were very quick and close, it would startle him so much he would even tremble afterwards, so that when he went on he was forced to swagger a little and assume the mask of the emerging fighter. Each time, however, the movement would prove to be just another of the little, dark birds making its sudden escape, leaping up and flitting and dipping away. Some of them, once they were hidden at a safer distance, chirped for a long time, adding another alarm to the tocsin of silence. Life on the plateau was not deceived about which power he was representing now. It knew he had gone over to the enemy. Gradually, because of these bird warnings, he began to realize that the multitudes that watched him were no longer sprites or the hunted parts of himself, but traitorous outposts of his new party, hostile, perhaps, to the brightness he had deserted, but also suspicious and envious of any new power among themselves.

Thus, tiringly alert, yet not in full possession of himself either, he went very slowly north over what seemed a long way, without seeing a single proper target. He passed inland around the washed sandstone heads of two ravines, through which the faraway talking of the surf came up to him distinctly. Gradually he became so nervously anxious to try the trigger that he had several times to repress an angry impulse to shoot at the sentinel birds. A few times he even started to raise the twenty-two, but he never quite gave in to the impulse, and each success in restraint left him with a pleasing sense of having conserved his power for a greater purpose.

At last he came to a place where the bench-land was severed by a ravine much longer and deeper than those before it. The trail he had been following dipped into the ravine and went down under him toward the head of it. Small, separate clouds of fog still clung here and there to the sides of the ravine, as if caught in the dark brush, or swam free in the great air between its walls, making the dark bottom crevice and the visible bits of sandy path going down toward the ocean on the other side appear very far below him. The sound of the surf came up the ravine like soft, gigantic sighing. For Buck, to whom any sound of ocean was always a profoundly suggestive, if mysterious, speaking, the ravine appeared at once an awful and exciting depth, a part of the geography of another world. As he gazed down into it, the wakefulness he had been so long striving to maintain was forgotten. He even forgot, for a moment, that the twenty-two lay in his arm. His attention, exhausted by long straining after particulars, drowsed out of touch, and formless, cosmic wonderings stirred slowly in him.

Yet it was out of this very instant of beginning to expand and lose himself that he was quickened for the first time by a really promising movement, a tiny, ground-fast leaping on the far side of the ravine, a twitch like an illusion created by his own pulse, which was altogether different from the aerial tossing and dipping of the birds. He struggled against the other-worldliness in his eyes, but then, in hunting out the movement, moved himself. At once the tiny pulsing way across there in the pale grass between the dark bushes ceased. It was only by a long, careful searching that he discovered the rabbit sitting there, scarcely darker than the grass it sat in, yet unquestionably, once he found it, a rabbit, bolt upright and with its ears erect and attentive.

Buck forgot his awe of the big ravine and swept out of mind with one kingly gesture all the wearying confusions of his first expedition in the new alliance. All the while watching the rabbit, without, he believed, once blinking, he very slowly raised the twenty-two to his shoulder and sought to steady it and take precise aim. This was a long-familiar exercise, but the first time he had applied it to a living target, and that, he discovered, made a difference. Old warnings and instructions came up, but as if into airy spaces in his mind, floating free, like the fog clouds in the ravine, and with a voice of their own, or a voice like his father's, save for the unwonted urgency. Among them entered observations drawn from the particular moment, and much longer and more emotional than the instructions.

"A gully is always wider than it looks," the voice like his father's reminded him. "It must be an awful big rabbit to show that clearly across such a big gully," the voice of the moment put in, and added, getting clear down into his belly, "which is practically a crack in the globe, which is twenty-five thousand miles around—" "So aim a little high," the voice like his father's went on. "Now take a full breath, let half of it out, hold it." "—and floating free in space," put in the new, excited voice, "belted with cloud and spinning so that it must hum like a top and everything on it be fearfully and perpetually dizzy and clinging, and yet it is actually but a motionless, soundless speck in the dark abyss of eternity, too faintly lighted even to show among the other stars, and what does that make you, who are less upon it, far, far less upon it, and as brief of being too, compared with it, than those tiny, practically invisible red spiders you saw climbing in and out of the craters in the skin of that orange in the copper bowl in the middle of the table Sunday."

"Squeeze the trigger; don't jerk it," admonished the calm, familiar voice.

"My God, what a canyon," cried the other, "opening right under your feet like the dark abyss of eternity."

Buck tried to shut it out in order to hear the final admonition of the practical voice before the rabbit over there, which must be as big as an elephant to appear so distinctly upon the far side of the abyss of eternity, decided to hop again and go off with his chance, with the very proof of his right to the new trust.

"You can't hold a sight steadily when you're standing up," said the practical voice. "Don't try to. Put it into slow motion. Sight below the target and squeeze as you come up. Only come up smoothly, and remember, you have to aim high, so leave the last little squeeze till just the top of the bull's-eye or even a hair above it."

The twenty-two, all by itself, so that it startled Buck, made a sound that was scarcely more than a sharp, short crackle above the gulf of the ravine and under the wide pall of the rising fog. It seemed to Buck, however, after his long silence, to make an indecent and violent uproar, a kind of sacrilege against the stillness of the bench-land and the ravine. The report was followed almost at once by a second report in the depths below, not nearly so sharp, but deeper, heavier and more protracted, like the distant firing of a much heavier weapon. Then, quickly, there came a second echo, shorter and fainter. It was as if two enemies were firing at each other across a considerable distance, down in the bottom of the ravine and toward the ocean.

Buck was astounded, when he lowered the twenty-two after these three reports, to discover the rabbit still sitting there, unchanged except that its right ear was no longer erect. For an instant he was chiefly, within the confusion left by the two voices, vexed because he had missed. Then it occurred to him that perhaps his eyes had deceived him, that perhaps he was seeing a rabbit only because he had been so long expecting to see a rabbit, where actually there was only a dead root or a small bush or grass clump that had, at that distance, something the shape of a rabbit. Peer as he would, however, it remained a rabbit to his eyes.

Quickly he ejected the empty shell and took aim again, very carefully. The voices resumed their opposed monologues in his head, but now he was hardly aware of them, save as a small panic of haste which he had to control in order to shoot well. He separated them from the act, leaving them to argue with each other, while he, quite alone, did the shooting, reminding himself of the necessary steps in a third voice, which was his own. This time, as he heard the crack of the real report, and then the soft, separated roars of the two echoes, he also saw, right through the notch of the rear sight and over the little point of the front sight, the rabbit's left ear drop. It dropped suddenly, not as if the rabbit had lowered it, but like a semaphore arm abruptly deprived of the current which had held it aloft. Yet the rabbit again just continued to sit there. The ear dropped by itself, and the rabbit didn't move.

For the first time there occurred in Buck a sudden and profound feeling for the rabbit as a rabbit, rather than as a target, an abstract object of his aim. It took the form of a violent revulsion in his middle, during which he was divided into two beings, as he had been previously divided between himself walking with the gun and himself watching from behind every bush and sharing the consternation of the birds. One part of him was still the hunter upon the south rim of the ravine, disturbed by his ineptitude, but the other part of him entered into the rabbit upon the north rim, patiently and inexplicably awaiting a third shot, and perhaps even, if that also proved a bad shot, the Lord only knew how many more for the Lord only knew what reason, if any. The hunter part of him was filled with a kind of desperation at the thought of the protracted cruelty. The two voices clamored incomprehensibly in his head, but he didn't even hear them. The third voice was unable to say a thing; the third speaker was choked up and very near to crying, and hadn't a single suggestion to make if he had been able to speak. For a moment

Buck, the body, longed to throw the vicious twenty-two into the brush and run away, as far as he could, from the place where he had done such a thing. He didn't, though. Instead, without the least feeling that he had decided to do so, he shucked out the second shell and automatically, hastily, almost blindly, lifted the twenty-two and fired at the rabbit a third time. He didn't even hear the report and its sunken echoes this time, and he was more bewildered than anything else, to see the rabbit slump a little, as if it had gone soft and boneless, then leap feebly upon its side, twice, and stretch out slowly and lie still. Its stillness became a very important fact, the single most important fact in the universe, around which all other being and meaning, like an enormous, concerned audience, was gathered without motion and without sense of self.

At that instant a hawk rose out of the bench-land, two, or perhaps even three, ravines farther north, but almost directly above the rabbit. In the moment it required to rise against the sea-wind that was beginning now, and then curve back on rigid wings and sink away inland to vanish against the dark brush of the hills, it seemed, so tiny, quick-rising and unexpected, to be ominously related to the rabbit, to have risen, indeed, directly out of it, and so to be the other, the enduring, portion of the creature against whom the crime of murder, in a peculiarly lengthy, deliberate and despicable form, had been committed. It went up toward God with word of an unforgivable sin.

Then, in a typhoon of emotion within which thoughts were innumerable but none of them decipherable or important, Buck was running down the trail into the ravine. When he reached a point below where the rabbit should be, he scrambled, in the same panting, driven confusion, as nearly straight up as he could go among the bushes and through the dry, rustling grass. The steep slope and the weight of the twenty-two, however, slowed him down in spite of all he could do, and as he slowed down, the whirling confusion in his mind slowed down too, and he recognized among his feelings a surprising eagerness to lay hands upon his first kill. Because of the visions of abysses, inter-stellar loneliness and a small, hawk-shaped soul rising straight up, but then curving away and downward out of sight, as if it too, even it, had somehow been mortally wounded, he was very glad of this eagerness. He strove to give it strength. He fed it with fragments of worldly maxim and bits of thick-skinned, male, public attitude, hoping it would grow big enough to defend him. The result was not altogether satisfactory. Instead of pushing out the many disturbing notions, the eagerness first, though it seemed to become much larger, was transformed into a mere hollow imitation of experienced indifference, a sensation akin to the one that went with coming out like a prize-fighter. This, in turn, still didn't push out the disturbing notions, but rather blended with them to make an all-pervading, uneasy defiance against glimpses of souls of any kind, all transient ecstasies, the regrets of mothers, the silent disapproval of fathers, the superior smiling of sisters, the unimpeachable delicacy of red-headed loves and in particular against gods of every category, inherent, mythical and metaphysical.

When finally he came up to the rabbit and stood there, staring down at it, this too-widespread defiance was no longer able to sustain him at all. It vanished, leaving him empty and incredulous while, all unknown to him, the enormous, primal chaos engendered by his act slowly shrank and was reshaped toward reality.

It was not a big rabbit at all, not by any means the elephant-sized, well, at least large dog-sized, creature he had been rushing up to see. On the contrary, it was a very small rabbit, a baby cottontail. Slowly, as he gazed down upon it, he was informed, in the reasonable marksman's voice of another, that it was not the wideness of the ravine that had made the rabbit seem small, but the smallness of the rabbit which had made the ravine seem wide.

The small rabbit lay flat upon its side, extended in a grotesque, straining arc, the motionless imitation of a desperate leap. Only its downy fur stirred a little when the sea-wind lightly, tenderly caressed it. At each touch of the sea-wind, also, the nearby grasses bowed a little in suppressed agony, and the topmost leaves and twigs of the bush close above trembled stiffly in unison. There was no confusion any more, and no haste. The world was its own size again, its own tangible self, everything in it real and believable, if holding a little aloof from Buck. Time had stopped, and in its fixity there was no progression, no change, no possible escape. This dead creature, not as large as his own two hands, capable, with room to spare, of being cradled in his own two hands, which lay there soft upon the harsh grass of almost the same color, had only begun to savor the ecstasy and dread and infinite, curious variety of life. He had been able to kill it only because it was so young that it simply couldn't move when it was scared. It was

so very young, indeed, that it had not learned even that
first of all lessons very well, for it had forgotten to
lower its ears.

One black-rimmed bullet hole, with only a very little
blood seeping up around the edges of it, showed just
above and in front of the alarmed, protuberant eye.
It was a neat, exact orifice, a most improbably tiny
entrance for death, yet the eye was already losing its
alarm, closing out the last look at the world with a
filmy shutter being let down just inside, between the
eye and the mind.

Buck knelt and lifted one of the leaf-shaped ears
upon his fingers. The ear was disturbingly warm and
soft, and when thus extended, it revealed just what
Buck had most hoped not to see. There was another
little, neat, dark-rimmed hole through the base of the
ear, not half an inch above the head. Through this hole
Buck could see the color of his own finger. The delicate
whorl of the fingertip was made distinct by gun oil and
a little blood in its grooves. He wished desperately to
end his examination with this one ear, but was unable
to do so. As if by itself, while something tiny and important in his mind raced toward the back of his skull,
away from where he could find it, his hands reached
farther under and lifted the other ear, still not by pinch-
ing it between thumb and finger, but upon the flat of
the palm, as if the ear might be reassured by such gentle
handling, and feel able to rest in such a position. The
tiny hole, which he could feel now as if it were pierced
in himself, was in this ear also, though a little farther
up from the head. The dark awe again moved faintly

but fearfully within him, as at the first glimpse of the rising hawk.

The hole in front of the eye became almost a comfort. At the same time, Buck felt the power of the twenty-two as never before, and with loathing. A rebellion within the congress of his insides sought to place the whole blame upon the cold, slick, heavy, sharp-working twenty-two, as if it might by itself not only have sent forth the three tiny monsters of doom, but also made the fatal decision, so empty of understanding and so criminally stupid about visible sizes and distances. The twenty-two was easily able, without a sound or a movement, just by lying there across his thigh, to turn this false accusation and put it home where it belonged.

Then Buck was compelled to go even farther, to lift the small rabbit by its wounded ears, in the full grip of his fist, and turn it. He must see all that had happened. The hole in the other side of the head was not nearly so neat. Most of the eye was gone, and on the yellow grass where the head had been lying, there were clots and streaks of shiny, new red. Buck was not sick, not from the belly and out at the mouth sick, anyway. He hardened his middle and benumbed his mind; that was all. He felt only the warm, short-furred, gristly ears in the clutch of his fist, and considered only the surprising heaviness of the small rabbit hanging from them.

Death is awful heavy, he thought, on the surface of his mind, not letting the notion in where it would stir feelings. That's all it is, just heavy. It's all there, but it's done, so it's just heavy.

But then he saw again, upon the small, traitorous screen of his memory, the sudden ascent of the hawk, and could not help wondering if the thing which made lightness and ecstatic loveliness in life had fled up out of the rabbit by way of the hole made by the third bullet. His mind began to open and let the feelings up. He closed them under again, resolutely. He thought, like someone else, like his father's voice arguing with him, that he should stand up, make himself expressionless, and attentive to nothing going on inside himself, but only to the safe, fixed things about him, and continue to hunt, carrying the small rabbit with him. At the same time deeper, if less orderly, counsel assured him that he would not do so. He looked around quickly, feeling that he wasn't alone in the ravine or on the bench-land, that somewhere, not very near, but near enough, certainly, to see him and be curious and perhaps even to guess, there was a man standing, a quiet, watchful, judging man, almost, but not quite, a stranger. There was no man, though. The watching was there, but not the man to do it. There was nothing in sight, really, but the fog, still lifting and thinning, and the withdrawn, silently lamenting bushes and grass of the ravine. He was free to retreat, to stand up and glide silently away from this place, leaving behind him, with the body of the small rabbit, the fear and shame of what he had done.

He stood up, holding himself dead-pan against this wish to run away. With the rabbit still in one hand, and the twenty-two in the other, he looked for the first time at the ravine whole, and all at once knew where he was. The world had changed, but not in appearance.

It had changed only because it was dead inside, and because it had shut him out, because it was no longer unceasingly quivering and shimmering with the multitude of invisible lives. Outwardly it was the same as ever, and he was not upon the edge of an abyss in the plateau of Tibet, but at the head of his own particular ravine, the ravine by which another Buck, back in another life, had usually gone down to the secret beach which had been the chosen resort of sprites and the charge of the benevolent spirit of the cliffs.

The outlaw Buck knew then what he wanted to do, and felt a relief at the knowledge, though a grave and somewhat dreamy relief, composed of a decision, with a trace of penitential eagerness, at the center, surrounded by a great holding-off of questions and feelings. Now that he had thought of it, indeed, it was not even what he wanted to do, but convincingly, blessedly, what he had to do, as if somone else, a trusted and much older and wiser someone, had ordered him to do it. He had to go swimming at the secret beach.

Still carrying the rabbit by its ears in one hand, and the twenty-two in the other, so that he had to go very slowly, balancing himself, and testing each foothold, he descended the steep side of the ravine. When he reached the trail, he turned down toward the beach. The smell of the sea was strong in the ravine, and the quiet seemed thickened and closed in, only the more complete for the pulsing whisper of the surf, which sent small, communicative ghosts of itself up along the brushy slopes above, and among the shelves and caves of bare sandstone in the chasm below. When he had gone a short way along the trail, Buck lifted the small rabbit against his sweat-shirt and worked his hand around under it, until he could carry it safely upon his forearm. This relieved him greatly, removing a painful strain from his own ears.

5

It occurred to Buck, after a time, that he should be running. He always ran on the canyon trail, once he was out of sight from the top. Farther down, when he was running so fast that it was like half flying, and his bare feet seemed to have eyes of their own to sail him over reaching bushes and to pick the clear spots among the black pebbles that rolled like shot, he should begin to sing in the high, quick way that went with downhill running. When he came hurtling around the last big bend and saw, all at once, between the high wings of the canyon-mouth, the whole blue dome of ocean swelling away into the west and sparkling everywhere, and felt the cool breeze straight in his face, there should arise in his breast, whatever sound actually came out, a great, martial delight of brass and drum, equal to the near crashing of the surf, and sufficient to lift him instantly into the god that could not be reasoned about. It made him uneasy that the running and the martial music now seemed a far-back, improbable conduct. He felt as if he were already late coming down to the beach, too, because here he was still walking, when usually he began to run just a few yards down from the very top of the trail, where the last vestige of authority, the last thread to the house, let go, and the ravine became his own, a kind of extension of the secret beach and its guardian portal. The will of the benign spirit of the cliffs prevailed in it also, and its lesser deities had much the same meanings as those of the beach.

Even this remembered security and the nudge of time, however, could not start Buck flying now. He continued to feel behind time, but that only gave the greater power to the forces which restrained him, forces alien here, but so wholly in control this morning, and because of his deed, that the native spirits had withdrawn, and even the will of their benign chief seemed only doubtfully in force. It was steadily growing lighter in the ravine, but the fog had not broken overhead, and it was only a cold, gray, wet kind of lightness. There was no question, in the extreme silence between the dark walls and under the fog, that the god of conscience had taken over, and that Buck was being kept under observation.

The same spy who had stood on the other edge of the ravine and watched him, with anything but approval, while he examined the little rabbit, was now moving down invisibly along the walls of the ravine, first upon one side and then the other, keeping Buck always in sight. It was evident that this spy was a deputy of the fog god, and that Buck was not trusted. It even seemed as if the whole business of getting the twenty-two for his own had been a trick. He had lost the bright gods; he had even made himself their enemy, a result he had not foreseen, though it now appeared perfectly logical. And hadn't he even been warned of just this result, before he ever saw the rabbit? When he first gave up trying to be Kit Carson, and became a real hunter, with a real,

loaded rifle in his arm, hadn't he seen only dark, frightened birds, birds ominous as legendary warnings, and
nowhere any sprites? And hadn't he felt innumerable
bits of himself hiding along the hillsides, filling the
places of the betrayed beings of light and exultation?

He had lost the bright gods, and he had not been
accepted by the dark. He was in no soul's land, and in
its isolation his own soul was withdrawn, small and heavy
as a stone within him, and closed about his evil deed.
No wonder it could not take wing and make the heralding music. That was the whole of reality now, the little
stone inside, and outside the cold, dark ravine and the
inescapable watcher. His knees felt weak and his body
deeply chilled, even with the red sweat-shirt on, and the
twenty-two and the rabbit were beginning to feel so
heavy that he knew he couldn't have run with them
even if his heart had been light and quick. Several
times, when he felt himself most closely watched, as if for
an immediate purpose, he looked up quickly, thinking,
"There's really somebody in here watching me." He
could never discover the watcher where he believed him
to be, however, and each time, when he went on, after
the first quick look, to search the side of the canyon,
there would be only the still, black bushes and the narrow side-washes coming down into the ravine, and the
sky of fog beginning to move and take shapes above the
rim. Then he would realize that the watcher had slipped
over onto the other side.

The rabbit, small though it was, became the particular
burden. All the other impressions of his plight were
fleeting as compared with his concentration upon the
rabbit, and at times it seemed as if the rabbit and the

small, inactive stone of his soul were the same thing. He wished very much that the rabbit were alive on his arm, nestling there of its own choice, like a pet cat. Several times he thought, with a small, imitation leap of ecstasy, of a miraculous resurrection of the rabbit. It would move on his hand and gather itself together, and then, when he knelt down to bring it closer to the earth, its small, strong hind legs would propel it out of his arm. Not at all afraid of him, but only glad to be back to what it knew, it would hop slowly away, sitting up now and then to look around or pull at a leaf and chew it. When it chewed it would work its mouth and nose the way rabbits always did, in both directions, side to side and up and down. At last, after he had watched it a long time, it would hop out of sight among the dark bushes, removing with itself all that Buck had done to transform the world so miserably.

None of these minor resurrections, however, helped against the unquestionable death that became heavier and heavier on his arm. The rabbit would not really draw itself warmly together and snuggle. On the contrary, it kept growing cooler and stretching out more, and now and then it rolled limply, as flexible but uncontrolled as jelly, and threatened to fall off. Each of these loose shifts within the rabbit weakened Buck like a failure of his own muscles. When he came around the third turn, where the ravine widened and the sound of surf was noticeably louder, Buck stopped and leaned the twenty-two against the wall of the trail and used both hands to arrange the small rabbit more compactly in the hollow of his arm. Despite his wish to close his eyes against the bullet holes in them, he also tenderly and painstakingly arranged the rabbit's ears to lie flat along its back. The act comforted him somewhat. It made, to the knowledge of his arm and hand, and his breast under the red sweat-shirt, a considerable decrease in the difference between the living and the dead. The small stone of his soul enlarged and softened somewhat, and began to move within, so that it felt more like a stubborn egg, nearly ready to hatch. Something unknown, but of great importance because it was alive, could be felt pecking at the thick shell of self-accusation. Very gently he stroked the undamaged forehead of the small rabbit, and back along its ears, and still farther, smoothing the fur over its hind quarters. He became intensely aware, though for the first time, of the silky fluff of the tail, scarcely more substantial than air, against his hand.

"Poor damn little old rabbit," he murmured. "What did you ever do to anybody?"

The unexpected sound of his own voice suddenly brought tears to his eyes, and the rabbit dissolved and spread and contracted and solidified ridiculously, like something seen through heat waves. It was a queer, amusing movement, as if the rabbit were trying to dance on his hand, and Buck made a short laugh and sniffled. It frightened him, then, to realize that he was standing alone on the trail in the very quiet ravine, with the watcher somewhere above him, and laughing and sniffling out loud. He wouldn't look for the watcher this time, but he spoke for the ears of the watcher, defiantly, and more loudly than he had spoken to the rabbit.

"Well, there's no use crying about it, baby. It ain't gonna help the poor damn rabbit any for you to cry about it, is it?"

The "ain't gonna," which was no part of his usual way of speaking, was as useful, at the moment, as the "damn." Both of them, and the accusation as well, went a good way to make him someone who was not Buck. His body felt less numb and useless, and the stirring within the egg increased. He picked up the twenty-two again, and started on down.

Having broken the barrier of silence, he was a little less alone, and the world was a little less remote and sterile. He went on talking to the rabbit. He argued to it that the shooting had not been in any way personal. He also assured it of his affection and regard, and confessed to it that he had been a fool not to see how small a rabbit it was, and also that he was a damned poor shot, and should never be allowed to touch a gun again. Finally there were moments when the rabbit replied in a small voice in the back of Buck's mind. He could not yet exactly hear the words of the replies, but he believed that the rabbit, in its separated, still perceptive part, was moved toward forgiveness.

In the intervals of his conversation with the rabbit, he began to consider the practical implications of the murder. They resolved themselves eventually into two opposed views, which he argued out alternately with the points of his confession to the rabbit, so that sometimes the two discourses became one, as when he told the rabbit, "I guess maybe I should bury you and say a prayer."

When he thought of the prayer, he saw himself upon his knees beside a very small grave with a pile of stones on it and a little cross standing up out of the stones, and he thought of the prayer as being offered up for the undying, miniature-hawk part of the rabbit. Buck seldom prayed upon his knees. He felt, with a quick wing-beating of the prisoner in the egg, that to pray openly, upon his knees, for the hawk-soul of the rabbit, would be to act in a manner that would go very far, nearly all the way, to satisfying the rabbit part of the rabbit.

The flutter in the egg was quickly stilled, however, by the dry-voiced counsel for the opposition, who chose to regard rabbits as of so little consequence that it made no difference whether they were dead or alive, and who pointed out a variety of unfortunate events which might be anticipated in the future of a Buck who sniffled over a dead rabbit and gave serious consideration to the notion of burying it with religious ceremony. Such a burial, he suggested, leering, would actually be a little difficult to tell from concealing evidence. The counsel for the opposition did not speak with Buck's voice at all, but with the voice of the world, and that fact gave him an undue influence in the court, so that his specious, when not downright cowardly, arguments stood up against those of counsel for atonement far better than they should have. Nonetheless, here in the silent ravine, with the rabbit still upon his arm, Buck was so ashamed of this half of the debate that during it he sat, so to speak, flushed and with his head bowed before a judge who seemed likely to regard rabbits and men as having many characteristics, and many rights, in common.

Gradually, since the argument remained short of settlement, the audible plea to the rabbit ceased, and its intentions became insensibly fused with the case of the counsel for burial and prayer. Buck went on down the trail, but even more slowly now than at first, and almost as silently, as if the prolonged indecision had affected his body also. Only once did any part of the struggle come out for his actual ears to hear.

"Lordy," he said, "would Evelyn ever give me a rough time if I came home without anything."

It helped only a very little to increase the moral stature of this revelation, that behind the smugly smiling face of Evelyn, he saw also the gaze of his father, silent, speculative and inscrutable.

Thus, with his head bent and the rabbit reduced to a point of contention within him, he followed the trail down and around two more buttresses of the ravine wall, passing, between the two buttresses, a sandstone shelf across the gorge below, that made a jumping off place, and in the spring a muddy, frothing waterfall. Beyond the second buttress he found himself in a wide passage almost on the level of the stream-bed. Here the black, sweet brush grew larger and closer together, and crowded down against the path on both sides, like a hostile multitude waiting for him to run the gauntlet. Buck emerged at once from the monotony of the court room, where the case had fallen entirely into circling repetitions, and saw the hollow before him with shocking clarity. He stopped abruptly, and stood there, looking around. After a moment he remembered the waterfall ledge he had passed above, and saw how, at the lower side of the hollow, the water course vanished over another sandstone ledge and the trail bent right and steeply downward and went along the cliff again. Then he understood why he had stopped. This was where he had almost stepped on the rattlesnake, and he had stopped here every time since, and each time he had got across to where the trail

went down along the cliff again, he had felt tremendously relieved. He had considered, every time, going
high up around the side of the hollow instead of through
it, though he had never permitted himself to do so. The
hollow had become, especially its farther edge, the very
spot, a kind of dangerous watch-gate, to be entered in
the spirit of Bunyan's Pilgrim. Each time he came
around the bend and saw the hollow now, he felt how
vulnerable bare feet were, and how defenseless a body
with nothing on it but a pair of shorts, and the feeling
made him live the escape over again.

He had been running so fast down the steep pitch
above the hollow that he could hardly keep his legs
under him and the quick singing was reduced to broken,
breathless snatches. He came around the buttress preparing himself joyously and with complete concentration
to let his feet and legs dodge through the closing bushes
like those of a clever broken-field runner. Indeed, he
stopped the chanting entirely in order to grit his teeth,
narrow his eyes and become Christman, State College's
star sprinter and tailback, darting upfield from the kick-
off among the huge, fierce, Western U tacklers. He
curled his left hand tensely over the nose of the ball—it
would never do to fumble when he was running away
from his blockers like this—held his right hand a little
forward and out to the side, preparing, the instant he
must swing left, to extend it in a jolting straight-arm.
So intent was he, as he came racing down among them,
on transforming each outstanding bush into a giant
tackler, and so exultant did he become as he avoided each
of them with full Christman virtuosity and approached
the goal line, which was the lower edge of the hollow,

with the screams of the multitude beating upon him from the slopes of the ravine, that he forgot to look where his feet were going. It was only because his right foot rolled on a loose pebble, so that he had to glance down as he writhed to keep his balance, that he saw the snake at all. His eyes saw the snake, and his body responded at once, though his mind was so far gone in triumph that it was quite incredulous, and wanted more time to make sure. It was a large, heavy rattlesnake, and it was already prepared for his coming, lying coiled on the right edge of the path, half under the bush that an instant before had been Western's number 39, a stocky, wily quarter-back, and the last man to be passed. The snake's head lay balanced with purposeful lightness upon the drawn spring of its neck. Its chin just touched the dusty scales of the uppermost coil, and its square nose was aimed directly at Buck's bare legs. There, too close to be dodged, and in the only opening, and with the treacherous pebble and the sharp dip and turn of the path just beyond it furnishing problem enough without it, the snake appeared to be of mythical proportions and wholly unavoidable. Buck felt that it was not even a natural rattlesnake, for it was as silent as it was motionless. Only its black tongue flickered in and out of the stony head like a small, separate life. It was the coiled spring of evil, the agent of the dark meaning, the very perfect, appointed conductor in the gateway to the other side.

All this came to Buck in the time of a single stride, and despair came with it. His bare right foot and the calf of his right leg could already feel, as if they had a separate and mordant imagination of their own, the fat, cold body sinking under them, and the impact of the horny nose, followed instantly by the tiny double-burning of the fangs. His mind heightened the effect by choosing that moment to remember the big, graying man, a friend of his father's, who had walked in the brown hills with them, stooped to pick up a stone which interested him, and then suddenly straightened up with a brief exclamation and held out his right arm, regarding it as if it didn't belong to him, and revealing the rattlesnake hanging from it, an incongruous, scarf-like ornament of doom. In his one gasping glimpse of this memory, Buck was again most impressed by the expression on the man's big, adult face, with its heavy, black brows, the expression of a startled child who needs only a moment more to begin weeping. Buck's right leg at once expected to lunge on down the path with the fangs jerking in its calf and the long weight of the snake thumping and coiling about it. It cried its fear to the left leg, which had not stumbled, and together they took desperate action while Buck's mind was still staring at the face of his father's visitor, and still seeing through it a phantom of the 39 on the broad chest of the bush. The right leg, foreseeing that its foot would otherwise be plunged directly into the entangling coil, made a stride only inches long, just touched its toes down, uncertain upon what in that blind rush, and threw the whole duty over to the left leg, which launched Buck upward and forward in the longest, highest leap it could possible manage alone.

Even as he leapt, Buck's mind was cleared at a single wipe of the big face and the last vestige of the ghostly 39. He saw only that the enormous snake was striking.

As it passed from sight under him, he believed that he felt his right ankle brushed, almost tripped, by the harsh, sedentary body, and a small, quick stab just where the muscles of his calf began to bulge. Then the right leg was forced into action again. There was a wild flurry of half-steps, which still could not quite support him or turn him back into the path. Under the impetus of the swerving straight-arm, the rolling pebble and the lopsided leaped all at once, he careened off to the left just where the path swung the other way, and crashed headlong into a laurel bush. The whole thing happened so quickly that it was only as he began to dive that his left hand and arm stopped hugging the imaginary football and reached to break the tumble. As his body struck, feeling everywhere the digging and scratching of the laurel twigs, and the tiny, cool hands of the leaves making mock comfort, he even had a last impression of the fumbled ball flying on over the bush ahead of him.

Then the game was entirely gone, from his muscles as well as his mind. The laurel bush had stopped him, but he was lying deeply imbedded in it, half over on his belly, and he had come so close to diving clear through it that he was looking down over the waterfall ledge into the basin of sand twenty feet below. He was not even aware of this height, however. He was concerned entirely with the enemy in the rear. His mind gave a dozen confused and hasty orders at once, so that the moment he stopped falling, he began a struggle to extricate himself, flailing out like a panic-stricken swimmer in a rip-tide, and at the same time trying to double himself up into the heart of the bush, pull all his extremities out of reach, turn over onto his back and free his hands and feet. Above all, though, he wanted to pull himself out of reach and turn over and be able to see the rattlesnake, which he believed to be only inches behind him, tossed there by his own foot, and coiling to strike again, into his leg or his buttocks, or even, for such a reach was not beyond it, into the naked, cringing small of his back. A series of chills coursed through him from each of those vulnerable points, but with his intentions thus simplified, he began to succeed. He turned onto his back, drew his knees up to his chest, got his arms free and rolled forward into a crouch, suspended precariously in the swinging heart of the laurel bush.

The snake, large enough still, Lord knows, but of less than mythological proportions after all, was coiled once more, sure enough, with its head aimed in his direction, and the little serpent-soul of the tongue flickering at him, but it was out in the middle of the path, and eight or ten feet away. In fact it was still right beside bush number 39, farther away than the length of Buck's body, or even its own. To Buck, with the branches swaying under him and the wiry fingers of the twigs still clutching him, this was not a safe distance, but it was promising. It was a distance which created great hope.

At once the haste of the frenzied swimmer was transformed into slow, searching withdrawals of one hand and one foot at a time. The caution of these maneuvers was increased by a sound which renewed the chills just as they had begun to pass off. Whether or not the snake had been rattling before, it was certainly rattling now. The small, dry, multiple percussions of its challenge were so exceedingly rapid as almost to blend into a single, shrill whining. They filled the ears and occupied, with tremendous import, the whole width and depth of the ravine.

Never looking away from the snake, Buck felt his way slowly sideward until one hand reached into the free air. Then, risking a single quick glance down, to make sure that he wouldn't be setting his foot on another snake—it had become possible during the retreat to conceive of the whole laurel as underlain by a squirming carpet of snakes—he stepped gingerly out of the bush and onto the edge of the path, just where it turned and went down. One final, widespread chill passed over him, and the goose-pimples began to diminish behind it. Retreat was now possible along an open and visible route. Also, the guardian of the gate was no longer in a position to surprise him or to take advantage of the insidious co-operation of the laurel bush.

The snake had not moved, save for its tongue and the small, frenetic gourds of its tail, and now the rattling was subsiding. It no longer screamed in the ears. It rose again, slightly, when Buck straightened up in the path, but only into a blurred buzzing, and then, since Buck stood still, it dropped away into a soft, slow, final shaking, in which it seemed almost possible to hear each separate seed in its papery shell.

Gradually Buck's mind resumed full charge of his doing. By means of quick glances away from the snake, he made sure that there were not two tiny drops or ribbons of blood under his right calf. There were moments of doubt during this examination, because he had been scratched in so many places by the laurel bush, but he was able to reassure himself concerning each suggestive mark.

After that, he was too much relieved to be very angry at the snake, but it seemed necessary to drive it out of the path, if only to give the incident a tolerable conclusion. Making sure it was still coiled and safely distant, he stooped and picked up a pebble, and then, with rapidly increasing confidence, half a dozen more. Before he could straighten up again with his ammunition, however, the snake, as if warned of the intended indignity, relaxed slowly out of its coils, almost melting into extension. Holding itself ready to recoil, its head lifted toward Buck and its tongue working rapidly and unceasingly, it began to slither away at an angle, up-trail and toward bush 39. So Buck just stood there watching, after all, with the first insulting pebble still held in his right hand. Smoothly and silently the snake gathered speed, and finally, turning its head away for the first time, it glided under the bush. Imperceptibly, like the blending into silence of a final, diminishing violin note, its tail shrank out of sight. Only then, and simply to relieve the long-pent impulse, Buck tossed the one pebble idly in the general direction of the disappearance.

Now, as Buck stood above the scene of this adventure, with the small rabbit in his arms, he was assailed by a conviction that the snake and the rabbit were related within the intentions of the gods concerning himself. In one motion of his mind and spirit, released, for the time being, from their conscientious squabble, he felt the rabbit to have been a ward, if not a companion, of the forces of light and air and life, as the rattlesnake had long been a servant of the fog god. Yet the rattlesnake had been set against him, who had proven the enemy of the rabbit. It had made this place of the waiting bushes an arena of repeated trial. Its nature lay always coiled in wait for him here, to break his running celebration and bring him chastened to the sacred beach. The snake was the defender of the rabbit. It followed that the powers of light and darkness were not wholly and always opposed to one another.

Buck, however, was unable to grasp so momentous a union all at once. It rather appeared to him, alone in the foggy ravine and struggling for his first hold of idea upon the feeling of unity, to have resulted from an absorbing victory for darkness. His sensation of guilt increased proportionately with this increase in the hostile power. He felt the need of appeasement.

"It should have got me," he said aloud, and then, looking down upon the huddle of fur in his arm, added bitterly, the connection now clear to his own mind, "Poor damn little rabbit. What did you ever do?"

This confession, accompanied by his first full recognition of the fact that the rabbit was incurably dead, gained him time, but he understood that the deed was required to prove the word.

"The hell with what they think," he said stoutly, and against his entire family. He buckled his determination against the ghost of the snake and advanced among the waiting bushes. Several times his eyes and his conscience together made a serpent where there was none, but each time he stared the vengeance out of being without even breaking his slow, processional walk.

When he came at last to the turn and onto the clear trail along the wall of the ravine, his relief was like forgiveness, or at least like a seal of approval upon his intention.

"Don't worry," he said to the rabbit. "We'll find you a good place. We'll find you the best place there is," and he began to walk a little faster because of the weight that had been lifted from him and because of his eagerness to commence the penitential act.

At first he thought he would just go down the trail far enough to get into the stream-bed easily, and then work back up the sandy bottom and bury the rabbit under the second fall. The gesture, however, didn't seem adequate. There were four such falls in the ravine, with little save their order to distinguish them one from another. Besides, the narrow, year-long darkness below any of the falls was all wrong for this once gay, hopping, nibbling creature with a milkweed tail and a soul like a bug-sized hawk. The thought of the darkness under the falls, reminded him of how the brown torrent poured, slick as grease, over those ledges in the spring rains, and churned and lathered in the basins.

"Wouldn't anything stay buried there for a minute," he said aloud, and grimaced because he could see the little rabbit churned and lifted out of its quiet sand, and borne, tossing and bumping, down the narrows and over two falls, and at last rolled down the final incline to the beach. There it would lie in the wet channel in the sand, all sodden and disarranged, with the muddy water still splattering down on it, or it might even be rolled and nudged on down the channel until the sea got hold of it and unrelentingly dragged it up and down the beach and slowly southward toward the whale rocks. More than once, in the spring floods, he had run down along the trail, the mud splattering at every step up onto his bare legs, to follow some floating bit of wood or small, uprooted bush down, and he could picture clearly what would happen to the rabbit.

His mind, having rejected the basin below the fall, began to hunt at random along the high slopes of the ravine for a suitable burial spot. Having started in the mouth of the ravine, after following the rabbit down, it discovered the look-out almost at once.

"That's the place, rabbit," Buck said aloud, and almost joyously. "I wouldn't mind being buried there myself. It's way up, nearly to the top; a swell place. You can see everything from there. You can see the village over on the point, and the long beach, and part of my beach, and the pier, and you can see the sun the longest of any place."

Once more, stimulated by his own generosity, he had increased his pace.

"The sea-gulls go by there all the time too," he told the rabbit, "and the pelicans, only the pelicans are always way down, sort of sliding along practically right on the water. Sometimes you even see a school of porpoises. It's a swell place; the best place there is."

This inspiration, which brought with it the memory of the lookout on a sunny, windy day, and which entailed much labor, and a gift that was a personal sacrifice, so much further lightened his burden that his legs took it upon themselves to skip twice, preparatory to running, and his chest and throat and mouth felt a strong urge to start a song. He barely remembered in time the solemnity of his mission and the crime which made it necessary. He held himself down again, under the somewhat relenting gaze of the watcher, to merely walking quickly, and instead of singing, said, "And I'll come up there to see you pretty near every time I come down to my beach."

He conceived a necessary final touch. "And I'll make a prayer for you every time," he promised.

It was thus, half floating in golden expectancy, and wanting very much to run, that he went down past the third fall and started around the last blind buttress onto the point of the trail from which the whole blue, sparkling Pacific would open before him and the music like cymbals and trumpets and drums burst forth.

What actually opened before him, then, was like a vast and dignified rebuke to his backsliding. There, almost immediately below him, was the last of the four falls, the one so narrowly enclosed and so high that someone had stood a notched driftwood timber up in one corner as a kind of ladder, and below it was the biggest sandstone basin of all, swept clean of sand by the ultimate force of the floods. And there, going up clear to the sky on both sides, were the great, angled walls of the ravine. But across this familiar and inspiriting V there stretched a completely strange ocean of slow, black, oily swells, an ocean which receded, before the eye had even begun to reach, into a lingering fog, which gradually veiled it from sight. The wind was not strong and clear, either, but slow and chill and heavy. Buck thought, one after another, of four of the darkest, deepest, least populous Doré prints in his father's copy of the *Inferno*, and at once perceived his secondary sin and the great distance between the actual present and the imagined past. He stood there on the point of the trail for a full minute, staring out at this indifferent, underworld sea, while the anticipatory glow faded within him and the funeral of the rabbit became a grim, necessary and inadequate penance.

6

He turned aside at the notched timber and climbed diagonally toward the lookout. The track was very steep, and with the dissolution of his forgiveness, excitement and lack of sleep began to have their effect. The rabbit and the twenty-two became heavier than ever, and because they kept him from using either hand to catch at bushes or act as a third leg, he often wavered and stumbled and even slid back, so that he had to stand still to get his breath and his balance. Despite the fog and the strengthening wind, he began to sweat before he was half-way up the slope. He thought yearningly of sitting, or even lying down to rest, and began to consider a swim as an active and soothing pleasure rather than as a cleansing duty not altogether pleasant in the darkness and chill of the fog. By the time he finally reached the lookout, after a dozen panting halts, he no longer had any feeling whatever about the burial, or even about the vast change in the world which had occurred while he stood remembering the snake. He wanted only to be done with this necessary-because-promised act, and to rest. The nature of the world could take care of itself, and as to what it made of him, he was completely indifferent.

He stood for some time in the center of the lookout,

panting and with his head bowed, waiting for the pounding of his heart to soften and slow down, and the
swimming, circling motes to go out of his eyes. He
could feel the sweat trickling down the sides of his jaw
from his hair, and down his ribs and the channel of his
back under the sweat shirt. When he could open his
eyes and see the lookout clearly, the gentle slope of
cratered sand with the ring of reddish-black rocks
around it and the three clumps of black brush above it,
he straightened himself and gazed up at the silhouettes
of the bushes on the rim of the canyon, against the sky,
and then at the edge of the cliff to his left, with the
great gulf of air beyond it, and then, so far below that
it seemed hardly to wrinkle or stir, the dark ocean.
Always before, merely to come up to the lookout had
been a joy to make him hug himself and invent frag-
mentary poems of praise. To see so far had been to
possess the world, to become capable of embracing it
before the obliterating ecstasy, so that memories remained that might be used to beget ecstasy in lesser
places. It was something to celebrate that the great pier,
nearly two miles south, was tiny and frail as a spider-
web ladder, and a source of heroic legend that he could
look straight across the bay at the village on the point,
with the narrow, white rim of surf around it, and consider it only as a kind of tropical garden for the delight
of Janet Haley. He always felt, squatting in the lookout,
with the sea a great swoop below and the point a clean,
arrowy flight across, that he was akin to the cormorants
that nested on the high, shadowy ledges of the village
cliffs, where the rollers boomed in caves under them,
and to the white gulls in their shining play with wind

and light. Now, for the first time, it was not so. He felt a little uneasy to be so near the edge of the cliff, and when he looked down beyond it, he wanted to draw back and hold onto something.

"For God's sake," he muttered against this fear. "Like some scaredy-cat girl."

He considered, just to try himself, going out to the very edge, so that he could look straight down at the toy rubble of the giant's building stones, with the edge of the sea foaming softly among them. His whole body resisted the test, and complained desperately of the encumbering rabbit and twenty-two. He excused himself aloud.

"You're all pooped out, that's all," he said, and turned around and sat down carefully in the center of the lookout, with the rabbit across his lap and the twenty-two propped against his shoulder. Thus secured, he looked down into the ravine and out at the whale rocks, like small, black fingers in the surf, and felt nothing about them, and south at the spider-web pier, and felt nothing, and across at the point, still dim with a mist of fog, and with a great nothingness of fog beyond it, and felt only that it was lonesome, and that it was improbable that Janet Haley, somewhere in it, was anything but a figure from one of his own less convincing tales. Later, for no reason at all, and out of a blank mind, he remembered his father saying, "Thank God," and "if you live to be as old as Methuselah." For a moment it seemed as if the full meaning behind those expressions were about to be unfolded within him, but when, with an effort, he sought to drive his mind to the understanding, the moment passed. Finally, when he was quite steady, and the edge of the cliff didn't seem so dangerously near, he began to feel that he was malingering, and again that it was necessary to propitiate the enormous dark power.

Because of the malingering, he said aloud, "Well, you can't sit here all your life," and because of the dark reminder he spoke defiantly, and then added, in full Promethean resentment, "Bury the damn rabbit, if you're going to."

The counsel for burial and prayer revived sufficiently to point out to him both the blasphemy of this utterance, and its profound unfairness to the rabbit. He looked down quickly, and stroked the rabbit's head and ears. They were quite cold now.

"It's all right, rabbit," he said. "I didn't mean it."

There returned a sufficient sense of his crime against the rabbit to set him in motion. He drew off the old, red sweat-shirt, pulling it carefully out from under the barrel of the twenty-two, and spread it on the sand beside him. He laid the small rabbit gently on its side in the middle of the sweat-shirt, and straightened its ears and smoothed its fur. The dimly outlined arm of Red Ryder was raised in salute from behind the rabbit's head. With the sweat-shirt off, the gray wind felt very cold on Buck's wet ribs. It put life into him, and he got up and leaned the twenty-two into one of the bushes above the lookout, and returned. He knelt beside the rabbit and looked at it, and touched its shoulder.

"We'll fix you up pretty quick now, rabbit," he said.

He began to dig a hole in the sand beside the red sweat-shirt. The sand, however, proved to be only three or four inches deep. He would have to pile it up to cover the rabbit, and then the first rain or wind that came along would uncover it again. Under the sand, there was the solid sandstone of the ledges. He sat back on his heels and thought for a moment. Then he got up and went slowly around the ring of stones until he found one stone that had something like a point on it, and wasn't too heavy to use. With this he came back and knelt again, and began to chip at the sandstone, pausing every few minutes to clear out the loosened pieces with his hands. He had it in mind to make the grave big and deep compared to the rabbit. Every once in a while he paused and looked across at the rabbit, to measure his work by it.

It was during one of these pauses that he became aware that the watcher was present once more, standing up on the edge of the sky and looking down at him. Again it seemed to Buck that he was not violently hostile, or altogether a henchman of darkness, but that, like the detestable counsel for the opposition, he was more amused than anything else. It seemed to the watcher a little ridiculous that a boy of twelve, who had just inherited a twenty-two, presumably because he was near enough a man to be trusted with it, should be spending all this labor and planning all this ceremony just to bury a rabbit. Since this attitude made him no more than a condescending intruder into matters wholly private to Buck and the rabbit, Buck wouldn't even give him the satisfaction of looking up.

When this contemptuous resistance had continued for several minutes, however, counsel for the opposition spoke again, in his dry, belittling voice. At first Buck replied for himself, as angrily and stubbornly as he continued to dig. But when, after rehearsing once more Buck's empty-handed entrance into the kitchen, and his passage under the eyes of his mother and sister, counsel for the opposition removed his pince-nez, and with a smile not unlike Evelyn's, and in a voice smoothly derisive, brought up the father for the first time, Buck was forced to withdraw and turn his case over once more to the counsel for burial and prayer. He stopped digging and sat back on his heels, staring into the little grave and feeling his face burn, while counsel for the opposition, now quite clearly representing the interests of worldly opinion, drew a picture, wonderfully visible in its every detail, of Buck entering the living room and finding his father there, as he often was, sitting in the chair by the ocean window and working on a writing board. The father looked up, with that wholly enigmatic attentiveness in his eyes that had been there ever since the death of the rabbit. He put his hand with the pen in it on the arm of the chair, as if preparing for a considerable discussion, and asked, in that casual manner proper to men, as if there were nothing in the world worth any particular fuss or attention, "Well, how did it go the first time out?"

At this point, counsel for the world leaned over toward Buck in the most ingratiating manner, and inquired gently, "And just how is the prisoner going to reply to that? Is he going to say, perhaps, 'I killed a rabbit, but I was sorry, so I buried it, and,' he added with particular emphasis, 'prayed over it'?"

"He doesn't have to say anything," began the defender of the rabbit. "All he has to do is . . . ."

"Or," interrupted counsel for the opposition, in the

same politic tone, "is he simply going to lie, and maintain, before the quite penetrating, I assure you, gaze of his father, that he saw no rabbit whatever? Obviously not. His only possible seemly reply is to hold up the rabbit to be seen, saying not a word, and revealing not a thing by his expression. Am I right, Buck?"

And Buck had to admit he was right.

At so great a disadvantage, and already put out by the interruption, counsel for burial replied more angrily than convincingly, and the whole interminable argument was on again. Apparently the period of seeming agreement under the influence of the rattlesnake spirit had been merely a truce or a recess. Buck could only sit helpless under the contention, as he had before. Gradually, however, he became aware of an important difference in the proceedings. The nameless, inscrutable judge seemed to be paying no attention whatever to the bickering counsels, but to be keeping his gaze, enigmatic and attentive, constantly upon Buck himself. As time passed and this gaze did not waver or vary, Buck became uncomfortably aware also that the arguments of the counsel for burial, ill-tempered and faulty though they were, nonetheless represented quite fairly an obscure but vital truth within himself, and that they were being seriously weakened by his passivity and his tendency to hope, even, that he might be permitted to act by the cowardly but superficially more logical code of the opposition. Worst of all, he was sure that the judge understood all this.

After a time, however, since the debate produced little that was new, he began to chip fitfully at the sandstone of the grave again. Without his even knowing it, the grave became a good deal deeper and wider one than the small rabbit needed. Meanwhile the debate, through mere exhaustion, had thinned away nearly out of his hearing, when suddenly it ended in a most unexpected move by the counsel for burial, who made a point so simple and final that it seemed at once the first thing that should have been said.

"Even allowing the worthy opposition's argument for the necessity of bearing home some token of prowess," he said, adopting a manner disturbingly like that of counsel for the world, "is the defendant's manliness to be demonstrated to women in the eyeless corpse of a rabbit no bigger than his two hands? Or his skill demonstrated to his father, unquestionably an excellent marksman, by exhibiting in the ears of that tiny rabbit, the holes made by two cruel and clumsy shots which failed to kill?"

This argument was recognized at once as a basis for agreement and a means to action. The two counselors shook hands and departed, blending, at the door of Buck's soul, into something disquietingly near one being, and that one a good deal more like counsel for the world than like the advocate of burial, whose previous appearance had been much like that of one of the bearded prophets in robe and sandals in the blue book of Old Testament stories.

Only the judge made no move, but continued, on his high, fog-borne bench, to lean forward upon his folded hands and gaze down at Buck with that enigmatic attentiveness, so disturbingly familiar. He said nothing, but Buck was unable to deny, under the burden of his eyes, that the agreement, though it permitted the better action, had been arrived at by the most despicable means.

He attempted to conciliate the judge by exhibiting a busy devotion to the interests of the rabbit. He worked energetically for a few minutes longer at enlarging the grave still further beyond need. Then he cleaned it out to bare, hard sandstone walls and floor, and crumbled the last fragments of sandstone as he piled them on the mound between his knees and the grave. This done, he paused for a minute, keeping a busy, preoccupied expression, and considered the matter of protection for the rabbit in its grave. He could bring down aromatic leaves from the bushes, and sheaves of the dry grass, and mold them into a nest in the hole. That would probably be a good deal like the rabbit's natural home. On the other hand, a covering of grass and leaves wouldn't keep out the dirt he'd have to pile on top. He looked at the rabbit, as if it might express a preference, and immediately, because of the renewed need for atonement, experienced a minor inspiration.

"I'll give you my sweat-shirt, rabbit," he said. "It'll keep the dirt out, and keep you nice and warm, too."

He worked over on his knees until he was kneeling before the rabbit, and began to fold the sweat-shirt over it and tuck it together. A voice, certainly his own, which was some relief, but also certainly out of the nature of counsel for the opposition, spoke in his mind.

"What will your mother say if you come home without that sweat-shirt?" it asked.

He ignored the question for the moment, because it had just occurred to him that he should put grass and sweet leaves into the sweat-shirt with the rabbit, both for hominess and incense. He clambered up onto the headland and gathered them, bruising the leaves with his fingers as he picked them, to make them smell stronger. Then he returned, undid the sweat-shirt and slipped the grasses under the rabbit and scattered the leaves over it. When the sweat-shirt had been folded closed once more, and bound around by its sleeves, he answered the question.

"I'll say I got too hot and took it off, and then I couldn't find it when I came back."

"But that is obviously untrue."

"I gotta say something," Buck said truculently. He was encouraged to this boldness because the lie, being made for the rabbit, seemed no lie at all, but only the final ornament to the final sacrifice of the sweat-shirt.

"You'll have to wait till the sun comes out to make that excuse work."

"So I'll wait till the sun comes out."

"That may be a long time, my young friend. You've already been out a long time, and so far there's not the slightest sign of the sun coming out. Are you going to be late for your own birthday dinner after all, and that to support a lie?"

Buck looked up uneasily at the sky. It was still gray everywhere, though lifted well above the headland now, and thinned a good deal too, he thought. He looked out at the ocean, and saw that it was not quite so dark now, only slaty gray, and that real waves were beginning to move on it, and that it was visible all the way to the horizon, or at least to so far west that he couldn't be sure it wasn't the horizon.

"It'll come out," he said boldly, but then added,

because of his doubt, "And I can't help it if it doesn't. Rabbit needs the sweat-shirt more than I do."

This reply, like all his present attitude and activity, seemed a little faked, intended more to influence the judge than to please the rabbit.

"I'm sorry, rabbit," he said aloud, "but this is about as good as I can do."

He laid the sweat-shirt, with the small, limp weight in it, gently in the grave, paused for an instant to give the moment its proper dignity, though with no specific thought or word, and began to fill the grave. First, in order not to disturb the rabbit, he carefully filled all around the sweat-shirt with fragments of sandstone. Then, a little at a time and lightly, he sifted on the first covering of sand. Only when no part of the sweat-shirt was any longer visible did he begin to take big handfuls and pour them in more boldly. He piled the sand on until it made a rectangular mound, and patted it down as firmly as he could with his hands. After another pause, he brought rocks from around the lookout and piled them against one another up the two sides of the mound, so that they made a kind of black, stone tent over it. It seemed to him that already the judge was relenting a little.

"You gotta have a cross, rabbit," he said aloud.

He thought about that for a while too, and then climbed up onto the headland once more, and searched in the black brush until he found two branches long enough and nearly enough straight to suit him. He broke them off, stripped them of twigs, and tried them across each other, held high in front of him. They made a pleasing, narrow, black cross against the gray sky.

There came then, however, the problem of binding them together. First he tried several stalks of the yellow grass, twisted together, but even wet with the fog as they were, they proved too brittle. He considered pulling threads out of his shorts, but gave that up without a trial because he knew he couldn't get them out long enough. Finally he tried to peel strips of bark from one of the bushes, but they wouldn't come off long enough either, and they tore when he tried to knot them. Reluctantly he abandoned the idea of a wooden cross.

"You gotta have some kind of marker, though," he said, and then, after a moment, "It'll have to be a stone, I guess. I can make a cross on the stone."

He went back down to the lookout and worked his way slowly around it, trying the remaining stones in his mind. None of them was really good, with flat sides and a rounded top, but he selected the one that came nearest to that shape. It was longer than any of the others, so it would stand up above the stones on the grave, and it came to a kind of point and had one nearly flat side. He laid it flat side up in the sand beside the grave, worked it down in until it was quite firm, and began to scratch a cross on the upper half of it, using his digging stone as a chisel. While he worked, he thought of also scratching a name and the date below the cross.

"Peter Rabbit," he said to himself, but discarded it at once. It was too childish, a kind of insult to a real rabbit who had really died. He tried others in his mind, but they all seemed false. He decided, at last, that just Rabbit would have to do.

However, when he had done as well as he could with

the cross, and still had only a wavering, scarcely visible figure on the black stone, it was evident that he could never write the whole of even Rabbit. He worked for a long time more, digging down and scraping with all his weight, until his hands were sore and his arms weary, and produced, at last, a single, scratchy R under the cross. He gave up the idea of the date, and set the headstone at the top of the grave, working it into the sand until it was steady. Finally he got slowly to his feet and stood looking down at the grave and the stone. He felt better about it then. It looked like a real grave, and a pretty special one, with that stone tent, and it stood out darkly against the sand. Also, looked down on from above, the gray scratches of the cross and the R showed quite clearly. He looked around, desiring to establish a suitable order all about the grave. The gaps in the ring of stones disturbed him, and he shifted those that were left until their intervals, though a little too wide, maybe, were regular. When this was done, he smoothed the sand of the whole lookout circle the best he could, and stood up, in the top of the grave, like the tin cans holding flowers he had seen in cemeteries, a single sprig of the sweet-brush.

There remained, then, only the prayer.

This final ceremony, however, didn't turn out to be so easy, after all. He stood up beside the grave and bowed his head and clasped his hands together, but then discovered that all truly prayerful feeling about the rabbit was gone. He had used everything up making the grave, or in the long argument with the bad ending. He tried to make himself feel something by thinking of the rabbit as he had first seen it, sitting up across the ravine from him, and as he had knelt beside it, feeling the bullet holes in the ears with his fingers, and as it was now, so alone in the red sweat-shirt under the sand, but it remained quite separate from him. A small motion occurred within him at the memory of the hawk-soul, but it turned out to be nothing but a weak imitation of the ascent and falling away of the real hawk, and when he tried to stimulate it into something more inclusive, even the motion ceased. Then, because he had remembered kneeling beside the dead rabbit, he was reminded of his promise to kneel when he prayed for it. The idea of kneeling was now repulsive to him, but nevertheless he forced himself down. It made no difference. Everything inside him was dead, or anxious to escape. After a minute or two of this dull struggle on his knees, he was still further weakened because a notion he had been repressing ever since the end of the trial, just by keeping busy, spoke itself clearly in his mind. "You aren't going home without anything to show them, are you? There's still plenty of time to hunt before dinner. You could probably get a real, full-grown rabbit, just on the way home, if you kept your eyes open. And this time you wouldn't make any mistake. You'd take your time and make one clean shot."

He rejected the suggestion violently, but he knew perfectly well that all he was really trying to do was keep such ideas out of the little rabbit's funeral. He wasn't really promising he wouldn't hunt again. And he knew that he was simply avoiding the real point when he made it all a matter of the size of the rabbit and the skill of the shooting. He was doing all over again, just what he had done to end the trial.

It was clear, after that, that real prayer would not happen. He decided at least to speak a prayer of words, to complete the ceremony, if nothing better. There was no being to whom a prayer in words could be made except the inconceivable head-god, from whom no response was to be expected. For once, though, since his relations with the lesser deities had become so confused, he found a kind of comfort in this separation. It came to him, as he began to select the words of the prayer, that there might even be some understanding of his difficulty and some tolerance for his shortcomings in this most impalpable of gods, who had to supervise the activities of the gods of both light and darkness, and at this thought, the head-god moved in him toward reality, borrowing from Poseidon and the god of the cliff, who looked a good deal alike, something of the appearance of Michelangelo's Moses or Blake's God, but assuming a nature of his own, very close to that of the judge. The indignity of kneeling increased before such a god. It seemed that he must regard self-abasement as cowardice, and perhaps even as an affront to himself, as if the petitioner hoped to use him as David had used Jehova. Buck stood up and went around to the other side of the grave in order to face the ocean across it. He stood with his arms down straight at his sides and lifted his face to the sky. He prayed aloud.

"O Lord and Father, take this little rabbit unto You. Give him back, O Father, the life that I have taken away. Make him forget how it hurt, and keep him with You forever and ever. Amen."

He looked down at the grave. It was not a good prayer. He understood that. It had a borrowed, church-going flavor quite unsuited to this high headland over the gray sea in the enormous, gray morning. It was almost as bad, in its inconsequence, as the talk of some men he had heard on the village beach in the early afternoon, when everybody came down, and the sand was crowded and unclean, men with too much stomach and clumsy walks, who would rub themselves all over with smelly oil and put on dark glasses and then sit there, with the salt wind in their faces and the whole blue bay sparkling before them and the magnificent sun freely making them warm and good-feeling and brown, and talk the whole time about business and taxes and politics. He was not in the least moved by the words himself, except perhaps a little when he said "how it hurt." It was not even faintly a prayer for which the god of light would have granted ecstasy, or the god of conscience some ease from the strain of having done wrong. There was, nevertheless, a comforting hope possible that an attentive and two-sided thinker like the judge-god would take account of its one small virtue of begging only for the rabbit. He had no sooner thought of this, however, than even that virtue was lost in the discovery that only the words had been for the rabbit, while actually, as in his first, too-busy digging of the grave, the real intention had been to influence the judge-god in his own favor. The faint mockery which was sometimes to be felt in his father's look before he said something distracting and incomprehensible was now in the judge-god's eyes, along with the enigmatic attentiveness.

Buck stood there for a minute, staring down at the grave, but not seeing it. He felt quite unhappy about this puny and dismal conclusion, but there seemed to be no way to improve on it without just getting himself in deeper. He turned and climbed out of the circle of the lookout, walking carefully, in order not to disturb the smoothed sand any more than he had to. He picked up the twenty-two out of the bush, cradled it in his arm, and started down the slope, going around outside the lookout, which now seemed to belong entirely to the rabbit. A few yards below the lookout, he stopped and turned around. He couldn't bear this emptiness and incompleteness. He looked back up at the small grave, with the pointed, black headstone standing at the top of it, and saw suddenly, as if his eyes had cleared and his vision opened out, how small and real it was on the great slope of the ravine, with the pale sky over it and the dark ocean filling the west. The bushes above the grave were jerking nervously in the wind, as the bushes had jerked above the rabbit when it died.

"Well, so long, Rabbit," he said. "I'm sorry I did it. Honest to God, I am."

Suddenly he was filled with a great sense of loss. The tears sprang to his eyes, blurring the black stone, so that it did a little, ridiculous dance, like the dance the rabbit had done.

"Well," he said, blinking hard, "there's not much I can do about it now, but I'll be up to see you again tomorrow."

He turned away and started down again, rubbing angrily at his eyes, and resolutely refusing to look back even once more. For a brief time the ceremony seemed at least a little cleaner and more honest. Even before he reached the bottom of the ravine, however, the calculating voice spoke again, just as he had known it would.

"You aren't going home without anything at all to show them, are you?" it began. By the time he was working his way down the last ledges onto the wave-row of driftwood and black kelp, a second debate, desperately like every instalment of the first, was going on full voice within him. He sought now only to quell it, to put off deciding.

"Oh, forget it," he said aloud.

His first look around at the secret beach furnished a kind of reply in itself. The tide had gone down until nearly all the rocks stood out of the water, but the long incline of the sand was still dark and wet from the fog. He always felt the unimaginable age of the ocean and its shore much more profoundly on foggy days, but this was the first time he had seen the secret beach that way. The kind of sea-weed that had antlered heads and long, anchor-line tails with little, clutching hands at the ends of them, lay scattered along the shore like prehistoric monsters that had crept up into the present to rest. The cliff above him seemed much higher and more forbidding than usual, and was only pale and cool, giving off no glow and holding none. It was not impossible that in the cliffs farther north, beyond the giant's stones, tooth-billed pterodactyls perched and stared down soullessly, awaiting the passage of equally soulless serpent fish through the underworld sea below them. There were no presences of any sort to be named or greeted over the whole beach, but only one sad, in-definable something, a kind of gentle but limitless reprimand. The wind was moving the sea a little, but still it wasn't really attacking the shore, but only ap-proaching it in slow, melancholy rollers and breaking

weakly at the last possible moment, with a soft, prolonged sound like the tearing of paper. The whale rocks
lay black and indolent above its farthest reach.

Buck went across to the nearest of them and leaned
the twenty-two against it, and took off his shorts. He
folded them as carefully as if he had to wear them to
an uninteresting party later, and laid them on the
rock beside the barrel of the twenty-two. Then he
walked slowly down the beach until the last turning
edge of the waves would cover his feet, and stood there,
motionless, for several minutes, staring down at the
foam sliding around his ankles, and not thinking or
feeling anything in particular that he could have discovered. He knew without looking that there was no
benign overseer in the cliff behind him, no far-looking
Poseidon on the last point in the north, no single
mermaid of any kind, let alone a red-headed one, riding
up in those melancholy rollers. The new presence was
greater and more inclusive, perhaps, than all his old
friends put together, but it was a stranger, and not
in the least interested in him, or in any single being,
probably.

At last, however, he felt the coldness of the water
around his ankles, and then the timid, used-up feeling
of his whole body, within which some great change was
rolling and growing by itself, silently as a new fog bank
rises from the ocean horizon, and no more comfortingly.

"Golly, I'm pooped," he said aloud.

He looked down at his chest and belly and thighs,
and then held out his arms and looked at them also,
hunting for the faint traceries that were left from the
scratches the laurel bush had made on him. Because he

had done the same thing in the same way the morning he had escaped the snake, and because that now seemed like this morning too, or rather because it seemed that he had shot and buried the rabbit on the same morning, a long time ago, he thought of the same thing he had thought of then, when the scratches were still red and some of them bleeding. He thought of the colored plates his father had of some of the Spanish and Mexican Christos, the very thin wooden ones that were painted chalky white with heavy blue veins and scarlet lines of blood as regularly spaced as the arms of a candelabra or the branches of childish tree without leaves. Also he remembered his father's incomprehensible but obscurely moving remark about them, "The Christian idols are at once the most beautiful and the most terrible of all. The old ones, that is. The things they make these days are door-stops." The remark had not been made to him. It seemed important now, for some reason, that the remark had been made to the big man with the heavy eyebrows on the same day he was bitten by the rattlesnake, only before he was bitten, of course. It was the words "beautiful" and "terrible" together that hadn't seemed right, but now, remembering the pictures and his own newly scratched body and the same colored blood of the little rabbit on the bleached grass, he felt that he nearly understood. But no, when he began to try to get it in words even the feeling escaped him again, as it had in the matter of "Thank God," and "Methuselah." He felt merely sad and tired and lonely. He let his arms down to his sides again, remembering that when the scratches were fresh, he had felt ashamed because such unimportant injuries, and on himself, had reminded him of the Christos.

The treacherous voice spoke unexpectedly in his mind. "You aren't going home without anything at all . . ." it said, before he could stop it.

Aloud and defiantly he said, "I gotta remember to give Arthur the red gun, first thing when I get home."

He looked out at the dark ocean under the low, gray sky. He was more than ever reluctant to enter it. His body had grown cold standing there in the increasing wind, and now it felt narrow and stiff and unusable. He began to tell himself the Kit Carson story again, but still the people would not speak their own words, and their faces, even Janet's, kept changing into the faces of others or bleaching out into white, dead faces that were all the same and a little like the faces of the Spanish Christos. After four failures, he abandoned the chronicle, saying, "Oh, the hell with it. Always thinking about some old girl."

At the very sound of that denial, however, he was more deeply moved than ever before, so that it hurt as if his insides were being twisted, by remembering as if she stood before him, as if he might reach out and touch her, the proud, cool beauty of the real Janet to whom he could not speak.

It was at this point that he noticed that everything was turning bright around him, with a faint, diffused shining that came from nowhere in particular. He looked north along the coastline and saw that way up, beyond the cliffs and almost to Poseidon's headland, the sun had broken through the fog and was reaching out to sea in a long, slanting column of white light. He was searched by this surprising magnificence in a way that was like the new feeling about Janet, only more so. It made him at the same time wish to weep and to burst out into triumphant song. He closed his hands into tight fists and pressed the fists into his ribs to stop the pain.

"O God, God," he cried out in a shrill voice that was quite strange to him.

He was shamed by the vehemence of this outburst. He looked away from the shaft of light in the north, to the ocean right in front of him. After a moment he assumed the expressionless countenance of the fighter advancing from his corner, and began to wade slowly out into the dark water, which was now faintly brightened upon all its ripples by the distant splendor.

The betraying voice spoke again in his mind. "You aren't going home . . ." it began, but he cut it off there.